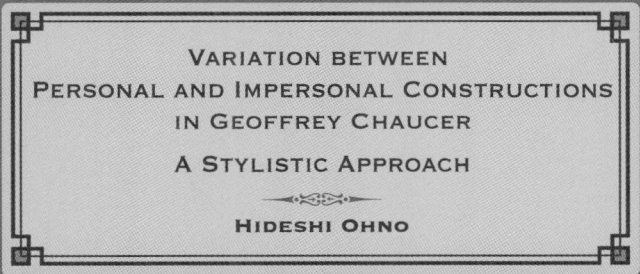

VARIATION BETWEEN
PERSONAL AND IMPERSONAL CONSTRUCTIONS
IN GEOFFREY CHAUCER

A STYLISTIC APPROACH

HIDESHI OHNO

UNIVERSITY EDUCATION PRESS

VARIATION BETWEEN
PERSONAL AND IMPERSONAL CONSTRUCTIONS
IN GEOFFREY CHAUCER
A Stylistic Approach

© 2015 Hideshi Ohno

All rights reserved. No part of this publication may be reproduced, stored in a retrieval system, or transmitted, in any form, or by any means, electronic, mechanical, photocopying, recording or otherwise, without the prior permission in writing of the publisher.

Published by
UNIVERSITY EDUCATION PRESS Co., Ltd.
855-4 Nishiichi, Minami-ku, Okayama-shi,
Okayama 700-0953

Printed in Japan

ISBN 978-4-86429-337-2

Preface

The aim of this book is to analyse Chaucer's use of the impersonal and personal constructions from the viewpoint of syntax and stylistics. The book is based upon the doctoral dissertation which I submitted to the Graduate School of Letters, Hiroshima University in 2010.

In publishing this book I have derived invaluable academic suggestions from many people. I am particularly indebted to Professor Toshiro Tanaka, who exposed me to the world of English philology when I was an undergraduate at Hiroshima University. I would like to express my profound gratitude to Professor Akiyuki Jimura, the supervisor of my dissertation, and Professor Yoshiyuki Nakao, who have both advised me constantly on Middle English language and literature, and on linguistics as well. They have also given me several opportunities to speak at the symposia organized by them. I wish to acknowledge my indebtedness to Professor Yoshihiro Shinoda, who spared no pains to read Middle English texts with me. I am highly indebted to Professor Ken Nakagawa for encouraging me to complete my dissertation on this subject. I am much indebted to Professor Osamu Imahayashi for encouraging me to publish this book. I am also obliged to the members of the English Research Association of Hiroshima for giving me invaluable suggestions at its annual and monthly meetings.

I wish to thank Mamoru Sato, President of University Education Press Co., Ltd. for his cooperation and assistance in publishing this book.

My hearty thanks also go to my wife, children, and parents for their love, encouragement, and support.

Kurashiki
February 2015

Hideshi Ohno

Contents

Preface	iii
Abbreviations	ix
Introduction	1
Part I Synchronic Variation in Chaucer's Texts	7
Chapter 1 Verbs of Pleasing and Liking	9
1. Syntactic and Prosodic Aspects	11
1.1. Complement Types	11
1.2. Grammatical Persons of Experiencer	13
1.3. Word Order	14
1.4. Rhyme	16
1.5. Clause Types	17
2. Semantic and Pragmatic Aspects	20
2.1. Personal Construction	21
2.1.1. *Liken*	21
2.1.2. *Listen*	23
2.1.3. *Longen*	26
2.2. Impersonal Construction	27
2.2.1. *Liken*	27
2.2.2. *Listen*	28
2.2.3. *Longen*	29
3. Summary	30
Chapter 2 Verbs of Grieving and Regretting	31
1. Syntactic and Prosodic Aspects	35
1.1. Complement Types	35
1.2. Word Order	41

1.3. Clause Types	42
1.4. Grammatical Persons of Experiencer	44
1.5. Rhyme	46
2. Semantic and Pragmatic Aspects	47
2.1. *Greven*	47
2.2. *Smerten*	48
2.3. *Reuen*	48
2.4. *Repenten*	49
2.5. *Recchen*	51
3. Summary	53
Chapter 3 Verbs of Obligation and Necessity	55
1. Syntactic and Prosodic Aspects of *Ouen*	59
1.1. Complement Types	60
1.2. Word Order	61
1.3. Clause Types and Rhyme	62
1.4. Forms and Significations	64
1.5. Grammatical Persons of Experiencer	64
2. Semantic and Pragmatic Aspects of *Ouen*	66
3. Analysis of Other Verbs	70
4. Summary	73
Chapter 4 Verbs of Remembering and Thinking	75
1. *Remembren*	75
1.1. Syntactic and Prosodic Features of *Remembren*	77
1.1.1 Complement Types	80
1.1.2. Word Order and Rhyme	80
1.1.3. Grammatical Persons of Experiencer and Clause Types	82
1.2. Semantic and Pragmatic Aspects	83

1.2.1. Impersonal Construction	83
1.2.2. Personal Construction	85
2. *Thinken / Thenken*	87
2.1. Syntactic and Prosodic Features of *Think*	88
2.1.1. Complement Types	88
2.1.2. Clause Types	91
2.1.3. Word Order and Rhyme	93
2.1.4. Grammatical Persons of Experiencer	95
2.2. Pragmatic Aspect of Parenthetical *Think*	97
2.2.1. Types of Parentheticals	100
2.2.2. Positions of Parentheticals	101
2.2.3. Function of Parenthetical *Think* in Chaucer	102
3. Summary	106
Chapter 5 Verbs of Dreaming	109
1. Syntactic and Prosodic Aspects	114
1.1. Complement Types and Word Order	114
1.2. Grammatical Persons of Experiencer	117
1.3. Clause Types	119
1.4. Rhyme	121
2. Semantic and Pragmatic Aspects	122
2.1. Complement Type 1: IC	122
2.2. Complement Type 2: NC	125
2.3. Complement Type 3: SC	127
3. Summary	129
Summary of Part I	131
Part II Diachronic Variation in Chaucer's Manuscripts	141
Chapter 6 Tendencies of Variation	143
1. Brief Sketch of Transition by Previous Studies	145

Contents

2. Ordering of Superiority of Two Uses in Chaucer's Texts	146
3. Overall Picture of Variation in Manuscripts	148
3.1. Statistical Data of Variation	150
3.2. Syntactic Aspects of Variation	153
3.3. Other Types of Variation	154
3.4. Dative Experiencer in Rhyme	155
3.5. Manuscripts with I-P Variants	156
4. Syntactic Analysis of Individual Verb	157
4.1. *Liken* and *Listen*	157
4.2. *Greven*, *Recchen*, *Repenten*, *Reuen*, and *Smerten*	159
4.3. *Bihoven*, *Moten*, *Neden*, *Ouen*, and *Thurven*	163
4.4. *Remembren* and *Think*	167
4.5. *Dremen* and *Meten*	169
5. Summary	171
Chapter 7 Explanations for Variation: Case Studies	173
1. Examination of Examples	174
1.1. *Listen*	174
1.2. *Ouen*	177
1.3. *Thurven*	178
1.4. *Recchen*	179
1.5. *Think*	180
2. Summary	181
Conclusion	183
Bibliography	187
Index	197

Abbreviations

I. Works Cited in This Book

1. The works of Chaucer

ABC	*An ABC*
Anel	*Anelida and Arcite*
BD	*The Book of the Duchess*
Bo	*Boece*
ClT	*The Clerk's Tale*
CT	*The Canterbury Tales*
CYT	*The Canon's Yeoman's Tale*
FranT	*The Franklin's Tale*
GP	*General Prologue*
HF	*The House of Fame*
KnT	*The Knight's Tale*
LGW	*The Legend of Good Women*
MancT	*The Manciple's Tale*
Mars	*The Complaint of Mars*
Mel	*The Tale of Melibee*
MerT	*The Merchant's Tale*
MilT	*The Miller's Tale*
MkT	*The Monk's Tale*
MLT	*The Man of Law's Tale*
NPT	*The Nun's Priest's Tale*
ParsT	*The Parson's Tale*
PF	*The Parliament of Fowls*
PhyT	*The Physician's Tale*
Pity	*The Complaint unto Pity*
Rom	*The Romaunt of the Rose*
RvT	*The Reeve's Tale*
ShipT	*The Shipman's Tale*
SNT	*The Second Nun's Tale*
SqT	*The Squire's Tale*
SumT	*The Summoner's Tale*
Thop	*Tale of Sir Thopas*

Tr	*Troilus and Criseyde*
Truth	*Truth*
Ven	*The Complaint of Venus*
WBT	*The Wife of Bath's Tale*

2. The work of Gower
CA	*Confessio Amantis*

3. The work of Langland
PPl	*Piers Plowman*

II. Manuscripts of *The Canterbury Tales* (Manly and Rickert 1940)

Ad[1]	Additional 5140
Ad[2]	Additional 25178
Ad[3]	Additional 35286
Ad[4]	Additional 10340
Ar	Arundel 140
Bw	Barlow 20
Bo[1]	Bodley 414
Bo[2]	Bodley 686
Cn	Cardigan
Cx[1]	Caxton, First Edition
Cx[2]	Caxton, Second Edition
Ct	Chetham
Ch	Christ Church CLII
Cp	Corpus Christi 198
Dd	Cambridge Dd.4.24
Dl	Delamere
Ds	Devonshire
Ds[2]	Devonshire Fragment
Do	Douce d.4
Ee	Cambridge Ee.2.15
En[1]	Egerton 2726
En[2]	Egerton 2863
En[3]	Egerton 2864
El	Ellesmere

Abbreviations

Fi	Fitzwilliam McClean 181
Gg	Cambridge Gg.4.27
Gl	Glasgow Hunterian U.1.1
Ha^1	Harley 1239
Ha^2	Harley 1758
Ha^3	Harley 7333
Ha^4	Harley 7334
Ha^5	Harley 7335
Hl^1	Harley 1704
Hl^2	Harley 2551
Hl^3	Harley 2382
Hl^4	Harley 5908
Ht	Hatton Donat 1
He	Helmingham
Hg	Hengwrt
Hk	Holkham 667
Hn	Huntington HM 144
Ii	Cambridge Ii.3.26
Kk	Cambridge Kk.1.3 (No.20)
La	Lansdowne 851
Ld^1	Laud 600
Ld^2	Laud 739
Lc	Lichfield 2
Ln	Lincoln 110
Ll^1	Longleat 257
Ll^2	Longleat 29
Ma	Manchester English 113
Mc	McCormick
Me	Merthyr
Mm	Cambridge Mm.2.5
Mg	Morgan 249
Np	Naples XIII.B.29
Ne	New College D 314
Nl	Northumberland
Ox	Oxford (Manchester English 63 and Rosenback)
Ps	Paris Anglais 39

Pp	Pepys 2006
Pw	Petworth
Ph[1]	Phillipps 6750
Ph[2]	Phillipps 8136
Ph[3]	Phillipps 8137
Ph[4]	Phillipps 8299
Py	Physicians 13
Pl	Plimpton
Ra[1]	Rawlinson Poetry 141
Ra[2]	Rawlinson Poetry 149
Ra[3]	Rawlinson Poetry 223
Ra[4]	Rawlinson C.86
Ryl	Royal 17 D.XV
Ry[2]	Royal 18 C.II
Se	Selden Arch. B.14
Si	Sion College
Sl[1]	Sloane 1685
Sl[2]	Sloane 1686
Sl[3]	Sloane 1009
St	Stonyhurst B XXIII
Tc[1]	Trinity College Cambridge R.33 R.33
Tc[2]	Trinity College Cambridge R.3.15
Tc[3]	Trinity College Cambridge R.3.19
To	Trinity College Oxford Arch.49

Introduction

This book is about the use of the impersonal and personal constructions in the verbs which describe mental activities. The verbs are categorised in five groups according to their semantic field: verbs of (1) pleasing and liking, (2) grieving and regretting, (3) obligation and necessity, (4) remembering and thinking, and (5) dreaming. In the age of Chaucer, the transition from the impersonal to the personal use was in progress, and in many instances the two uses can be found in a single verb. In this book, mainly from the syntactic and stylistic viewpoints, I will explain the significance of this variation and consider what interpretations the variants make possible in his works.

What is the impersonal use? There are some fluctuations in its definition. Denison (1993: 62) comments as follows:

> The strictest syntactic definition of impersonalness would apply only to clauses (presumably subjectless ones) whose verbs have no personal argument at all. The term is often extended, however, to subjectless clauses whose verbs do have personal arguments. A further extension brings in clauses which do have a subject but whose subject is not a (characteristically) personal one for that verb. And the widest usage employs 'impersonal' for any verb which *can* appear in any of the previously mentioned clause types, even when it is being used 'personally'.

Dealing with the verbs describing mental activities, I focus on the grammatical case of the "experiencer" (Ex). The term "experiencer" is used "to refer to the CASE of an entity or person psychologically affected by the action or state expressed by the VERB" (Crystal 2003: 171). When a verb occurs with an Ex in the oblique case, sometimes with a preposition before it, it is classified as "impersonal". However, even so, when a verb also takes a nominative subject which functions as a Cause, the example is classified as "Cause-Subject". Finally, when the case of the Ex is obscure or when a verb in question is non-finite, the example is not classified into any use.

According to the books about the history of the English language, the impersonal use had existed in Old English (OE) and the number of verbs in the impersonal use increased in Middle English (ME) because of some verbs which had newly acquired the impersonal use, and of some borrowings from Old French and Old Norse. However, the impersonal use underwent transition to the personal use during the Middle English period with some exceptions. What has been traditionally thought to be the cause of the transition, is the reanalysis of the (pro)noun before the verb as the subject, which is caused by the establishment of word order and the levelling of inflexions.

Many scholars have conducted research on the two constructions. From the diachronic viewpoint for instance, van der Gaaf described the transition in each type of the impersonal construction. Elmer showed the relationship between the complement types and the constructions. There are also many other syntactic and linguistic studies on this topic, such as Allen, Fischer and van der Leek, Denison, Fischer, Ikegami, Tripp, etc. Among them Allen says (1995a: 321):

> the grammatical compromise of making the topical Experiencer a subject but marking it with dative case to express the non-volitionality of the Experiencer was a favoured option.

Fischer and van der Leek also argue that in the personal use "the animate experiencer is nominative subject and therefore the initiator of the 'action'" whereas in the impersonal use "the experiencer, bearing dative or accusative case, is only passively related to what is expressed in the verb" (1983: 351). Jespersen not only takes a syntactic approach to the transition, but also argues that the psychological point of view is an important reason for the transition. Ogura explains the transition from the syntactic and semantic points of view and says:

> I still believe that the choice between 'impersonal' and personal expressions is a choice between indirect and direct ways of describing, and the choice, therefore, is stylistic as well as syntactic. (1996: 143)

Synchronic studies seem to have a shorter history, but have shown successful results. Allen researched the data from Shakespeare from a pragmatic perspective, and Tani focused on the grammatical persons of the Ex. Thus, they have raised questions about a general idea that newer and older expressions are used interchangeably at one stage of the language change.

While the above-mentioned studies are usually based on large cross-genre corpora, it is necessary to look at a passage in detail, where the context may give key factors differentiating the two uses in one author. Jimura (1983, 2005) illustrates the narrative effects of the verbs of happening in *Troilus and Criseyde*. Among others, Elliott (1974: 52) makes the insightful comment on the impersonal construction, although he lacks statistical data to support it. Adducing a few examples of *longen*, he says:

> The latter [= the personal construction] denotes a straightforward desire, but the former [= the impersonal construction] ... connotes an element of helplessness, a passive surrender to physical or psychological urges ....

Considering those previous studies, Part I will analyse the data from various perspectives and show what explications the variation of the use can provide, which is not mentioned by Horobin (2007). After overviewing a diachronic transition of each verb, Part I will look at syntactic and prosodic factors, such as the type of complement, the word order, the type of clause, the grammatical person of the Ex, the position of the Ex in one line, etc. In this process, the data, mainly from Chaucer's contemporaries like Gower and Langland,[1] will be used for comparison. Thus, I will show what kind of relations these factors have with the two uses. Then, I will try to give some semantic and pragmatic explanations of the results of the previous process. In particular, referring to the speakers' frame of mind about a proposition, their volition, their attention to the addressee(s), etc., I will deduce what interpretations the uses allow in context.

Part II, based on the results of Part I, investigates how the two constructions were accepted in the manuscripts of *The Canterbury Tales*. The manuscripts were produced during the fifteenth century, when the transition from the impersonal to the personal use was reaching its final phase. The major task of the scribes is to follow their exemplar(s), but there are many variant readings in their manuscripts. The main theme of Part II is what kind of tendencies those readings display and what they can mean.

The corpus of Chaucer consists of "all the undoubtedly Chaucerian works in the Riverside Chaucer" (Benson 1993: ix). Therefore, "Chaucer's texts" refer to Benson's edition. There is no extant manuscript of Chaucer's own writings, and his works are edited on the basis of the manuscripts produced by scribes. Examining "the language of the manuscript tradition of Chaucer's *Canterbury Tales*", Horobin sees "how Chaucerian language has been

---

[1] Although the themes of the three poets are not the same and Langland's *Piers Plowman* is an alliterative poem, it is inferred that they shared some varieties of the language in London. Gower was "Chaucer's friend and fellow poet" (Gray 2003: 217) and "it would seem that Langland had spent some time in London" (Gray 2003: 277). Concerning the relationship between Chaucer and Langland, according to Gray, "Earlier modern critics ... dismissed the possibility of contact between them. More recent critics have suggested that this view may need revision" (2003: 277).

treated in printed editions of his works" (2003: 77) and makes sceptical comments on Benson's edition as follows (2003: 95):

> The *Riverside* edition does not represent a fundamentally new edition, and its primary significance lies in its widespread adoption as the principal reference work by Chaucer scholars. ... The major difference between this edition and that of Robinson lies in the greater scepticism with which the editors treated readings unique to El [= the Ellesmere manuscript], although the editors state clearly that they were 'especially chary of deserting El completely because we remain unconvinced ... by Manly and Rickert's argument that El represents a text "editorially sophisticated"' (1120). ... However the adoption of much of Robinson's language and text has ensured that the language of the El manuscript has remained the basis for critical discussions of Chaucer's work. Despite the reservations about its textual and linguistic accuracy that have been voiced by scholars, the language of El has come to be considered synonymous with Chaucer's language.

His argument may be reasonable, but in view of the present situation, no one can say that a particular manuscript records Chaucer's genuine language. Therefore, I think it rational to use the widely-adopted edition.

In Part II, differences found between the edition and the Hengwrt manuscript, the earliest one of *The Canterbury Tales*, are noted as the need arises. The textual information of the manuscript is from Manly and Rickert, Ruggiers, and Stubbs.

Part I

Synchronic Variation in Chaucer's Texts

Part I, from a synchronic viewpoint, will carry out syntactic, prosodic and semantic research into the impersonal and personal uses of a single verb in Chaucer. After finding some syntactic tendencies peculiar to either use, I will apply semantic and pragmatic explanations to them.

The verbs dealt with in each chapter are as follows:

Chapter 1: *liken*, *listen*, and *longen*
Chapter 2: *greven*, *recchen*, *repenten*, *reuen*, and *smerten*
Chapter 3: *bihoven*, *neden*, *moten*, *ouen*, and *thurven*
Chapter 4: *remembren* and *thinken/thenken*
Chapter 5: *meten* and *dremen*

There are some other verbs which have the impersonal use in Chaucer such as *anoien*, *athinken*, *eilen*, *forthinken*, *gamen*, *shamen*, and *tikelen*. However, the number of their occurrences is not large enough for statistics.

Chapter 1

Verbs of Pleasing and Liking[1]

This chapter refers to the verbs of pleasing and liking, especially *liken*, *listen* and *longen*. They also belong to Elmer's "PLEASE/DESIRE class" (1981: 107-20). According to diachronic studies such as Elmer's and Allen's, in early Middle English the plural nominal experiencer (Ex) began to conjugate an impersonal verb, and in late Middle English, especially in the fourteenth century, these three verbs appeared with the nominative pronominal Ex. The two tables below summarise Elmer's research (1981: 108, 109, 113, 116, 118, 119, and 120).

Table 1. Constructions of *Liken*, *Listen* and *Longen* with Sentential Complements

	OE	12c.	13c.	14c.	15c.	16c.	17c.	18c.	19c.
liken	●	●	●○	●○△	●○△	●○△	△	△	△
listen	●	●	●	●△	●○△	●△	●○△	●△	●△
longen	●	●	●	●△	●△	●△	△	△	△

NB ●: Type S [= dative Ex + V + complement]; ○: *it*-construction; △: personal construction

Table 2. Constructions *Liken*, *Listen* and *Longen* with Nominal Complements

	OE	12c.	13c.	14c.	15c.	16c.	17c.	18c.	19c.
liken	●	●	●	●△	●△	●△	●△	●△	●△
listen	○◎	○	○◎	○●◎	○●◎	●◎△	△	△	-
longen	○	○	○◎	○●◎	○●◎	◎	◎	◎	◎

NB ○: Type N (*him reweth of* NP); ●: Type I (*him reweth* NP); ◎: Type II (*he reweth of* NP); △: Type transitive (*he reweth* NP)

These tables help to overview the diachronic transition, however they do not give much synchronic information about the tense relations between the personal and impersonal constructions.

---

[1] This chapter is based on Ohno (1995) and (1996b).

Before turning to a closer examination, it is essential to first define the classification among "impersonal", "personal", and others. In [1] the Ex *yow* is in the oblique case. This kind of example is classified as "impersonal".

> [1] And if *yow liketh* to hunte to roos, ye ne gon nat to the foordes of the watir that highte Tyrene. (*Bo* 3 m8.7-9)[2]

Next, in [2] the verb means "to please", as pointed out by the *MED* (s.v. *liken* (v.(1)) 1a. (a)) and Davis et al (s.v. *lyke(n* v. 1.), and not the nominative *he* but the oblique *me* is the Ex. Also in [3] the verb means "to please" and the Ex *Troilus* is the object of the preposition *to*. These kinds of examples should not be treated together with *liken* meaning "to like". In these cases, I will use the term "cause" to refer to an argument such as *he* and *This counseil*, and classify these examples into "Cause-Subject" (CS)

> [2] I took no kep, so that he *liked me*,
> How poore he was, ne eek of what degree.   (*WBT* 625-26)
>
> [3] This counseil *liked* wel *to Troilus*,   (*Tr* 2.1044)

Finally, when the case of the Ex is obscure as per *Fortune* in [4] and when the verb occurs in non-finite forms, these kinds of examples are not classified as "personal" or "impersonal".

> [4] For certein, whan that *Fortune list* to flee,
> Ther may no man the cours of hire withholde.
> (*MkT* 1995-96)

These verbs are used both personally and impersonally in Chaucer and his contemporaries. The frequency of each use in them is tabulated in Table 3.

---

[2] All emphases are mine.

Table 3. Frequency of *Liken, Listen,* and *Longen* According to Use

		Impersonal (I)	Personal (P)	CS	Not Classified
liken	Ch	106	1	7	18
	Gw	58	2	2	3
	Lng	26	2		14
listen	Ch	299	8		41
	Gw	95	6		8
	Lng	12			
longen	Ch	2	4		4
	Gw	5	2		2
	Lng				

NB The "Ch", "Gw", and "Lng" denote Chaucer, Gower, and Langland respectively.

This table shows that the impersonal use is still dominant, even in *listen*, which introduces the personal use in the thirteenth century, however I cannot say anything decisive about *longen* because of its small number of occurrences.

The following sections deal with the two constructions from the syntactic, prosodic, semantic, and pragmatic aspects.

1. Syntactic and Prosodic Aspects

Firstly, some syntactic aspects are dealt with: complement types, word order, and grammatical persons of the Ex. This section uses the data from Gower and Langland as well for comparison.

1.1. Complement Types

Table 4 below shows the frequency of *liken*, *listen*, and *longen* according to the complement type. While the three verbs are almost always used in the impersonal construction as in [5], several examples of the personal use are found, especially in Chaucer's and Gower's *listen* with a non-finite clause as in [6]. A few other examples of the personal use take a nominal complement (including a prepositional phrase) as in [7].

Table 4. Frequency of *Liken*, *Listen*, and *Longen* According to Complement Type

		Complement	I	P	CS
liken	Ch	Implied (IC)	41		
		Nominal (NC)	34	1	7
		Sentential (SC) (non-finite)	25		
		SC (finite)	6		
	Gw	IC	14		
		NC	13	1	2
		SC (non-finite)	31	1	
	Lng	IC	21	1	
		NC	4	1	
		SC (non-finite)	1		
listen	Ch	IC	157	1	
		NC	39		
		SC (non-finite)	100	7	
		SC (finite)	3		
	Gw	IC	18		
		NC	23		
		SC (non-finite)	54	6	
	Lng	IC	6		
		NC	1		
		SC (non-finite)	5		
longen	Ch	NC		2	
		SC (non-finite)	2	2	
	Gw	IC	1		
		NC		1	
		SC (non-finite)	4	1	

NB What is called "impersonal *it*" or "dummy *it*" is not considered a complement.

[5] "And after hym by ordre shul ye chese,
After youre kynde, everich as *yow lyketh*,
And, as youre hap is, shul ye wynne or lese.   (*PF* 400-02)

[6] Suffiseth me thou make in this manere:
That thou reherce of al hir lyf the grete,
After *thise olde auctours lysten for to trete*.   (*LGW* 573-75)

[7] *She longed so after the king*   (*BD* 83)

The examples with a non-finite clause include those in which *listen* is juxtaposed with another personal verb, which is one cause of the transition from the impersonal to the personal construction (van der Gaaf 1904: 33-36). In

[8] the subject of *listen* is juxtaposed with *han* in the previous line.

[8] Delyte nat in wo thi wo to seche,
As don thise foles that hire sorwes eche
With sorwe, whan thei han mysaventure,
And *listen* naught to seche hem other cure.   (*Tr* 1.704-07)

These kinds of examples are found in three out of seven occurrences in Chaucer, and in two out of six in Gower.

When the tables are taken as a whole, it is noteworthy that *liken* and *listen* are more frequently used with an IC than with the other complements.

1.2. Grammatical Persons of Experiencer

Next, the grammatical person-perspective of the Ex is examined. Table 5 shows the frequency of the three verbs in each grammatical person-perspective of the Ex.

Table 5. Frequency of *Liken*, *Listen*, and *Longen* According to Grammatical Person of Ex

	Person of Ex	Chaucer I	P	CS	Gower I	P	CS	Langland I	P
liken	1st	26*		1	5			5	
	2nd	45		2	13			5	
	3rd	36*	1	4	40	2	2	16	2
listen	1st	37			10	1		1	
	2nd	132	1		24	1			
	3rd	131	7		61	4		11	
longen	1st	2			3				
	2nd		1						
	3rd		3		2	2			

NB   Concerning the figures marked with an asterisk, one example has two Exs in the 1st- and 3rd-person, counted twice.

Table 5 indicates that although the impersonal construction is significantly dominant, the personal construction is found in the examples with a 3rd-person Ex. This tendency was identified in late Middle English and early Modern English drama texts by Tani, who says as follows (1997:

59):

> The results of the study being reported here show a type of "person hierarchy" in the variation between the personal and impersonal uses of *like*. According to this hierarchy, the verb (i.e. *like*) with 1st- and 2nd-person experiencers is more likely to take the impersonal than the personal construction, while that with a 3rd-person experiencer shows the preference for the personal to the impersonal construction. In addition, the verb when used with a 1st-person experiencer shows a stronger tendency toward using the impersonal construction than when used with a 2nd-person experiencer. As for *list*, no differentiating tendency according to person could be found in this corpus.

As far as my corpus is concerned however, *listen* shows this tendency more clearly than *liken*.

1.3. Word Order

The three verbs belong to the same semantic field, but as far as the word order in which they appear is concerned, *liken* takes a much wider variety than the other two verbs, as Tables 6-8 below indicate.

Chapter 1 Verbs of Pleasing and Liking

Table 6. List of Word Orders in Which *Liken* Appears

Word Order	Chaucer I	Chaucer P	Chaucer CS	Gower I	Gower P	Gower CS	Langland I	Langland P
EV	18 (12)			10			21	1
VE	3 (2)							
V *to* E	2 (1)							
it EV	2 (2)			2				
it VE	9 (8)			2				
it V *to* E	7 (4)							
EXV				1			1	
EVX	18 (16)	1 (1)		18	1		2	1
XEV	9 (5)			10	1	1	2	
XVE	17 (12)		2 (2)	1				
VEX	6 (6)			1				
XV *to* E			5 (3)					
to EXV						1		
it EVX				1				
E *it* VX				2				
it VEX	10 (7)			7				
it VXE				1				
X *it* EV				1				
X *it* VE				1				
it V *to* EX	4 (1)							
it to EVX	1 (1)							

NB The "E", "V", and "X" denote "Ex", "verb", and "complement" respectively. The brackets itemise the number of the examples in verse.

Table 7. List of Word Orders in Which *Listen* Appears

Word Order	Chaucer I	Chaucer P	Gower I	Gower P	Langland I
EV	153 (146)	1 (1)	17		6
it EV			1		
it VE	3 (3)				
it V *to* E	1 (1)				
EVX	88 (81)	7 (6)	51		5
EXV			1		
XEV	42 (41)		22	6	1
VEX	10 (10)		1		
to EVX	2 (2)				
X *it* VE			1		
it VEX			1		

Table 8. List of Word Orders in Which *Longen* Appears

Word Order	Chaucer I	Chaucer P	Gower I	Gower P
EV			1	
EVX	1 (1)	2 (2)	2	2
EXV		1 (1)		
VEX	1 (1)	1 (1)		
XEV			2	

It is noteworthy that *liken* often appears in the word order where the Ex comes at the end, especially in Chaucer, as in [9].

[9]   "Sire," quod this squier, "whan it liketh *yow*,
       It is al redy, though ye wol right now." (*FranT* 1215-16)

This fact is associated with rhyme, which is dealt with in the next section.

1.4. Rhyme

As seen in Section 1.3, the fact that Chaucer uses *liken* in various word orders is likely to be associated with his use of rhyme. Table 9 indicates that in Chaucer *liken* frequently appears with the Ex in rhyme position.

Table 9. Number of Ex in Rhyme

		I	P	CS
liken	Chaucer	22 (18) / 77	1 (1) / 1	3 / 5
	Gower	0 / 58	0 / 2	0 / 2
listen	Chaucer	1 / 283	0 / 7	
	Gower	0 / 95	0 / 6	
longen	Chaucer	1 (1) / 2	0 / 4	
	Gower	0 / 5	0 / 2	

NB   The brackets itemise the number of personal pronouns. The figure after the slash indicates the total number of the examples in verse.

In the 18 examples where the dative Exs of *liken* appear in rhyme position, 10 have the Ex *me*, five *yow/you*, and three *the(e)*. The frequent use of *me* in rhyme position is identified by Masui (1964: 49).[3]

Alternatively, it is quite noteworthy that the only example of the personal use of *liken* has the Ex *she* in rhyme position.

> [10] And, for he was a straunger, somwhat *she*
> Likede hym the bet, ...   (*LGW* 1075-76)

The nominative *she* is also "extremely frequently used at the end of the line" (Masui 1964: 46),[4] while the dative *hire* is used only four times in Chaucer's whole verse. This fact means that the choice of the personal use here is very likely to be determined by the demands of rhyme.

However, unlike *liken*, *listen* appears dominantly in the word order in which the verb comes at the end, as Table 7 shows. That means not the Exs, but the verb frequently appears in rhyme position: in 112 out of 332 examples in verse, while *liken* appears in 17 out of 100 examples. In this case the position of the verb itself does not affect the choice of either use, but the reasonably limited number of word orders may be connected to set phrases.

1.5. Clause Types

This section deals with the clause types where *listen* and *liken* appear. As Table 10 shows, among adverbial clauses, *liken* is frequently used in an *if*-clause by all the three poets, but Chaucer differs by using it in an *as*-clause as frequently.

> [11] "Come and, *if it lyke you*
> To dauncen, dauncith with us now."   (*Rom* 801-02)

---

[3] More precisely, according to Oizumi and Yonekura (1994: 1283-309), among 8,550 rhyme words in Chaucer's poetical works, *me* is the second most frequent (392 times), *thee* being the 24th (123 times) and *yow/you* being the 66th (47 times).

[4] *She* is the fifth most frequent rhyme word in Chaucer's poetical works (Oizumi and Yonekura 1994: 1283).

[12] "The tersel egle, as that ye knowe wel,
. . .
Which I have formed, as ye may wel se,
In every part *as it best liketh me* —
It nedeth not his shap yow to devyse — (*PF* 393, 396-98)

Table 10. Frequency of *Liken* in Each Clause Type

Clause	Chaucer I	Chaucer P	Chaucer CS	Gower I	Gower P	Gower CS	Langland I	Langland P
main	29	1	2	9	1		1	1
if / but (if) / and	18		1	11			6	
as	18			5			6	
relative	14		1	13				
that	5		3	7		1		
whan (so)	7			3			3	
syn / sith	5							
there / where(soever)	3						7	
for				4				
what							2	
while							1	
after								1

NB The lists of Chaucer and Gower contain the clause types which have more than three examples. The "main" includes an apodosis, and the "relative" includes *what*.

As for the relationship between the frequent clauses and rhyme, the statistics on Chaucer show that in *if-/but (if)*-clauses 7 of 14 examples have the Ex and two have the verb in rhyme position in his verse, while in an *as*-clause 2 of 12 has the Ex, and four have the verb in rhyme position.

As for the relationship between the grammatical person of the Ex and the clause types, Chaucer uses *liken* with the 2nd-person Exs in an *as*-clause more frequently (9 of 18 examples) than his contemporaries (Gower: 1/5 and Langland: 1/6).

Table 11. Frequency of *Listen* in Each Clause Type

	Clause	I	P
Chaucer	*as*	76	
	if / but (*if*)	62	1
	relative	48	3
	whan	32	1
	main	31	1
	ther (*as*) / *wher* (*so/as*)	17	
	that	9	
	for	7	
	while	5	
	syn	3	
	thogh	3	
Gower	relative	24	1
	if	15	1
	as	13	
	that	10	2
	main	9	1
	whan	7	1
	ther as / wher (*as*)	7	
	for	6	
	whil	2	
	though	1	
	which	1	
Langland	*if / and*	5	
	as	3	
	til	2	
	main	1	
	what	1	

NB The list of Chaucer contains the clause types which have more than three examples. The "main" includes an apodosis and the "relative" includes *what (so)*.

Table 11 gives an indication that *listen* is also frequently used in *as*-, *if-/but* (*if*)- and *whan*-clauses. As for the relationship between the clauses and rhyme in Chaucer's verse, the verb is placed in rhyme position in 35 of 74 examples in an *as*-clause, 26 of 58 in *if-/but* (*if*)-clauses, and 9 of 31 in a *whan*-clause, while no example has the Ex in rhyme position. The typical examples are [13]-[15] below.

[13] Dooth with my lyf and deth right *as yow lest*. (*WBT* 1248)

[14] For wel I woot, lord Phebus, *if yow lest*,
Ye may me helpen, save my lady, best.   (*FranT* 1041-42)

[15] She with hym spak, *whan* that *she* dorst or *leste*; (*Tr* 3.452)

So far, Section 1.5 has highlighted that *liken* and *listen* are frequent in certain adverbial clauses used as set phrases, and that those clauses are associated with rhyme.

As observed above, Section 1 has depicted the syntactic and prosodic conditions concerning the impersonal and personal uses of *liken*, *listen* and *longen*. Chaucer is different from the two other poets in that he frequently uses *liken* and *listen* in an *as*- or *if*-clause with a 2nd-person Ex and an IC, as shown in [11], [13], and [14]. Those phrases are often utilised in rhyme, functioning as a rhyme clause, as Masui says (1964: 180, 181, and 184). Rhyme is likely to be one determinant for the choice of either use, for the only example of personal *liken* has the Ex *she* in rhyme position. Tables 6-8, which list the breakdowns by verse and prose, seem to show no difference according to the writing styles.

These kinds of objective information can solve the fluctuation in the two constructions to some extent, but they have not fully discussed the personal use of *listen*, for instance. It is necessary to introduce other viewpoints, which will be dealt with in Section 2.

2. Semantic and Pragmatic Aspects

This section investigates the personal and impersonal uses in Chaucer's works from the viewpoints of semantic[5] and

---

[5] According to the *OED*, the three verbs have some similarity in the chronology of their senses. *Liken* had the meaning "to please, be pleasing, suit a person" (s.v. *like*, v.[1] 1. a.) in OE, which survived until about 1800, while the current sense (s.v. *like*, v.[1] 6. a.) appeared around 1200. *Listen* had the meaning "to be pleasing to" (s.v. *list*, v.[1] 1.) from OE, which can be found even in the seventeenth century, while the sense with the personal construction appeared about 1200 (s.v. *list*, v.[1] 6.). *Longen* also had the impersonal use in OE and the sense with the personal use "to have a yearning desire; to wish earnestly" appeared around 1300 (s.v. *long*, v.[1] 6.). As to the chronology there are different opinions. Tripp lays emphasis on the psychological element, saying as

pragmatic aspects, with some reference to the findings of the previous section. Concerning the agentivity[6] of a subject, Fischer and van der Leek (1983: 351) suggest that a nominative Ex functions as "the initiator of the 'action'". Thus, this section will explore a possible reading of either use in context.

2.1. Personal Construction

2.1.1. *Liken*

In her article Allen (1986: 400) quotes [16] and [17] as the first with a nominative Ex. As mentioned in Section 1.4,

---

follows:
> Psychological movement into ego-consciousness is a constant, growing, and all-pervading force modifying and reshaping all levels of language directly and simultaneously. (1978: 181)

To the contrary, Fischer denies the "change of meaning", saying as follows:
> The basic difference between our account and Jespersen's and other's is the suggestion that impersonal verbs have one basic meaning which is modified according to the different constructions in which they occur. We reject the postulated semantic change in a verb like *lician* from Old English causative 'to please' to Middle English receptive 'to like'. Instead, we suggest that the verb *lician* simply indicates the 'existence of pleasure'. This core meaning is present in all constructions in which *lician* appears; it is made more specific by the alternative argument structures in which the verb can appear. In general, each Old English impersonal verb can appear in three different argument structures (one without a syntactic subject — the 'true' impersonal construction — one with the experiencer as subject, one with the cause/source as subject), which give it a neutral, a receptive or a causative meaning respectively.
>
> In our view, therefore, the change concerning the impersonal verb in Middle English does not involve a change of meaning, but a loss of one or usually two constructions with their concomitant meanings. (1992: 236-37)

It is irrelevant to the main subject of this book to investigate the cause of the transition from the impersonal to the personal use, but it is important to examine the relationship between the form and the meaning when the data in the middle of the transition are treated.

[6] The term "agentive" is used "to refer to a FORM or CONSTRUCTION whose typical FUNCTION in a SENTENCE is to specify the means whereby a particular action came about" (Crystal 2003: 16).

[16] has the Ex *she* in rhyme position. According to Masui (1964: 45-51), the nominative *she* frequently occurs in rhyme, but the oblique *hire* does not; that is, the nominative may be preferred as the rhyme word.

> [16] For after Venus hadde he swich fayrnesse
> That no man myghte be half so fayr, I gesse;
> And wel a lord he semede for to be.
> And, for he was a straunger, somwhat *she*
> *Likede hym* the bet, as, God do bote,
> To som folk ofte newe thyng is sote.
> Anon hire herte hath pite of his wo,
> And with that pite love com in also;
> And thus, for pite and for gentillesse,
> Refreshed moste he been of his distresse. (*LGW* 1072-81)

In [17] the Ex *she* directly governs *gan enclyne*, not *like*. Although this present study does not classify [17] as either of the two uses because the verb *like* is the infinitive governed by the verb *enclyne*, this quotation can be considered to be personal because the complement *him* is not in the nominative but in the oblique case.

> [17] For I sey nought that she so sodeynly
> Yaf hym hire love, but that *she gan enclyne*
> *To like hym* first, and I have told yow whi;   (*Tr* 2.673-75)

By contrast, from the contextual point of view these two examples can be explained as follows: in [16] *she* liked *hym* the better, for the reasons described in the first four lines, and this sentence expresses her love for him. In [17] the italicised part follows the passage "I sey nought that she so sodeynly / Yaf hym hire love" and means that *she* began/did incline to like *hym*. This clause also expresses her affection for him. As to this kind of emotion, McCawley says, "nothing is so deeply EGO-centered as the notion of 'love and hate' as well as that of 'hunger and thirst'" (1976: 200), although this verb, compared with *listen*, shows spontaneous and uncontrollable emotion of the Ex, as their definitions in the *OED* (s.v. *like*, v.[1] and *list*, v.[1]) show.

The quotation [18] is seemingly an example of the personal construction:

> [18] For God so wys be my savacioun,
> I ne loved nevere by no discrecioun,
> But evere folwede myn appetit,
> Al were he short, or long, or blak, or whit;
> I took no kep, so that *he liked me*,
> How poore he was, ne eek of what degree   (*WBT* 621-26)

However, as the *MED* (s.v. *liken*, v.(1) 1a.) says, the verb *liked* here, unlike [16] or [17] above, means "to give pleasure to, make happy, please," and the Ex is *me* and the nominative *he* is the Cause. The nominative *he* is the object of the desire of the speaker, the Wife of Bath; in other words, she likes not a specified person but whoever/whatever gives her pleasure. This clause vividly shows that she gives full swing to her desire.

Considering the syntactic aspect of [18], the animate *he* is exceptionally used as the Cause, for the Cause is usually an inanimate NP. However, it may be noteworthy that the verb *liken* appears with the nominative animate subject, even though it is not the Ex but the Cause.

2.1.2. *Listen*

As van der Gaaf (1904: 33-36) points out, one reason *listen* is used in the personal construction is that the verb is joined to a personal verb. Here are cited three examples:

> [19] She with hym spak, whan that *she dorst or leste*; (*Tr* 3.452)

[20] Delyte nat in wo thi wo to seche,
  As don *thise foles that* hire sorwes *eche*
  With sorwe, whan thei han mysaventure,
  And listen naught to seche hem other cure. (*Tr* 1.704-07)

[21] And if that *he* noght *may*, par aventure,
  Or ellis *list* no swich dispence endure,
  But thynketh it is wasted and ylost,
  Thanne moot another payen for oure cost,
  Or lene us gold, and that is perilous. (*ShipT* 15-19)

The verb *listen* is juxtaposed with *dorst* in [19], with *eche* in [20], and with *may* in [21].

In [22] the Ex is the plural noun *auctours* and this phenomenon appeared first in early Middle English as noted at the beginning of this chapter.

[22] Suffiseth me thou make in this manere:
  That thou reherce of al hir lyf the grete,
  After *thise olde auctours lysten* for to trete.
           (*LGW* F 573-75)

Here the God of Love, the speaker, is telling Chaucer to write the old stories in accordance with what their authors intended to do. The personal construction here seems to emphasise their intention.

In [23] the Ex *he* is separated from the verb by the insertion of *to vertu* between them.

[23] I have a sone, and by the Trinitee,
  I hadde levere than twenty pound worth lond,
  Though it right now were fallen in myn hond,
  He were a man of swich discrecioun
  As that ye been! Fy on possessioun,
  But if a man be vertuous withal!
  I have my sone snybbed, and yet shal,
  For *he to vertu listeth nat entende*;
  But for to pleye at dees, and to despende
  And lese al that he hath is his usage (*SqT* 682-91)

In his suggestion to me, Norman Blake says, "By putting something in between, it allows both [= *he* and *listeth*] to be stressed. I think this is important for the SqT example since the 'he' refers back to 'my sone' in the previous line and allows the 'he' to carry stress". The Franklin, the speaker, is complaining of his son by emphasising his prodigality.

Also in [24] the Ex *I* and the verb *leste* are separated, and the verb is in rhyme position. In regards to this phenomenon Masui (1964: 149) says, "There is observed in Chaucer such a wide and growing tendency to end the lines with these verbs, etc. as to suggest that he may have liked the verbal rimes, whatever reason there may be". However, here in his long speech Troilus, the addresser, uses the 1st-person singular pronoun very frequently and tells Pandarus, the addressee, that he will die because of his lamentation, though he will not tell that to anyone. The personal construction here conveys Troilus' flat refusal. The nominative Ex *I* is also likely to appear in parallel with *I*'s repeated in his speech.

> [24] "What cas," quod Troilus, "or what aventure
> Hath gided the to sen me langwisshinge,
> That am refus of every creature?
> But for the love of God, at my preyinge,
> Go hennes awey; for certes my deyinge
> Wol the disese, and I mot nedes deye;
> Therfore go wey, ther is na more to seye.
>
> "But if thow wene I be thus sik for drede,
> It is naught so, and therfore scorne nought.
> Ther is another thing I take of hede
> Wel more than aught the Grekes han yet wrought,
> Which cause is of my deth, for sorowe and thought;
> But though that *I* now *telle it the ne leste*,
> Be thow naught wroth; I hide it for the beste."
>
> (*Tr* 1.568-81)

2.1.3. *Longen*

One example of the personal use is:

> [25] Thanne *longen folk* to goon on pilgrimages,
> And palmeres for to seken straunge strondes,
> To ferne halwes, kowthe in sondry londes; (*GP* 12-14)

To borrow Elliott's phrase, the personal construction in the example "denotes a straightforward desire" (1974: 52) for the pilgrimage. Also in [26] below the Ex *she* wants to meet her sister, whom she has not seen for as long as five years.

> [26] But shortly of this story for to passe,
> For I am wery of hym for to telle,
> Fyve yer his wif and he togeder dwelle,
> Til on a day *she gan so sore longe*
> *To sen* hire sister that she say nat longe,
> That for desyr she nyste what to seye (*LGW* 2257-62)

The *longen* in the following quotation appears with the preposition *after*.

> [27] This lady, that was left at hom,
> Hath wonder that the king ne com
> Hom, for it was a longe terme.
> Anon her herte began to [erme];
> And for that her thoughte evermo
> It was not wele [he dwelte] so,
> *She longed so after the king*
> That certes it were a pitous thing
> To telle her hertely sorowful lif
> That she had, this noble wif,
> For him, alas, she loved alderbest (*BD* 77-87)

According to the *OED* (s.v. *long*, v.[1] 5.) and the *MED* (s.v. *longen*, v.(1) 2. (d)), the impersonal use also occurs with the preposition *after* in late Middle English, but there is no instance of this kind in Chaucer. This example, with the nominative Ex *she*, also conveys her ardent desire to meet her beloved husband, who has been away on a voyage for a long time.

2.2. Impersonal Construction

This construction occupies most of the examples in this group of verbs, as Table 3 shows above.

2.2.1. *Liken*

One interesting example of the impersonal use is:

[28]   "For certes, lord, so wel *us liketh yow*
       And al youre werk, and evere han doon, that we
       Ne koude nat us self devysen how
       We myghte lyven in moore felicitee,   (*ClT* 106-09)

Here, both the Ex *us* and the Cause *yow* are in the oblique case, and, as T. Nakao (1972: 300) points out, this shows the blending of the impersonal and personal uses; in this passage one subject is offering counsel to his marquis. In regard to the 1st-person dative pronoun occurring with an impersonal verb, Allen (1986: 403) says, "the first person singular pronoun was the most frequently occurring preposed dative" and shows that *me* appeared also with the verbs in other classes, such as *thinken*, even after 1500. Applying this to the 1st-person plural pronoun and considering the hierarchical relationship between the addresser and the addressee in this quotation, it can be said that the addresser's self is displayed modestly. This fact may show that in contrast to the personal construction, the impersonal construction is a polite way of expressing the speaker's own feelings or thoughts.

In the next quotation Criseyde, the Ex, is affected by Troilus' features, but she does not begin to like him yet.

[29] Criseyde, which that alle thise thynges say,
To telle in short, *hire liked* al in-fere,
His persoun, his aray, his look, his chere,

His goodly manere, and his gentilesse,   (*Tr* 2.1265-68)

Later in the story (*Tr* 3.85-6), the verb *loven*, instead of *liken*, is used to describe the development of her love for him.

2.2.2. Listen

As said in Section 2.2.1, the impersonal construction in the following quotation is a polite way of expressing the feeling of the knight, the narrator.

[30] Therfore I stynte; I nam no divinistre;
Of soules fynde I nat in this registre,
Ne *me* ne *list* thilke opinions *to telle*
Of hem, though that they writen wher they dwelle.
(*KnT* 2811-14)

The extremity of this construction is a hackneyed phrase such as *if/as yow liste*, as mentioned in Section 1. The phrases usually show negative politeness,[7] and as Masui (1964: 180ff) points out, are frequently found especially in *Troilus and Criseyde*, where the level of the language is courtly, as in [31]. In this quotation, Criseyde is telling Troilus to trust in her promise that she will come back to him later.

[31] And Attropos my thred of lif tobreste
If I be fals! Now trowe me *if yow leste*!   (*Tr* 4.1546-47)

---

[7] "Negative politeness ... is essentially avoidance-based, and realizations of negative-politeness strategies consist in assurances that the speaker recognizes and respects the addressee's negative-face wants and will not (or will only minimally) interfere with the addressee's freedom of action" (Brown and Levinson 1987: 70).

Another example is:

[32] For with ful yvel wille *list hym to leve*
 That loveth wel, in swich cas, though hym greve.
 (*Tr* 5.1637-38)

This passage shows a general tendency of lovers. According to various notes and glossaries such as Baugh (1963: 207n), Benson (2008: 582n), Davis et al (s.v. *wil(l)/wille* n.), Donaldson (1984: 991n), Fisher (1989: 536n), and Windeatt (1984: 549n), the phrase "with ful yvel wille" means "unwillingly" or "reluctantly" and matches with the relatively passive nature of the impersonal construction.

2.2.2. *Longen*

One example of the impersonal construction is:

[33] Now sire," quod she, "for aught that may bityde,
 I moste han of the peres that I see,
 Or I moot dye, so soore *longeth me*
 To eten of the smale peres grene. (*MerT* 2330-33)

Concerning this example, in comparison with [25], Elliott says that it "connotes an element of helplessness, a passive surrender to physical or psychological urges, which fit with appropriate irony into the strategy of 'this fresshe May' attempting to deceive her blind, doting husband" (1974: 52). Additionally, it is safe to say that his idea leads to May's deliberate politeness to her much older husband.

So far Section 2 has attempted to highlight some semantic and pragmatic features based on the contexts where the verbs appear. Although not fully supported with sufficient examples, the positive or negative mental attitude is associated with the choice between the two uses to some extent.

3. Summary

What has been said in this chapter can be best summarised in the following sentences. In the days of Chaucer the impersonal construction and the Cause-Subject construction are significantly dominant in this group of verbs. From the syntactic and prosodic viewpoints, it is likely that either construction is chosen from the necessity of rhyme and set phrases. In addition, the semantic and pragmatic research allowed us to fully understand that the impersonal use conveys a general or relatively temperate manner of speaking, while the personal use expresses the subjecthood or positiveness of the Ex.

Chapter 2

Verbs of Grieving and Regretting

This chapter researches the verbs of grieving and regretting: *greven, recchen, repenten, reuen,* and *smerten.* Their definitions in the *OED*[1] which cite examples from Chaucer's time show that *greven, smerten,* and *reuen* bear causative meanings, while *repente* and *recchen* do not.

A diachronic change of the verbs from the impersonal to the personal use has been observed by Elmer and van der Gaaf. Elmer refers to these verbs as "RUE verbs", to which also belong *anoien, shamen, forthinken,* and *eilen.* Elmer's research can be summarised as in Tables 1 and 2, although they do not cover all the verbs dealt with in this chapter. Van der Gaaf's study (1904: 163) can add that the personal *reuen* appeared by about 1320 and the personal *smerten* in 1377.

Table 1. Constructions of Elmer's RUE Verbs with Sentential Complements

	OE	12c.	13c.	14c.	15c.	16c.	17c.	18c.	19c.
rewen	●	-	●	●○	●○△	●○△	△	-	-
shamen	△●	-	●	●△	●△	○△	○△	○△	○△
greven			●○	●○△	○△	○△	○	○	○
forthinken			○	●○△	●○△	○△	-	-	
eilen	●	-	-	-	●△	●	-	-	-

NB ●: Type S (= dative Ex + V + compl.); △: personal construction; ○: *it*-construction

---

[1] *greven* (s.v. *grieve,* v. 1.-8.), *recchen* (s.v. *reck,* v. 1.-8.), *repenten* (s.v. *repent,* v. 1.-4.), *reuen* (s.v. *rue,* v.¹ 1.-12.), and *smerten* (s.v. *smart,* v. 1.-4.).

Table 2. Constructions of Elmer's RUE Verbs with Nominal Complements

	OE	12c.	13c.	14c.	15c.	16c.	17c.	18c.	19c.
rewen	○◎●	●	○◎●△	○◎●△	○◎●△	◎●△	◎△	◎△	◎△
shamen	○◎	-	○◎	○◎△	○◎●△	◎△	◎△	△	△
forthinken			○△	○◎●△	○◎●△	●△	△	△	
greven			●△	●△	●△	●△	△	△	△
eilen	●	●	●△	●△	●△	●△			

NB ○: Type N (*him reweth of* NP); ●: Type I (*him reweth* NP); ◎: Type II (*he reweth of* NP); △: Type transitive (*he reweth* NP)

Tables 1 and 2 show that the personal use with a nominal complement (NC) appeared in the thirteenth century and with a sentential complement (SC) in the fourteenth century. That means that most of the verbs are used impersonally and personally in Chaucer's time.

Before commencing with the main issue, let us confirm what the impersonal use is. In [1] the Ex *yow* is in the oblique case; this kind of example is classified as impersonal.

[1] And yf I pleyne what lyf that I lede,
  Yow rekketh not; that knowe I, out of drede; (*Anel* 302-03)

Next, [2] has the oblique Ex *yow* and the nominative Cause *I*, and in [3] the Ex *kinde* is the object of the preposition *to*. These kinds of examples are classified as "Cause-Subject" (CS).

[2]   ... And heer take I my leeve
  Of yow, myn owene lord, lest *I yow greve*." (*ClT* 888-89)

[3] And yit to kinde no plesance
  It doth, bot wher he most achieveth
  His pourpos, most *to kinde he grieveth*, (*CA* 3.8-10)

I should note that when the case of the NC is obscure, as *his nygardye* in [4], the example is classified as impersonal, whatever the word order may be.

[4] But yet me greveth moost *his nygardye*.   (*ShipT* 172)

Specifically, examples which apparently look like CS are classified as impersonal in this chapter.

Finally, in [5] the case of the Ex *som* is obscure, in [6] the verb *repente* occurs in a non-finite form, and in [7] the verb is in the imperative.[2] These kinds of examples, in which the case of the Ex is obscure or which do not have an overt Ex, are not classified as personal or impersonal.

[5] And dredelees, if that my lyf may laste,
    And God toforn, lo, *som of hem shal smerte*; (*Tr* 1.1048-49)

[6] And elles, God forbede but he sente
    A wedded man hym grace to *repente*
    Wel ofte rather than a sengle man!   (*MerT* 1665-67)

[7] *Rewe* on this olde caytif in destresse,
    Syn I thorugh yow have al this hevynesse.   (*Tr* 4.104-05)

As seen in Tables 1 and 2, *shamen*, *forthinken*, *anoien* and *eilen* are excluded from the analysis hereafter in this chapter because they, especially the former two, do not have sufficient examples and because the latter two have "a restricted range of collocation" (Higuchi 1990: 215), as Table 3 shows.

---

[2] In the imperative the subject *thou* or *ye* is conventional. However, they may affect the tendency of the examples with expressed Exs and therefore are not classified into either use.

Table 3. Frequency of RUE Verbs According to Use

		Impersonal (I)	Personal (P)	CS	?
greven	Chaucer	16	5	5	14
	Gower	17		14	25
	Langland	5		12	8
reuen	Chaucer	5	15		28
	Gower	1	3		6
	Langland	1	1		1
smerten	Chaucer	13	2		
	Gower				
	Langland	1	1		
recchen	Chaucer	10	39		19
	Gower	9	3		3
	Langland		5		5
repenten	Chaucer	4	24		14
	Gower	1	4		2
	Langland		9		3
shamen	Chaucer	1		2	4
	Gower				
	Langland			1	1
forthinken	Chaucer		1	2	1
	Gower	4	1		1
	Langland	1			
eilen	Chaucer	21			1
	Gower	7			2
	Langland	1			
anoien	Chaucer	1	1	23	12
	Gower				
	Langland			1	1

NB   The symbol "?" indicates "Not Classified".

Higuchi (1990: 215) details the restrictive collocation of *eilen* as follows:

> Of the twenty-two instances of *ail*, the collocation "what + ail" numbers twenty (twelve of which are used in the formula "what eyleth thee/you?"...). This frequency is high enough to deduce that the context in which *ail* was used must have been virtually restricted to "what + ail".

As in the previous chapter, this chapter will investigate the impersonal and personal uses of the verbs in question from syntactic, prosodic, semantic, and pragmatic aspects. Firstly, this chapter obtains an overview of their statistical

Chapter 2 Verbs of Grieving and Regretting

data (Section 1), and then adds semantic and pragmatic considerations to each verb (Section 2).

1. Syntactic and Prosodic Aspects

This section covers the syntactic aspects: complement types, word order, clause types and grammatical persons of the Ex. It also discusses the prosodic aspect: rhyme.

1.1. Complement Types

Before considering the statistical implication between the complement types and the impersonal and personal uses, I must draw attention to *what* and *nothing/noght*.[3] Firstly, according to Oizumi (2003: 1469 and 1475), *what* as used in [8] is a pronoun and in [9] is an adverb, while the *OED* (s.v. *reck*, v.) consistently comments that *what* co-occurring with the verb is a pronoun.

[8] "*What rekketh me* of youre auctoritees?
I woot wel that this Jew, this Salomon,
Foond of us wommen fooles many oon.   (*MerT* 2276-78)

[9] *What rekketh me*, thogh folk seye vileynye
Of shrewed Lameth and his bigamye?   (*WBT* 53-54)

In both these examples the verb *recchen* takes *what* and the Ex *me*, and in [8] it also governs the prepositional phrase (PP) *of youre auctoritees* as its nominal complement as well. When considering that the verb does not take two or more complements, it is plausible that *what* is an

---

[3] A particle *that* is also to be mentioned. As the *MED* (s.v. *that*, particle. 14.) and Oizumi (2003: 1084) observe, the italicised *that* in the quotation below, which follows *hou*, is a particle and not considered as a complement.
"Now trewely, hou soore *that* me smerte,"
Quod he, "to Atthenes right now wol I fare,
Ne for the drede of deeth shal I nat spare
To se my lady, that I love and serve.   (*KnT* 1394-97)

adverb in [8], but there is no apparent reason supporting Oizumi. Therefore, this section, following the *OED*, decides that *what* is usually a pronoun, but the PP in [8] is an adverbial and not regarded as a complement.

Next, *nothing* and *noght* are also problematic. The dictionaries and concordances agree that their functions vary in the impersonal use: *no thyng* in [10] is an adverb and *naught* in [11] is a pronoun. Concerning the personal use, they have almost the same opinion that they are adverbs as in [12].

[10] He wente his wey, as *hym no thyng ne roghte*,
But to Boloigne he tendrely it broghte. (*ClT* 685-86)

[11] "I have," quod she, "seyd thus, and evere shal:
I wol no thyng, ne nyl no thyng, certayn,
But as yow list. *Naught greveth me* at al,
Though that my doughter and my sone be slayn —
At youre comandement, this is to sayn. (*ClT* 645-49)

[12] And as she slep, anonright tho hire mette
How that an egle, fethered whit as bon,
Under hire brest his longe clawes sette,
And out hire herte he rente, and that anon,
And dide his herte into hire brest to gon —
Of which *she* nought agroos, *ne nothyng smerte* —
And forth he fleigh, with herte left for herte. (*Tr* 2.925-31)

Their agreement is closely based on the meanings and the complementation of the verbs.

However, there is one example which has two readings.

[13] "What is he more aboute, me to drecche
And don me wrong? What shal I doon, allas?
Yet of hymself *nothing* ne wolde *I recche*,
Nere it for Antenor and Eneas,
That ben his frendes in swich manere cas. (*Tr* 2.1471-75)

Benson (1993: 613) says that the italicised *nothing* is a

Chapter 2 Verbs of Grieving and Regretting   37

pronoun while Davis et al (s.v. *nothing/no thing*) state that it is an adverb. A close survey of the verb complementation of *recchen* reveals that it often appears in sentence structures shown in [14] and [15].

[14] Goth Pandarus, and Troilus he soughte
Til in a temple he fond hym al allone,
As he that *of his lif no lenger roughte*;   (*Tr* 4.946-48)

[15]   O destinee, that mayst nat been eschewed!
Allas, that Chauntecleer fleigh fro the bemes!
Allas, his wyf *ne roghte nat of dremes*!   (*NPT* 3338-40)

In [14] and [15] the verb occurs with an adverbial such as *no lenger* and *nat* and a PP such as *of his lif* and *of dremes*. From this fact, this section regards the *nothing* in question as an adverb.

Table 4 shows the frequency of *greven*, *reuen*, *smerten*, *repenten*, and *recchen* according to the complement type (and the word order for later use in Section 1.2.)

Table 4. Frequency of Each Use According to Complement Type and Word Order

	Complement		Word Order	Chaucer I	P	CS	Gower I	CS	Langland I	CS
greven	IC		E refl. V	4						
			EV	2			3			
			it EV	2						
	NC	NP	EXV					3		1
			EVX	1						
			XEV	3			12	7	1	2
			XV *to* E					1		
			XVE	4 (1)		5 (1)	2	2	2	9
			VEX	2					2	
			to EXV					1		
		PP	EXV		1					
	SC	non-finite	*it* VEX	1 (1)						
			X *it* VE	1						

Part I Synchronic Variation in Chaucer's Text

	Complement		Word Order	Chaucer I	Chaucer P	Gower I	Gower P	Langland I	Langland P
reuen	IC		EV		2	1	1		
			it EV	2					
			it VE	1					
	NC	NP	EXV		2	1	1		1
		PP	EXV		7				
			EVX	1	4		1		
	SC	finite	EVX	1					
smerten	IC		EV	9 (0)	2 (0)				1
	NC	NP	XVE	1 (1)				1	
			XEV	2					
		PP	XEV	1					
repenten	IC		E refl. V		2	2			
			EV	2	4 (3)				4
			EV refl.		5 (4)		1		2
			VE	1					1
			V refl.						1
	NC	NP	EVX		1				
			EXV				1		
			XEV			1			
		PP	E refl. VX		1				
			EV refl. X		2 (2)				
			EVX	1	1				
			XEV		2 (2)				
	SC	finite	EVX		1				
			EV refl. X		1				
		non-finite	EVX		1				1
			XEV		3				
recchen	IC		EV	2	7 (2)	1		1	
			VE		1				1
	NC	NP	XVE	2					
			EVX		1				
			EXV				1		
		PP	EXV		2				
			EVX	2	5 (2)	1	1		1
			XEV		3				
			XVE		1				1
	SC	finite	EVX	1	11 (2)	7			
			XEV		1	1			
			VEX		2				1
		non-finite	EVX	3 (1)	4				
			VEX		1				

NB The brackets itemise the number of the examples in prose. The "X" indicates a complement.

Table 4 shows the following: firstly, *greven* seems to appear frequently in the impersonal use, but as mentioned above, most of the examples have a noun of Cause whose case is obscure, as shown in [4], and they can be considered as CS as well. So, in addition to the examples with an IC, those like [16], where the verb co-occurs with an SC, are undeniably impersonal.

[16] But up I clomb with alle payne,
And though *to clymbe it greved me*,
Yit I ententyf was to see,
And for to powren wonder lowe,
Yf I koude any weyes knowe
What maner stoon this roche was. (*HF* 1118-23)

Some personal examples are found in Chaucer, and there the verb has a subject Ex and a reflexive pronoun as in [17].

[17] "Now, sires," quod this Osewold the Reve,
"I pray yow alle that *ye* nat *yow greve*,
Thogh I answere, and somdeel sette his howve;
(*RvT* 3909-11)

Even these examples show the causative meaning of the verb, and can be considered as CS as well. This idea is supported by Ogura, who surveys OE and ME verbs used both impersonally and reflexively and says (1991: 87):

> in active sentences the emphasis is put on the subject that performs the action, while in 'impersonal', reflexive, and '*be* + past ptc [= participle]' sentences the focus is on the person to whom the action is directed.

Therefore, it can be said that [18], with a PP, has the undeniable personal use, which can modify Elmer in Table 2.

> [18] But, tolde I yow the worste point, I leve,
> Al seyde I soth, *ye* wolden *at me greve*.   (*Tr* 1.342-43)

Repenten and *reuen* are often used personally, but some impersonal examples, especially with an IC are found in Chaucer, as shown in [19] and [20].

> [19] But afterward *repented me* ful soore;
> He nolde suffre nothyng of my list.   (*WBT* 632-33)

> [20] But sith I see that thou wolt heere abyde,
> And thus forslewthen wilfully thy tyde,
> God woot, *it reweth me*; and have good day!'
>   (*NPT* 3095-97)

Reuen frequently appears in the personal use with a PP in Chaucer, as in [21].

> [21] "Now, deere lady, if thy wille be,
> I praye yow that *ye wole rewe on me*,"
> Ful wel acordaunt to his gyternynge.   (*MilT* 3361-63)

In this case, the verb bears the active meaning "to feel pity or compassion" (*OED*, s.v. *rue*, v.[1] 12.), which feeling is channelled not to the Ex but to others.

Next, although the total number of examples is limited, *smerten* is almost always used impersonally in Chaucer. Especially, the impersonal use is predominant with an IC as in [22] and [23].

> [22] What wonder is, though that *hire* sore *smerte*,
> Whan she forgoth hire owen swete herte?   (*Tr* 5.62-63)

> [23] "Now trewely, hou soore that *me smerte*,"
> Quod he, "to Atthenes right now wol I fare,
> Ne for the drede of deeth shal I nat spare
> To se my lady, that I love and serve.   (*KnT* 1394-97)

There the verb appears in adverbial clauses beginning with

though and *hou*, and a *hou*-clause is often found in Chaucer, as referred to later in Section 1.3.

Finally, *recchen* is used both personally and impersonally by Chaucer and Gower, but only personally by Langland. In Chaucer, although both uses appear in all the complement types, the personal use is dominant with an IC, NC (PP), and SC. One example, with an SC, is [24].

[24] For douteles, to don his wo to falle,
He roughte nought what unthrift that he seyde.
(*Tr* 4.430-01)

Gower is different from Chaucer in that he uses the verb only in the impersonal use with an SC (finite), as in [25].

[25] Be so the bagge and he acorden,
Him reccheth noght what men recorden
Of him, or it be evel or good. (*CA* 5.4701-03)

As displayed above, each verb has a different attitude about personal and impersonal uses, and Chaucer and Gower seem to have their own preference in the use of *smerten* and *recchen* respectively. What is common among *repenten*, *reuen*, and *smerten* in Chaucer, is that their examples with an IC more frequently have the impersonal construction than those with the other types of complements.

1.2. Word Order

Next, it is also necessary to mention the word order in which the verbs in question occur. Table 4 above details the frequency of each use according to the word order. *Greven*, which has retained a causative meaning, has many examples with the complement preceding the other elements, although the word orders do not seem closely related to the choice between the impersonal and personal uses. As for *reuen*, *smerten*, *recchen*, and *repenten*, there are more examples with the Ex preceding the other elements. However, the two uses appear with the same word order. Thus, word order is not a decisive factor of the choice.

1.3. Clause Types

Thirdly, let us examine the types of clauses in which the verbs in question occur.

Table 5. Frequency of Each Use According to Clause Type

	Clause	Chaucer I	Chaucer P	Chaucer C	Gower I	Gower P	Gower C	Langland I	Langland P	Langland C
greven	*for*									1
	if				1	1				
	lest			1						
	main	9 (1)	1		3	3		4		8
	relative	2 (1)		1	9	3		1		
	syn			1						
	that	2	3	2 (1)	4	5				3
	thogh	3	1							
	whan						1			
	wherof						1			
reuen	*but / if*		3			1		1		
	for	1								
	main	3 [2/0/1]	4 [3/0/1]			2			1	
	relative		1							
	that	1	5		1					
	though		1							
	whoso		1							

Chapter 2 Verbs of Grieving and Regretting

	Clause	Chaucer I	Chaucer P	Gower I	Gower P	Langland I	Langland P
smerten	*for*					1	
	how	6					
	though	3	1				1
	relative	1 (1)	1				
	main	1					
	that	1					
	wherof	1					
repenten	*but / if*		1				1
	for		1				
	lest	1					
	main	2 [2/0/0]	10 (3) [8/0/2]		1		4
	relative		5 (5)	1			3
	that		6 (2)		3		1
	though	1	1 (1)				
recchen	*algate*		1				
	as	1					
	as if		1				
	for		2	1			1
	how		1				
	main	7 [3/2/2]	23 (2) [8/9/6]	4	3		3
	relative		1				
	that	2 (1)	7 (2)	4			1
	whan		2 (2)				
	prnth.		1				

NB The brackets itemise the number of examples in prose. The square brackets itemise the number of examples of "main clause only" / "main cl. + dependent" cl. / "dep. cl. + main cl." in Chaucer. The "prnth" stands for "parenthetical".

As shown in Table 5, all the verbs except *smerten* most frequently appear in a main[4] or *that*-clause, and that the personal and impersonal uses appear in the same clause types. *Smerten* is frequent in a *how*- or *though*-clause with an IC, and in that case it is used impersonally as [23] shows in Section 1.1. Here is quoted an example in a *though*-clause.

---

[4] *Recchen* has the personal use more frequently in a main clause with a subordinate clause, but *repenten* and *reuen* do not show a similar tendency. As far as all the verbs dealt in this book are concerned, this tendency cannot be found elsewhere.

[26] For many a man so hard is of his herte,
   He may nat wepe, *althogh hym soore smerte*. (*GP* 229-30)

Repenten occurs in the personal use in a relative clause (five examples). In one example, the Ex is a relative pronoun whose case is obscure, but the relative clause contains a reflexive pronoun; in two other examples the verb is juxtaposed with another personal verb; in the two other examples the relative pronoun refers to the object of the preposition which is a complement of the verb, as in [27].

[27] And Piers Alphonce seith, 'If thou hast myght to doon a thyng *of which thou most repente*, it is bettre "nay" than "ye."' (*Mel* 1218)

Relative clauses, which postmodify noun heads, emphasise the action or the agent inside them. This idea can explain this phenomenon. However, this tendency is not applicable to the other verbs.

As a whole, the clause types are unrelated to the choice between the two constructions.

1.4. Grammatical Persons of Experiencer

Chapter 1 has found that the verbs of pleasing and liking frequently occur in the personal use with a 3rd-person Ex. Table 6 describes the tendencies the verbs of grieving and regretting show in the same contexts.

Chapter 2 Verbs of Grieving and Regretting   45

Table 6. Frequency of Each Use According to Grammatical Person of Ex

	Person of Ex	Chaucer I	Chaucer P	Chaucer C	Gower I	Gower P	Gower C	Langland I	Langland P	Langland C
greven	1st	11 (1)			5			1		2
	2nd	4 (1)	4	3	2		1	2		1
	3rd	1	1	2 (1)	10		13	2		9
reuen	1st	4								
	2nd		10			2				
	3rd	1	5		1	1		1	1	
smerten	1st	6 (1)	1							
	3rd	7	1					1	1	
recchen	1st	2	17		2				1	
	2nd	1	6						1	
	3rd	7 (1)	16 (6)		7	3			3	
repenten	1st	1	8							
	2nd	1	6 (3)			1			4	
	3rd	2	10 (8)		1	3			5	

Firstly, concerning *greven*, which almost always has a causative meaning, the unquestioned impersonal example in Chaucer, [16], has the 1st-person Ex, and the undeniable personal example, [18], has the 2nd-person Ex. Also with the 2nd-person Ex, the personal examples occur with a reflexive pronoun, as seen in [17].

Next, *reuen* is used personally with a 2nd- or 3rd-person Ex, while impersonally with a 1st-person Ex. In Chaucer the personal examples with a PP, as in [21], almost always (9 of 11 examples) have a 2nd-person Ex. Even with a PP however, a 1st-person Ex co-occurs with the impersonal use, as in [28].

[28] So ferde another clerk with astromye;
   He walked in the feeldes for to prye
   Upon the sterres, what ther sholde bifalle,
   Til he was in a marle-pit yfalle;
   He saugh nat that. But yet, by Seint Thomas,
   Me reweth soore of hende Nicholas.   (*MilT* 3457-62)

Also, two of three impersonal examples with an IC take a 1st-person Ex.

Concerning *recchen*, the high frequency of a 3rd-person

Ex in the impersonal use in Gower seems due to his preference for the verb with a SC, as mentioned above quoting [25]. Conversely however, it is worth noting that six out of his eight examples with a SC have a 3rd-person Ex. In Chaucer there are seven impersonal examples with a 3rd-person Ex, although with different complement types. Those facts demonstrate a close relationship between the grammatical person of the Ex and the impersonal use.

About the two other verbs, the grammatical persons of the Ex seem to have no marked tendency towards a certain use.

1.5. Rhyme

Section 1.4 of Chapter 1 drew attention to the relationship between the demands of rhyme and the personal and impersonal uses. Table 7 shows that, unlike *liken* in Chapter 1, there is only one example with the Ex in rhyme position ([16] above). As seen in Section 1.5 of Chapter 1, rhyme is often associated with certain adverbial clauses, i.e. rhyme clauses. It makes sense that the verbs of grieving and regretting are difficult to use for a prosodic or colloquial purpose.

Table 7. Number of Ex in Rhyme

		I	P	CS
greven	Chaucer	1 (1) / 14	0 / 5	0 / 4
	Gower	0 / 17		0 / 14
reuen	Chaucer	0 / 5	0 / 15	
	Gower	0 / 1	0 / 3	
smerten	Chaucer	0 / 12	0 / 2	
recchen	Chaucer	0 / 9	0 / 33	
	Gower	0 / 9	0 / 3	
repenten	Chaucer	0 / 4	0 / 13	
	Gower	0 / 1	0 / 4	

NB The figures after the slash indicate the total number of the examples in verse. The brackets itemise the number of personal pronouns.

Contrarily, the verbs themselves are much more convenient as a rhyme word, as Table 8 shows. However, as seen in Section 1.4 of Chapter 1, the position of the verb is not a key factor in the choice between the two uses. It is clear that rhyme has no ties to the two uses.

Table 8. Number of Verbs in Rhyme

		I	P	CS
greven	Chaucer	4 / 14	5 / 5	4 / 4
	Gower	9 / 17		10 / 14
reuen	Chaucer	2 / 5	10 / 15	
	Gower	1 / 1	3 / 3	
smerten	Chaucer	11 / 12	2 / 2	
recchen	Chaucer	1 / 9	4 / 33	
	Gower	2 / 9	1 / 3	
repenten	Chaucer	0 / 4	8 / 13	
	Gower	0 / 1	3 / 4	

So far, Section 1 has statistically grasped the overview that certain complement types or grammatical persons of Ex bear some relevance to each of the personal and impersonal uses. However, as referred to earlier, the verbs in question are slightly different in their meanings, and need more careful observations separately.

2. Semantic and Pragmatic Aspects

Based on the findings of the investigation in Section 1, the discussion of the verbs *greven, recchen, repenten, reuen,* and *smerten* is extended with the addition of semantic and pragmatic aspects. Each verb is examined separately.

2.1. *Greven*

As a whole, *greven* has a causative meaning, and most examples are in the CS use. As Elmer points out, the verb "discontinues the personal construction, adopting the *it*-variant instead" (1981: 92); the verb is not productive in terms of a historical development.

There are some unquestioned impersonal examples with

an IC and with an SC (non-finite), as in [16], and there is only one undoubted personal example, [18]. I have no definite information on the choice between the two uses.

2.2. *Smerten*

Like *greven*, *smerten* has meanings related to mental pain and distress. It is used basically in the impersonal use with two exceptions in Chaucer: [12] and [29].

> [29]   A! Nay! Lat be; the philosophres stoon,
> Elixer clept, we sechen faste echoon;
> For hadde we hym, thanne were we siker ynow.
> But unto God of hevene I make avow,
> For al oure craft, whan we han al ydo,
> And al oure sleighte, he wol nat come us to.
> He hath ymaad us spenden muchel good,
> For sorwe of which almoost we wexen wood,
> But that good hope crepeth in oure herte,
> Supposynge evere, though *we sore smerte*,
> To be releeved by hym afterward.   (*CYT* 862-72)

In [12], the verb *smerte* shares the subject with the preceding personal verb *agroos*, and therefore, [29] "is the only instance of *smerten* where a pronoun in the nominative is used" (Kerkhof 1982: 82). The manuscripts[5] recording this line have no impersonal readings (Manly and Rickert 1940: VIII 88). A contextual explanation to this example may be possible: the personal use describes the infinite distress which those who search for "the philosophres stoon" (l. 862) suffer, but currently I do not have enough data to discuss the choice as a whole.

2.3. *Reuen*

This verb has mainly two meanings: (1) showing the Exs'

---

[5] As far as in Manly and Rickert, 56 manuscripts record this line, although the Hengwrt manuscript does not.

pity, compassion, etc. towards others and (2) showing their repentance, grief, sorrow, etc. to themselves. With the meaning (1), which shows the active mental attitude of the Ex, the verb almost always takes the personal use, with a PP as its complement. In contrast, with the meaning (2), the verb demonstrates a tendency to appear in the impersonal use with a 1st-person Ex, as in [30], and in the personal use with a 2nd- or 3rd-person Ex.

[30] But wyte ye what? In conseil be it seyd,
    Me reweth soore I am unto hire teyd.   (*MerT* 2431-32)

It is noteworthy that the three examples with the 1st-person singular Ex in the impersonal use, have the present indicative tense while almost all the others have modal auxiliaries *wol* or *shal* or the subjunctive mood. That means that in the three examples, the Exs feel regret at what has happened and the feeling can be spontaneous. In [30] Harry Bailly, the Host, is disclosing his secret to the pilgrims, and the impersonal "Me reweth soore", which shows his regret for the fact "I am unto hire teyd", also seems to depict his unwillingness to confess that. Following this idea, it can be said that in [28] the speaker John, the husband of Alison, is spontaneously feeling compassion for one of his boarders, Nicholas, without knowing he is beguiled by him.

By contrast, in almost all the other examples, especially the personal examples, the Exs will feel pity or compassion for what will happen, with the act of regretting a little more emphasised, as in [21].

Thus, the personal and impersonal uses with the meaning (2) seem to show the Exs' agentivity and the Exs' indirect way of expressing their own feeling respectively.

2.4. *Repenten*

Repenten is generally used in the personal construction.

50   Part I   Synchronic Variation in Chaucer's Text

Although it has a similar meaning as (2) of *reuen* above, no such person hierarchy as Tani (1997) finds in *liken* is observed. There are only four examples of the impersonal use. Three of them appear with an IC, as in [31], but they differ from each other as to the grammatical person of the Ex and the clause type.

[31] 'Ne be no felawe to an irous man,
     Ne with no wood man walke by the weye,
     Lest *thee repente*;' I wol no ferther seye.   (*SumT* 2086-88)

More interestingly is the other example, [32], in which the verb appears with a PP. This example is in the speech of the queen defending Chaucer, who is accused by the God of Love of writing stories against his will.

[32] And yf ye nere a god, that knowen al,
     Thanne myght yt be as I yow tellen shal:
     This man to yow may falsly ben accused
     That as by right *him oughte ben excused*.
     ...
     And eke, peraunter, for this man ys nyce,
     He myghte doon yt, gessyng no malice,
     But for he useth thynges for to make;
     Hym rekketh noght of what matere he take.
        Or *him* was boden maken thilke tweye
     Of som persone, and durste yt nat withseye;
     Or *him repenteth outrely of this*.
     ...
     Hym oughte now to have the lesse peyne;
     He hath maad many a lay and many a thing.
                    (*LGW* F 348-51, 362-68, and 429-30)

Her long speech to the God contains verbs which can be used both personally and impersonally in Chaucer's time,[6] but she uses them consistently in the impersonal use.[7] The

---

[6] *Oughte* will be dealt with in Chapter 3.
[7] "Alceste's story does not appear among the legends, but her importance in the prologue demands attention. Unnamed at first, she is

italicised 3rd-person pronouns refer to Chaucer. In order not to incur the displeasure of the God, she, in a moderate way, avoids any expression showing the poet's volition or activeness and emphasises his inevitable situations. The situation bears out the point that the impersonal use attaches more weight to the objecthood than the subjecthood of the Ex.[8] It may also be worth noting that the repetition of *Or him*, i.e. anaphora, is effective in a speech of defence or persuasion.

2.5. *Recchen*

As far as the data surveyed in this section are concerned, *recchen*, with meanings relevant to concern or anxiety, always appears in a negative sentence or a rhetorical question. As seen in Section 1.4 above, Chaucer and Gower share a phenomenon that the impersonal use is often found with a 3rd-person Ex. Some examples from Chaucer, in addition to [32], are as follows:

[33] Save this, she preyede hym that, if he myghte,
Hir litel sone he wolde in erthe grave
His tendre lymes, delicaat to sighte,
Fro foweles and fro beestes for to save.
But she noon answere of hym myghte have.
He wente his wey, as *hym no thyng ne roghte*,
But to Boloigne he tendrely it broghte.   (*ClT* 680-86)

[34] So wo-begon a thyng was she.
She al todassht herself for woo
And smot togyder her hondes two.
To sorowe was she ful ententyf,

---

the God of Love's 'queen' and intercedes him on behalf of the narrator, though the arguments she uses are hardly flattering" (McMillan 1987: 34).

[8] This is much more persuasive than the fact that the queen, being a person of the past, uses an older way of expression because her significance is rather that she "gave herself to death in place of her husband" (McMillan 1987: 34).

> That wolful recheles caytyf.
> *Her roughte lytel of playing*
> *Or of clypping or kissyng*;   (*Rom* 336-42)

> [35] And thus endureth til that she was so mat
> That she ne hath foot on which she may sustene,
> But forth languisshing evere in this estat,
> Of which Arcite hath nouther routhe ne tene.
> His herte was ellesswhere, newe and grene,
> That on her wo ne deyneth him not to thinke;
> *Him rekketh never wher she flete or synke.* (*Anel* 176-82)

In those quotations the Exs do not seem to disguise their concern or anxiety persistently. The action of caring is out of their mind, because of profound sadness in [34], for instance.

On the contrary, apart from [8] and [9] above, all the examples with a 1st-person Ex are in the personal use as in [36]. This citation is from *The Clerk's Tale* as [33] is, i.e. the same tale contains two different uses. In [36] the verb appears in Grisilde's speech, who, after hearing the truth from Walter, is feeling intense relief and pleasure. Here it is likely that the personal use conveys her strong emotion that she is not afraid of death at all.

> [36]   Whan she this herde, aswowne doun she falleth
> For pitous joye, and after hire swownynge
> She bothe hire yonge children to hire calleth,
> And in hire armes, pitously wepynge,
> Embraceth hem, and tendrely kissynge
> Ful lyk a mooder, with hire salte teeres
> She bathed bothe hire visage and hire heeres.
>
>   O which a pitous thyng it was to se
> Hir swownyng, and hire humble voys to heere!
> "Grauntmercy, lord, God thanke it yow," quod she,
> "That ye han saved me my children deere!
> Now *rekke I nevere to been deed right heere*;
> Sith I stonde in youre love and in youre grace,
> No fors of deeth, ne whan my spirit pace!   (*ClT* 1079-92)

The above-described phenomena may mean that the speakers take a definite stance towards the feelings harmful to them more easily than when talking about third parties, and that may cause the impersonal use to remain with a 3rd-person Ex. However, it should not be overlooked that the impersonal use is in the minority and there are much more personal examples even with a 3rd-person Ex. It is also true that almost all examples of this verb share strong negatives such as *never, nothing, not a myte*, etc.

3. Summary

The relationship between the impersonal and personal uses varies according to the semantic aspects of the verbs. *Greven* and *smerten* are almost always used in the impersonal use or in the CS use; *reuen* allows the two uses but their proportions are different according to the meaning; *recchen* and *repenten* also allows both the uses but with the decisive superiority to the personal use. From a chronological point of view, the first two verbs are undeveloped in the transition from the impersonal to the personal use, while the last two verbs have almost finished the transition.

Through the analyses of *reuen*, *recchen*, and *repenten* from various aspects, I have found their preference for the impersonal use according to the grammatical person of the Ex. Although *reuen* has a different tendency from the other two, what they have in common semantically and contextually is that in the impersonal use, the Ex functions as recipient and the feelings expressed by the verbs are spontaneous and the personal use seems to show the Ex's deeper involvement in the action. This can explain the personal use found in [29], in which the Ex will smart from what *will* happen as well as what *has* happened to them.

Chapter 3

Verbs of Obligation and Necessity[1]

Among verbs denoting obligation or necessity in Chaucer's works are *bihoven, neden, moten, ouen,* and *thurven.* The first two verbs were used in the impersonal use since the Old English period, and the following three began to be used impersonally in the Middle English period[2] on the analogy of the first two and other impersonal verbs (van der Gaaf 1904: 144, 146, and 154). Then, in the middle of the fourteenth century the first two acquired the personal use, and eventually in Chaucer's days these five verbs had both the impersonal and personal uses. Elmer (1981: 124) and Ono (1982: 203) show the historical change of the uses in *bihoven*[3] and *ouen* respectively as below.

Table 1. Constructions of *Bihoven* with Sentential Complement

	OE	12c.	13c.	14c.	15c.	16c.	17c.	18c.	19c.
bihoven	●	●	●○	●○△	●○△	●○△	○△	○△	○△

NB ●: Type S (= dative Ex + V + compl.); ○: *it*-construction; △: personal construction

---

[1] This chapter is based on Ohno (1996a) and (2007a).
[2] More precisely, according to Visser (1963-73: 26, 28, and 29) and the *OED* (s.v. *must*, v.¹ 10., *ought*, v. 6., and *tharf, thar*, v. 2.), the impersonal use of *ouen* and *thurven* appeared in the thirteenth century and that of *moten* in the fourteenth, and the impersonal use of the three verbs is recorded until the fifteenth century.
[3] Allen surveys the verb and says, "I believe that the increase in the non-nominative Experiencer was semantically motivated" (1997: 15).

Date \ Meaning / Form	owe	Impersonal ought pt.	ought prs.
	c1220 ｜ c1450	a1225 ｜ 1297 1470-85	a1225 ｜ c1500
Current Usage (*OED*)	*Obs.*	*Obs.*	*Obs.*

Figure 1. Impersonal Construction of *Ouen*

In this chapter, an example like [1], which has a nominative Ex, is classified as personal:

[1] ... '*we* oghte paciently taken the tribulacions that comen to us ... (*Mel* 1496)

An example like [2], which has an oblique Ex, is classified as impersonal:

[2] Yif thou abidest after helpe of thi leche, *the* byhoveth discovre thy wownde" (*Bo* 1 pr4.4-6)

An example where the case of the Ex is obscure or where the verb is in a non-finite form is not classified as personal or impersonal.

Thus, the statistical data of the verbs used by Chaucer and his contemporaries are tabulated below:

Chapter 3 Verbs of Obligation and Necessity

Table 2. Frequency of *Bihoven, Moten, Neden, Ouen*,[4] and *Thurven*

		Impersonal (I)	Personal (P)	Not Classified
bihoven	Ch	15 (7)	0	29
	Gw	1	0	9
	Lng	1	0	4
moten	Ch	4 (3)	314 (261)	154
	Gw	0	135	60
	Lng	0	20	20
neden	Ch	30 (26)	1 (0)	71
	Gw	16	0	21
	Lng	1	0	5
ouen	Ch	42 (22)	71 (39)	83
	Gw	15	5	27
	Lng	0	4	2
thurven	Ch	12 (11)	1 (0)	2
	Gw	2	0	1
	Lng	0	1	0

NB As for the examples of Chaucer, the brackets itemise the number of the examples in verse. This is applied to the following tables in this chapter.

Statistically speaking, *ouen* appears equally in both the personal and impersonal constructions while *bihoven*, *neden*, *thurven* are almost exclusively used impersonally and *moten* personally. When Chaucer is compared with his contemporaries, it is safe to say that he is different from Gower in the use of *ouen*: Chaucer's *ouen* is more frequently used in the personal construction while Gower's appears more frequently in the impersonal construction.

In the historical change of some linguistic features there can be a period when both older and newer uses co-occur. But a question now arises: is there any difference between the personal and impersonal uses when one person employs both uses? Some scholars have commented on the

---

[4] Examples of *ouen* meaning "to own" are omitted. The example "in this caas *yow oghten* for to werken ful avysely and with greet deliberacioun" (*Mel* 1298) has the verb with *-en* ending which indicates plural, although the Ex is in the oblique case. This is a hybrid between the personal and impersonal uses, as T. Nakao (1972: 299) points out, although it is noticeable that the Hengwrt manuscript reads *ye* for *yow*. This chapter, drawing focus to the case of Ex, classifies the example into the impersonal use.

use of certain impersonal verbs. Elliott, for example, explains Chaucer's use of *longen*, saying (1974: 52):

> The latter [= the personal construction] denotes a straightforward desire, but the former [= the impersonal construction] ... connotes an element of helplessness, a passive surrender to physical or psychological urges ...

Observing his opinion, this chapter mainly explores possible differences between the two uses of *ouen* in Chaucer from syntactic, prosodic and semantic points of view first. Then, based on the survey results, the other verbs are referred to when needed.

Before taking up the main subject, let us look into *ouen* from a chronological point of view. Table 3 gives the number of occurrences of *ouen* in each work.

Table 3. Frequency of Impersonal and Personal Constructions in Chaucer's Works

Work	Date	I	P
ABC	Before 1372	1	2
Rom	Before 1372	1	2
BD	Before 1372	0	1
HF	c. 1372-1380	0	1
Anel	c. 1372-1380	0	1
Pity	c. 1372-1380	0	1
PF	Early 1380s	0	1
Bo	Early 1380s	0	18
Tr	c.1382-1385/6	8	13
Mars	c. 1385	0	4
LGW	c.1386	6	5
CT	c.1387-1400	26	21
Ven		0	1

NB   The dates are from Windeatt (1992: 5).

The table shows that *ouen* appears only in the personal use in *Boece*. However, because it is used personally and impersonally in *The Tale of Melibee* and *The Parson's Tale*, one cannot say that the verb appears only personally in prose.

The table also indicates that while *ouen* seems to have a

tendency towards the personal use in *The Complaint of Mars*, moreover the verb is used both personally and impersonally in later works.

When one examines a single work, for example in *Troilus and Criseyde*, *ouen* is used in both ways by an elder character, Pandarus (four examples in the impersonal use and three in the personal), while only personally by younger ones, Troilus and Criseyde (five and four examples respectively). However, the number of examples is insufficient to conclusively link the two uses to the age of the characters.

1. Syntactic and Prosodic Aspects of *Ouen*

Since *ouen* takes a non-finite clause as its complement in Chaucer, it is necessary to take into consideration auxiliarisation as well as personalisation of this verb. Tajima, dealing with the texts in the fourteenth and fifteenth centuries, states that "the present-day situation with *ought*, in form as well as in function, was virtually reached by the middle of the fifteenth century, or at latest in the second half of the century" (2000: 212). According to Warner (1993: 153), it is in the Middle English period that some auxiliary features began appearing in the verb. He sets up 11 criteria distinguishing auxiliaries from full verbs (1993: 3-9), among which four below can be applied to Chaucer's *ouen*:

> (c) *Ellipsis*. Auxiliaries both finite and nonfinite may appear in elliptical constructions without their normal complement ...
> (i) Modals lack the third person singular present indicative inflection of full verbs.
> (j) Modals are followed by a plain infinitive ...
> (k) 'Tense' relationships in modals are not parallel to those of verbs.

In reference to these points, the following section inspects the use of *ouen*.

1.1. Complement Types

Firstly, let us look at the sentence structures *ouen* takes. Table 4 shows the numbers of impersonal and personal constructions of *ouen* according to its complement.

Table 4. Frequency of *Ouen* According to Complement Type

	Complement	I	P
Chaucer	Implied (IC)	13 (7)	2 (1)
	Sentential (SC) (non-finite)	29 (17)	69 (38)
Gower	IC	0	1
	SC (non-finite)	15	4
Langland	SC (non-finite)	0	4

The table shows that, unlike in Gower, in Chaucer the examples with an IC appear almost exclusively in the impersonal construction while those with an SC appear in the personal construction more frequently. Concerning *ouen* with an SC, Visser says (1963-73: 1817):

> That the pronouns *us*, *him*, etc. were subsequently realized as constituting the subject of the sentence in spite of their forms emerges from their use before *owe(þ)* + *to be* + past participle, where their interpretation as 'indirect objects' is absolutely ruled out.

Among Chaucer's examples which are classified into either use, there are seven examples with the complement referred to by Visser above, five of which having the personal use, as [3] shows.

[3] And that is she that hath, ywis,
So mochel pris, and therto she
So worthy is biloved to be,
That *she* wel *ought*, of pris and ryght,
Be cleped Rose of every wight.   (*Rom* 44-48)

Chapter 3   Verbs of Obligation and Necessity   61

In Gower there are two examples of this kind, which are in the personal construction. Borrowing Visser's words, I can assume that in these examples the choice of a nominative Ex is affected by the complement type and not by the verb, and therefore *ouen* undergoes not personalisation yet auxiliarisation.

Concerning the examples with an IC, however, all the 13 examples in Chaucer's *as*-clause are impersonal, as in [4], although there is one example of this kind in Gower, which is personal.

> [4]   ... they into halle hire broghte,
> And ther she was honured *as hire oghte.*   (*ClT* 1119-20)

Although, according to Warner's criteria (c), the ellipsis of complements is a feature of an auxiliary, I would rather think that such clauses become stereotyped and are used as rhyme clauses, as Masui (1964: 184) says. Gower has one example in an *as*-clause.

In addition to the above, the examples of *ouen* were explored concerning whether the complements are infinitives with *to*- or bare infinitives, or in what kinds of sentences (for example, negative sentences and rhetorical questions) the verb is used. These explorations, however, did not make any important findings.

1.2. Word Order

Next, let us look into the word order in which *ouen* appears. The table below summarises the frequency of the verb in each word order.

Table 5. List of Word Orders in Which *Ouen* Appears

Word Order	Chaucer I	Chaucer P	Gower I	Gower P	Langland I	Langland P
EV	13 (7)	1 (0)	1			
VE	2 (2)	3 (1)				
EVX	26 (12)	50 (21)	15	4		2
VEX	1 (1)	19 (17)				1
EXV						1

NB The "X" denotes a complement.

The table shows the following: (1) the "EVX" order is the most common, (2) the "EV" order is frequent in Chaucer, where the impersonal use is dominant, and (3) the "VEX" order is frequent in Chaucer, where the personal use is dominant especially in his verse.

As for the second point, 11 out of 13 examples have the verb in an *as*-clause, which will be dealt in Section 1.3. As for the third point, 12 out of 19 examples have the adverb *wel* just before the verb, as in [5] below.

[5] *Wel oughte I* sterve in wanhope and distresse.   (*KnT* 1249)

Although this order seems favourable for metrical purposes, yet I cannot say that the order is a determinant for using the personal or impersonal because the dative Ex (*me* in the case of [5]) could come instead of the nominative one.

1.3. Clause Types and Rhyme

As seen in the previous section, the clause type in which *ouen* appears and the demands of rhyme are likely to determine the choice between the two uses. This section fully examines their relationship. Firstly, let us look into the frequency of the verb according to its clause type.

Table 6. Frequency of *Ouen* According to Clause Type

Clause	Chaucer I	Chaucer P	Gower I	Gower P	Langland I	Langland P
as	13 (9)	0	0	1		
for	3 (3)	2 (2)	3	0		
hou	1 (0)	0	1	0		
if	0	1 (1)				
main	7 (6)	42 (26)	8	3	0	3
relative	3 (1)	11 (4)			0	1
syn	0	1 (1)				
than	2 (0)	1 (0)				
that	6 (2)	10 (4)	1	1		
ther as / wher as	2 (1)	0	1	0		
wherof			1	0		
which	0	1 (0)				
why	0	1 (1)				

NB The "main" includes an apodosis.

Table 6 seems to show mainly two things. Firstly, Chaucer frequently uses the verb in an *as*-clause and that in the impersonal construction.[5] This clause is closely related to rhyme. Like *listen* in Chapter 1, there are nine examples in which *ouen* appears impersonally in an *as*-clause, and six of them have the verb, *o(u)ghte*, in rhyme position, as shown in [4] above.[6]

Secondly, Chaucer (and Langland) more frequently uses the verb in the personal use in a main clause, while in Gower the verb more frequently appears in the impersonal use. More careful examination indicates the following. In Gower there are eight impersonal examples in main clauses, five of which are in apodoses. However, in Chaucer there are two examples in apodoses which are in the personal use. Therefore, the type of main clause does not seem to affect the choice.

---

[5] Many of them are found mainly in *Troilus and Criseyde* and *The Tale of Melibee*.

[6] In the Ranking Rhyme Element-Frequency List (Oizumi and Yonekura 1994: 1153-60), the elements *-oghte* (69 times) and *-oguhte* (33 times) are the 133rd and 204th most frequent among the 1,155 elements in total. That seems to mean that those elements are moderately frequent, although Masui (1964) does not mention them.

1.4. Forms and Significations

In the early Middle English period, the past-tense form *ought* began to be used with a present or future signification. Such a use became popular in Chaucer's days, and *ought* became established as an auxiliary in the fifteenth century (T. Nakao 1972: 178). In Chaucer's days, there were two uses mixed in *ought*, as Table 7 shows.

Table 7. Forms and Significations of *Ouen* in Chaucer

Form + Signification	I	P
Present + Present/Future	1	3
Past + Past	10	1
Past + Present/Future	31	67

From the table it is clear that the impersonal use is dominant when the verb forms accord with the significations, and the personal use is dominant when the forms do not. This fact shows a tendency of the verb towards auxiliarisation. However, the facts that among the examples of *ought* with a present or future signification 31 contain the impersonal use and that 30 out of 67 examples of the personal use have endings of the plural or the 2nd-person singular present tense, show that the auxiliarisation is still in progress.

1.5. Grammatical Persons of Experiencer

In his research on *like* in late Middle English and early Modern English, Tani (1997) points out that the grammatical person of Ex is responsible for the choice between the impersonal and personal uses. He concludes that the Ex in the 1st or 2nd person co-occurs predominantly with the impersonal use and the Ex in the 3rd person co-occurs predominantly with the personal use. This feature, however, cannot be applied to *ouen*, as Table 8 shows.

Chapter 3   Verbs of Obligation and Necessity   65

Table 8. Frequency of *Ouen* According to Grammatical Person of Ex

Person of Ex	Chaucer		Gower		Langland
	I	P	I	P	P
1st	6	21*			2
2nd	9	17*		2	2
3rd	27	33	15	3	

NB   Concerning the figures marked with an asterisk, *ought* in Chaucer (*Tr* 4.1265) has two experiencers: *ye* and *I*, which are counted separately.

According to this table, in Chaucer the personal use predominates in every case and the tendency is stronger with a 1st- or 2nd-person Ex, while the impersonal use is as frequent with a 3rd-person Ex. In particular, as for the 1st-person singular Ex, Kerkhof (1982: 160-61) states:

> In many cases ... it [= *oghte*] is accompanied by the oblique form. ... The only exception is the first person singular, which is always *I* ...

This is worth noting, because a survey of the *Helsinki Corpus* finds the Ex *me* in works contemporary with Chaucer and later, as shown in [6] and [7].

[6] for y loue ȝow as miche as *me oweþ* to loue my fader;
   (*The Brut or the Chronicles of England* (1350-1420))

[7] alas reynart what saye ye / sette ye so lytyl by hony / *me ought* to preyse and loue it aboue alle mete
   (*The History of Reynard the Fox* (1420-1500))

In association with the persons of the Ex, close attention should be paid to the relationship between the addressers and the addressees. There are two interesting phenomena: the queen uses *ouen* impersonally only when addressing the God of Love in *The Legend of Good Women*; all examples with the 2nd-person Ex *ye* (except those in quoted passages or in an *as*-clause) are in the personal use in *The Tale of Melibee*. In order to understand what they mean, it is necessary to consider the meanings of *ouen*.

2. Semantic and Pragmatic Aspects of *Ouen*

In Present-day English *ought* has the root meaning: weak obligation and the epistemic meaning: tentative assumption, and historically speaking, the latter has a more recent meaning of the modal auxiliary. As to Middle English, Warner negates the existence of the epistemic meaning, saying (1993: 175):

> *Mun* and *ouen* both occur as deontics, and *mun* is found as a future epistemic. But I have not noted clearly subjective instances with *ouen*.

However, the *MED* points out that *ouen* "as modal verb in subjunctive or conditional constructions" implies "doubt or uncertainty" (s.v. *ouen*, v. 6. (a)), quoting [8] below:

> [8] And we wol, lord, if that ye wole assente,
> Chese yow a wyf, in short tyme atte leeste,
> Born of the gentilleste and of the meeste
> Of al this land, so that it *oghte* seme
> Honour to God and yow, as we kan deeme. (*ClT* 129-33)

The citation is from the speech of one of Walter's people in *The Clerk's Tale*. The addresser is offering a suggestion to Walter politely, using *oghte* which has the epistemic meaning.

In addition, it is presumable that *ought* bears the epistemic aspect in the following examples:

> [9] "God woot, of thyng ful often looth bygonne
> Comth ende good; and nece myn, Criseyde,
> That ye to hym of hard now ben ywonne
> *Oughte* he be glad, by God and yonder sonne;
>   (*Tr* 2.1234-37)

This quotation is from Pandarus' speech to Criseyde in *Troilus and Criseyde*. Pandarus is surmising Troilus' sense

Chapter 3   Verbs of Obligation and Necessity   67

of joy, using *oughte* in the subjunctive mood.

Quotation [10] is from Boece's speech in *Boece*. The italicised *oughte* shows his speculation that he is safe against many other people although he earned the hatred of an accuser.

> [10] And for as moche as the peyne of the accusacioun ajugid byforn ne schulde noght sodeynli henten ne punyssche wrongfully Albyn, a conseiller of Rome, I putte me ayens the hates and indignacions of the accusour Cyprian. Is it nat thanne inoghe isene that I have purchaced grete discordes ayens myself? But I *oughte* be the more assured ayens alle othere folk, that for the love of rightwisnesse I ne reservede nevere nothyng to myselve to hemward of the kyngis halle, by whiche I were the more syker. But thurw tho same accusours accusynge I am condempned.
> (*Bo* 1 pr4.96-109)

Citation [11] is from Philosophie's speech. *Aughten*, along with *wolden*, represents her guess about the villains' thinking in the apodosis.

> [11] And eek the schrewes hemself, yif it were leveful to hem to seen at any clifte the vertu that thei han forleten, and sawen that they scholden putten adoun the filthes of hir vices by the tormentz of peynes, they ne *aughten* nat, ryght for the recompensacioun for to geten hem bounte and prowesse whiche that thei han lost, demen ne holden that thilke peynes weren tormentz to hem; and eek thei *wolden* refuse the attendaunce of hir advocattz, and taken hemself to hir juges and to hir accusours.   (*Bo* 4 pr4.274-85)

Quotation [12] is from Pandarus' speech to Troilus.

> [12] "Sith thus of two contraries is o lore,
> I, that have in love so ofte assayed
> Grevances, *oughte* konne, and wel the more,
> Counseillen the of that thow art amayed.   (*Tr* 1.645-48)

The meaning of *oughte* is likely to come under the influence of *konne*, of which there are various readings.[7] When *konne* means "to be able", *oughte* has the epistemic rather than root meaning, showing Pandarus' confidence in his ability to counsel Troilus. When its meaning is "to know how", *konne*, along with *counseillen* in line 648, is a sentential complement of *oughte*, and *oughte* is likely to denote the assumption as well as the obligation of the addresser, that is, it has both root and epistemic meanings.

Citation [13] is from Criseyde's complaint against a night.

[13] "O blake nyght, as folk in bokes rede,
That shapen art by God this world to hide
At certeyn tymes wyth thi derke wede,
That under that men myghte in reste abide,
Wel *oughten* bestes pleyne and folk the chide,
That there as day wyth labour wolde us breste,
That thow thus fleest, and deynest us nought reste.
(*Tr* 3.1429-35)

There is a possibility that *oughten*, with *bestes* and *folk* as its subjects, has both root and epistemic meanings. However, the grounds of her argument that a night does not allow people to rest are personal and subjective. Such subjective grounds of argument can also be observed in [14] below, where the addresser argues for the need to feel pity for Petro's death.

[14]   O noble, O worthy Petro, glorie of Spayne,
Whom Fortune heeld so hye in magestee,
Wel *oghten* men thy pitous deeth complayne!
(*MkT* 2375-77)

The seven examples above will suffice to show that *ought* with the epistemic meaning or the subjective aspect

---

[7] Benson (2008: 482n): "be able"; Fisher (1989: 414n): "know the reasons for"; Donaldson (1984: 733n): "be able to recognize causes of grief"; Windeatt (1984: 127n): "know how".

does not have impersonal use and it functions as a modal auxiliary instead.

Then, what makes the difference between the impersonal and personal uses of *ouen* with the root meaning? In all works of Chaucer, except *Boece*, where *ouen* is used only personally, it seems that the impersonal use is dominant when general ideas are based on objective grounds, such as in religious teaching, as in [15] or when the statements are based on the social status or standing of the Exs as in [4]. In [15] the Second Nun preaches about idleness, and in [4] the Ex is Grisilde, the marquise.

> [15] For he that with his thousand cordes slye
> Continuelly us waiteth to biclappe,
> Whan he may man in ydelnesse espye,
> He kan so lightly cache hym in his trappe,
> Til that a man be hent right by the lappe,
> He nys nat war the feend hath hym in honde.
> Wel *oghte us* werche and ydelnesse withstonde. (*SNT* 8-14)

In contrast, the personal use seems to be dominant when the statements come from personal judgements of the addressers as in [16] and [17].

> [16] Ne a trewe lover oght me not to blame
> Thogh that I speke a fals lovere som shame.
> *They oghte* rather with me for to holde
> For that I of Creseyde wroot or tolde,
> Or of the Rose; what so myn auctour mente,
> Algate, God woot, yt was myn entente
> To forthren trouthe in love and yt cheryce,
> And to ben war fro falsnesse and fro vice
> By swich ensample; this was my menynge."
> (*LGW* F 466-74)

> [17] Me thynketh thus: that nouther *ye* nor *I*
> *Ought* half this wo to maken, skilfully;
> For ther is art ynough for to redresse
> That yet is mys, and slen this hevynesse. (*Tr* 4.1264-67)

In [17], for example, Criseyde is cheering up Troilus, who is grieving over their separation, by saying that there is a solution to the crisis, but her statement lacks foundation.

It seems that the subjectivity or objectivity of the statement or its grounds is expressed in both personal and impersonal constructions respectively. That can explain the above-mentioned fact that the impersonal use is frequent in narrative or *as*-clauses and the personal use is frequent in examples with a 1st-person Ex. From this viewpoint, one may say that the impersonal use of *ouen* by the queen in *The Legend of Good Women* expresses her logical and convincing appeal to the addressee, the God of Love, as seen in [18].

> [18] For, syth no cause of deth lyeth in this caas,
> *Yow oghte* to ben the lyghter merciable;
> Leteth youre ire, and beth sumwhat tretable.
> (*LGW* F 409-11)

3. Analysis of Other Verbs

The survey of *ouen* has found that the meanings of the verb, the subjectivity/objectivity of the statement or its grounds, and the demands of rhyme are likely to affect the choice between the impersonal and personal uses. This section deals with the other verbs, sometimes trying to applying the findings. As shown in Table 2, among the other verbs in Chaucer, *neden* usually appears in the impersonal use with one exception, while *moten* is usually used personally with four exceptions. Those exceptions will be examined individually below.

> [19] Allas, kan a man nat bithynke hym on the gospel of Seint Luc, 15, where as Crist seith that "as wel shal ther be joye in hevene upon a synful man that dooth penitence, as upon nynty and nyne rightful men that *neden* no penitence."
> (*ParsT* 700)

Chapter 3 Verbs of Obligation and Necessity   71

Citation [19] is the only example of *neden* in the personal use in my data. The citation is in Chaucer's prose, which means rhyme or metre is not likely to be taken into consideration. *Neden* is not a modal but a full verb with an NC and the 3rd-person plural Ex. There are four other examples with the same sentence structure and there the verb *neden* appears in the impersonal use. In [19] the verb is in Christ's speech quoted by the Parson, the narrator, and the judgment about the need for penitence seems more religious than personal. Therefore, the result obtained from the survey of *ouen* cannot explain this example, and the number of examples is so limited that I cannot discuss the use of *neden* thorougly.

The idea about *ouen* might be applied to [20]-[22].

[20]   "Pardee," quod oon, "somwhat of oure metal
       Yet is ther heere, though that we han nat al.
       And though this thyng myshapped have as now,
       Another tyme it may be well ynow.
       Us moste putte oure good in aventure.
       A marchant, pardee, may nat ay endure,
       Trusteth me wel, in his prosperitee.
       Somtyme his good is drowned in the see,
       And somtyme comth it sauf unto the londe." (*CYT* 942-50)

[21]   Afterward, in getynge of youre richesses and in usynge of hem, *yow moste* have greet bisynesse and greet diligence that youre goode name be alwey kept and conserved. For Salomon seith that 'bettre it is and moore it availleth a man to have a good name than for to have grete richesses.'
       (*Mel* 1636-38)

[22]   Narcisus was a bacheler
       That Love had caught in his danger,
       And in his net gan hym so strayne,
       And dyd him so to wepe and playne,
       That nede *him must* his lyf forgo.   (*Rom* 1469-73)

In [20] an alchemist speaks to his master and colleagues,

comparing their business with merchants'. In [21] Prudence is advising his husband Melibeus, quoting the words of Solomon, who is "known for his great wisdom" (*MED*, s.v. *Salomon*, n.). In [22] Narcissus' predicament is being narrated objectively. However, it is true that there are considerably more examples of the personal use in the similar situations in Chaucer.[8]

Citation [23] is from Troilus' letter to Criseyde, where he complains of her delay in returning to him. Here *moot* seems to have the epistemic meaning showing his belief about love, which is not consistent with the fact that *ouen* with the meaning does not appear in the impersonal use as mentioned in the previous section.

[23] "But for as muche as *me moot* nedes like
Al that yow liste, I dar nat pleyne moore,
But humblely, with sorwful sikes sike,
Yow write ich myn unresty sorwes soore,
Fro day to day desiryng evere moore
To knowen fully, if youre wille it weere,
How ye han ferd and don whil ye be theere;
(*Tr* 5.1352-58)

In this case, I would rather consider Denison's opinion that "modal verbs ... are 'transparent' to verbal restrictions" (1990b: 144). That means the impersonal use in question is caused not by *moot* but by *like*. His opinion is also supported by Warner (1993: 122-24). Another example is [24] below.

[24] Savour no more than *thee bihove shal*,
Reule wel thyself that other folk canst rede,
And trouthe thee shal delivere, it is no drede.   (*Truth* 5-7)

---

[8] For example, Prudence speaks to Melibeus, using *moten* with 2nd-person Exs in the personal construction, seven times.

4. Summary

Auxiliarisation as well as personalisation is instrumental in the development of *ouen*. The two phenomena can be found emerging in Chaucer, but still there are some examples of the impersonal use, sometimes with morphologically-auxiliarised *ought*, which does not prove that the personalisation is closely related to the auxiliarisation.

The choice between the impersonal and personal uses depends rather on the meanings of the verb. Some examples in Chaucer's works have the epistemic meaning and within these cases the impersonal use does not appear, which evidences the auxiliarisation. Alternatively, when it has the root meaning, the personal use seems dominant when statements or their grounds about the agent's obligation are more subjective, as typified by the examples with the 1st-person singular Ex, and the impersonal use does so when the addresser's involvement in the obligation is slighter, as typified by the examples in *as*-clauses. This idea that the addresser's attitude determines the use might explain the impersonal examples of *moten* as well, although the number of examples is limited.

Chapter 4

Verbs of Remembering and Thinking[1]

This chapter is intended as an investigation of *remembren*[2] and *thinken/thenken*. Although they are seen as similar by Ogura (1996: 29), they are not necessarily in the same semantic field. The following analyses each of the verbs in order.

1. *Remembren*

The verb *remembren* is of Old French origin and appeared in English at the beginning of the fourteenth century

---

[1] Section 1 of this chapter is based on Ohno (1998).
[2] The verb group *remembren* belongs to may include *recorden* as well, which has the meaning "To call to mind, to recall, recollect, remember" (*OED*, s.v. *record*, v.¹ †4.). *Recorden* is considered personal (*OED*, s.v. *record*, v.¹ and *MED*, s.v. *recorden*, v.) and few scholars mention the impersonal use of the verb. Higuchi (1990: 211), however, shows that two examples in Chaucer are impersonal, although he gives no example. Judging from the pattern of sentence structure in his table, two examples below seem to square with his idea:
   "Remembreth the," quod sche, "that I have gaderid and ischewid by forseide resouns that al the entencioun of the wil of mankynde, whiche that is lad by diverse studies, hasteth to comen to blisfulnesse."
   "It remembreth me wel," quod I, "that it hath ben schewed."
   "And *recordeth* the nat thanne," quod sche, "that blisfulnesse is thilke same good that men requiren, so that whanne that blisfulnesse is required of alle, that good also is required and desired of alle?"
   "It ne *recordeth* me noght," quod I, "for I have it grely alwey ficched in my memorie." (*Bo* 4 pr2.47-61)
The *MED* quotes the former as an example of a reflexive use (s.v. *recorden*, 1(b)) and the latter as that of the verb meaning "to come to the mind of (sb.)" (s.v. *recorden*, 2). But as to the latter *recordeth* it is worth noting that in line 52 *remembren* is used in the impersonal construction "It remembreth me wel," which is similar to "It ne recordeth me noght." These two verbs mean both "to remember" and "to remind" and there seems to be similarity between them.

(*OED*, s.v. *remember*, v.¹). It denotes "psychological phenomena" (T. Nakao 1972: 297). Most of the impersonal verbs in Old and Middle English became personal over a period of time. *Remembren*, however, had been used only personally by Chaucer's time, that is, by the late fourteenth century, and he began to use it impersonally as many scholars such as van der Gaaf (1904: 144-45), T. Nakao (1972: 298), and Yoshikawa (1999) put it. To borrow Burnley's phrase, the impersonal construction was "coined" (1983: 229). Miura (2007) states that this use is attributed to Jean de Meun's Old French translation of *Boece*, corresponding to Mustanoja's comment that "The late ME *me remembreth* 'I remember' ... is a calque on OF (*il*) *me remembre*" (1960: 436). There is corroborative evidence to show this. The following passage, in which the verb is impersonal, is a near translation of *Le Roman de la rose*.[3]

[1]   But — Lord Crist! — whan that *it remembreth me*
Upon my yowthe, and *on my jolitee*,
It tikleth me aboute myn herte roote.   (*WBT* 469-71)

The fact that half the examples of the impersonal construction (7 of 14 examples) appear in *Boece* might lend to the fact, although I currently have no information about the original *De Consolatione Philosophiae*.

Many scholars have pointed out the peculiarity of Chaucer's impersonal use of *remembren*,[4] but only a few comprehensive surveys of the use seem to have been made.[5] Chaucer uses the verb both personally and imper-

---

[3] Christine Ryan Hilary, who writes the explanatory notes to the *Wife of Bath's Prologue and Tale* in Benson's edition, observes that in lines 469-73 "Chaucer follows RR 12932-48 very closely" (Benson 2008: 869).
[4] Yoshikawa says, "Now we cannot deem impersonal *remembren* peculiar to Chaucer, but it may have originated with Chaucer" (1999: 62).
[5] Yoshikawa (1999) and Miura (2007).

sonally and there may be some difference between the two constructions.

The following will survey syntactic features of the impersonal and personal constructions of the verb (Section 1.1), and examine what examples in the impersonal use can say from the semantic and pragmatic aspects (Section 1.2).

1.1. Syntactic and Prosodic Features of *Remembren*

The examples of *remembren* are classified syntactically. In reference to previous chapters, the case of the Ex is the basis for the classification. There are several points to notice. Firstly, this verb has largely two groups of meanings: "to remember" and "to remind" (*OED*, s.v. *remember*, v.[1] I and II) and to the latter group belong the two examples below:

[2] ... thou recordist and *remembrist* me thise thinges yet the seconde tyme; (*Bo* 3 pr12.2-3)

[3] And this was, as thise bookes me *remembre*,
    The colde, frosty seson of Decembre. (*FranT* 1243-44)

In each of these two examples the pronoun *me* is an Ex and the subject is a reminder. Therefore these examples are classified into "Cause Subject" (CS) in this chapter.

In addition, this verb has the reflexive construction. Ogura, who investigates Old English and Middle English verbs used both impersonally and reflexively, states that it is difficult to "distinguish a reflexive construction with the subject understood from an 'impersonal' construction, when the verb form is in the 3rd pers. sg." (1991: 79). She adds that "the element order is not a crucial factor to identify a certain construction even as late as the fifteenth century" (1991: 78). In each citation listed below, the pronoun *hym* may be a dative Ex or a dative pronoun for a reflexive use:

[4] This Eneas is come to paradys
Out of the swolow of helle, and thus in joye
Remembreth *hym* of his estat in Troye.　(*LGW* 1103-05)

[5] Thanne who so that sekith sothnesse, he nis in neyther nother habite, for he not nat al, ne he ne hath nat al foryeten; but yit *hym* remembreth the somme of thinges that he withholdeth, and axeth conseile, and retretith deepliche thinges iseyn byforne ...　(*Bo* 5 m3.47-53)

Nobody mentions [4], and only the *MED* (s.v. *remembren*, v. 1d.) refers to [5], considering this example impersonal. In this chapter [4] is classified into the reflexive use on the ground that the verb *remembreth* is joined to *is come* in line 1103, and [5] into the impersonal use on the grounds that the editor uses a semicolon,[6] which marks a stronger break than a comma. Thus, [5] is worth noting in that the personal verbs *axeth* and *retrethith* follow the impersonal construction, showing the subjecthood of *hym*.

There are 10 examples of the imperative in Chaucer, which may be classified into the personal construction for the reason that in the imperative the subject *thou* or *ye* is conventional. However, they may affect the tendency of the examples with expressed Exs. Therefore they are not classified into either use.

---

[6] Concerning the punctuation in his edition, Benson (2008: xliii) says as follows:
　For many readers such [= F. N. Robinson's] punctuation detracts rather than helps, and the texts have therefore been repunctuated in a style more nearly in accord with modern usage. Middle English differs from Modern English in ways that make it impossible to use a completely modern style of punctuation ... and works intended for oral recitation naturally differ from those intended solely for reading. The editors have endeavored to provide a punctuation that is as close as possible to contemporary usage but that takes account of the nature of the texts.

When an auxiliary accompanies the verb, the auxiliary is thought "transparent to verbal restrictions" (Denison 1990b: 144) and the example is classified into either construction according to the case of the Ex.

There are syntactically ambiguous examples. Firstly, in the citations below it is difficult to tell whether the *it* is impersonal *it* or not:

[6] ... this is a thyng that greetly smerteth me whan *it* remembreth me. (*Bo* 2 pr4.5-7)

[7] "And I have schewyd that God is the same good?" "*It* remembreth me wel," quod I. (*Bo* 3 pr12.67-69)

The *it* in each citation seen above may be an impersonal *it* or may refer to the preceding clause or NP. In Chaucer a complement is usually preceded by the verb and the Ex, except for the examples of the CS use, as shown in Table 2 below as well. There are two examples in which a complement precedes the two others ("XVE") and they are both in his verse, which means the word order is necessary for rhyme. As to "*it* VE" order, three out of four examples are found in his prose, the other appearing in his verse for rhyme. It is, therefore, plausible to consider *it* in that order as an impersonal *it*. Therefore, the *it* in question is treated as impersonal *it*, and should not be considered as a complement in this chapter.

Secondly, in the quotation below it may be ambiguous whether the impersonal construction occurs with a sentential complement (SC) (finite clause) or with an implied complement (IC). However, this chapter treats this example as the construction with an IC.

[8] 'but now it *remembreth* me wel, here was I born, her wol I fastne my degree, here wol I duelle.' (*Bo* 4 m1.37-39)

1.1.1. Complement Types

Table 1 shows the frequency of *remembren* according to the complement type.

Table 1. Frequency of *Remembren* According to Complement Type

	Complement	I	P	CS	?
Chaucer	IC	5 (2)	1 (1)		
	Nominal (NC) (NP)	3 (1)	8 (1)	2 (1)	
	NC (PP)	3 (2)	10 (2)		10
	SC (non-finite)		1 (1)		
	SC (finite)	3 (0)	7 (2)		
Gower	NC (NP)		1		2
	SC (finite)		1		

NB   No example of the verb is found in Langland. The brackets itemise the number of examples in verse.

This table shows the following. Gower uses the verb with an NC or SC, and with these complements the personal use is more frequent also in Chaucer. He more frequently uses the impersonal construction with an IC, as [9] shows.

[9] Than seyde he thus: "Lo, lordes myn, ich was
Troian, as it is knowen out of drede;
And, if that *yow remembre*, I am Calkas,   (*Tr* 4.71-73)

1.1.2. Word Order and Rhyme

Next, let us examine the word order in which the verb appears.

Table 2. Frequency of *Remembren* According to Word Order

Word Order	Chaucer I	Chaucer P	CS	Gower P
EV	1 (1)	1 (1)		
it VE	4 (1)			
E refl. VX		2 (2)		
EV refl. X		10 (0)		
EVX	4 (0)	12 (4)		1
it VEX	3 (1)			
XEV			1 (1)	1
XVE			1 (0)	
VEX	2 (2)	2 (0)		

NB   The "X" refers to a complement.

Chapter 4   Verbs of Remembering and Thinking

According to Table 2, the impersonal use occurs mainly in the "*it* VE(X)" orders, especially *it remembreth me*. Concerning this fact, Masui suggests that Chaucer's fixed expressions include the impersonal use (1962: 190-91)[7] and Mair also mentions the "formulaic expressions" (1988: 216). It is safe to say that the expressions with the 1st-person Ex are frequently used, therefore making them easier to remember. In addition to those word orders, the "EVX" order has many examples of the impersonal use. However, the order is also the most common in the personal use, some of which contain reflexive pronouns.

The important point to note is that in Chaucer's verse the impersonal use appears in "*it* VE" and "XVE": the order in which the Ex comes last. Each example has the Ex in rhyme position, as in [10] and [11]. The latter is the only example in which the SC precedes both the verb and Ex.

[10]   ... "Frend, in Aperil the laste —
    As wel thow woost, if *it remembre the* —
    How neigh the deth for wo thow fownde me,
    And how thow dedest al thi bisynesse
    To knowe of me the cause of my destresse. (*Tr* 3.360-64)

[11] Mars dwelleth forth in his adversyte,
    Compleynyng ever on her departynge,
    And what his compleynt was, *remembreth me*;
    And therfore, in this lusty morwenynge
    As I best can, I wol hit seyn and synge;
    And after that I wol my leve take,
    And God yeve every wyght joy of his make! (*Mars* 148-54)

The Ex is also put in rhyme position in the "*it* VEX" order, where the X is in the next line.

---

[7] Masui quotes "if the (yow) liste", "as the (hem), etc. leste", "as hym oughte", "Me were levere" and "I had levere" (1962: 190-91). See also Masui (1964: 180-87) and Ohno (1995: 4 and 1996: 5).

82   Part I   Synchronic Variation in Chaucer's Text

[12]   But — Lord Crist! — whan that *it remembreth me*
       Upon my yowthe, and on my jolitee,
       It tikleth me aboute myn herte roote.   (*WBT* 469-71)

As Masui (1964: 46 and 50) and Oizumi and Yonekura (1994: 1283) point out, the pronouns *me* and *the* are common rhyme words. Although the number of examples is limited, it can be said that Chaucer introduced the impersonal use to *remembren* when translating *Boece* and utilised the use for rhyme in his verse.

1.1.3. Grammatical Persons of Experiencer and Clause Types

As seen in the previous chapters, strong connectivity can be found between the grammatical persons of the Ex and the two uses. The frequency of each use according to the grammatical person is tabulated below.

Table 3. Frequency of *Remembren* According to Grammatical Person of Ex

Person of Ex	Chaucer I	Chaucer P	Chaucer CS	Gower P
1st	10 (3)	6 (3)	2 (2)	0
2nd	3 (2)	10 (1)	0	1
3rd	1 (0)	11 (3)	0	1

According to this table, most examples of the impersonal construction contain the 1st-person singular Ex *me* (10 of 14 examples) in Chaucer. The examples of the personal construction, by contrast, prefer a 2nd- or 3rd-person Ex (29 of 35 examples). In other words, the impersonal and personal uses are closely related to the 1st-person Ex and to a 2nd- or 3rd-person Ex respectively. The same tendency, that is Tani's "person hierarchy" (1997), has been found in the case of *liken* and *listen*.

Next, let us examine the clause types in which *remembren* appears.

Table 4. Frequency of *Remembren* According to Clause Type and Grammatical Person of Ex in Chaucer

Clause	Impers.			Pers.			CS
	Ex1	Ex2	Ex3	Ex1	Ex2	Ex3	Ex1
main	7	1	1	3	7	7	
if		2			2		
whan	2			2		1	
that	1				1	1	
as				1			1
ascaunce					1		
whoso					1		
for							1

NB The "Ex1", "Ex2", and "Ex3" stand for 1st-, 2nd-, and 3rd-person Exs respectively.

Table 4 gives some connection between the impersonal use with 2nd-person Exs and an *if*-clause, but the number of examples is inadequate to support this opinion.

1.2. Semantic and Pragmatic Aspects

This section will focus on the semantic and pragmatic aspects of the two uses in Chaucer, on the basis of the findings of the previous section.

1.2.1. Impersonal Construction

There are 14 examples of the impersonal use in Chaucer, eight of which are found in *Boece*, most of which "are clearly inspired by the occurrence of almost identical impersonal constructions in Jean de Meun's Old French translation" (Miura 2007: 223). With the remaining examples, five of the six are in Chaucer's verse, four of which having the Ex in rhyme position. Apart from rhyme, Section 1 has found that the choice of the impersonal use may be influenced by the Ex in the 1st person singular, the IC type, and an *if*-clause.

When the examples with the Ex *me* are considered from the viewpoint of Ex being either positive or negative, it can be said that the impersonal construction is an indirect or polite way of expressing the speaker's own feelings or thoughts, as stated in Chapter 1.

[13] Thanne seide I thus: "O norysshe of alle vertues, thou seist ful sooth; ne I mai noght forsake the ryght swyfte cours of my prosperite (that is to seyn, that prosperite ne be comen to me wonder swyftli and sone); but this is a thyng that greetly smerteth me whan it *remembreth me*. For in alle adversites of fortune the moost unzeely kynde of contrarious fortune is to han ben weleful." (*Bo2* pr4.1-9)

[14] The thridde cause that oghte moeve a man to Contricioun is drede of the day of doom and of the horrible peynes of helle. For as Seint Jerome seith, "At every tyme that *me remembreth* of the day of doom I quake;
(*ParsT* 158-59)

In each of the quotations [13] and [14], what comes across the speakers' mind is horrible and dreadful to them and they do not want to be reminded of it. In other words, the impersonal use in those quotations seems to express the negativity or unwillingness of the speakers.

Next, there are three examples with a 2nd-person Ex, one appearing in *Boece* and the other two in *Troilus and Criseyde*, as shown in [15] and [16]. It is noteworthy that the verb appears in an *if*-clause.

[15] And [Troilus] gan his look on Pandarus up caste
Ful sobrely, and frendly for to se,
And seyde, "Frend, in Aperil the laste —
As wel thow woost, *if it remembre the* —
How neigh the deth for wo thow fownde me,
And how thow dedest al thi bisynesse
To knowe of me the cause of my destresse. (*Tr* 3.358-64.)

[16] Than seyde he thus: "Lo, lordes myn, ich was
Troian, as it is knowen out of drede;
And, *if that yow remembre*, I am Calkas,
That alderfirst yaf comfort to youre nede,

>   And tolde wel how that ye shulden spede.
>   For dredeles, thorugh yow shal in a stownde
>   Ben Troie ybrend and beten down to grownde. (*Tr* 4.71-77)

In [15], after listening to Pandarus' plan for Troilus' assignation with Criseyde, Troilus is speaking to Pandarus in a grateful and friendly manner. In [16] Calkas, who has abandoned his city, is ingratiating himself with the Greeks. The speakers do not compel the addressee(s) to remember things, which they are going to rehearse next. In [15] *if it remembre the* seems to convey Troilus' affection and politeness towards his friend Pandarus. In [16] Calkas uses *if that yow remembre* to bring himself to the attention of the Greeks. In other words, the phrase conveys his (fake) friendliness towards them.

1.2.2. Personal Construction

When considering Chaucer's peculiar use of the impersonal use of *remembren*, the interpretation of the personal use may sound strange. There are, however, some examples which may be counterpoints to the impersonal use.

Firstly, when the verb accompanies the 1st-person Ex *me* (six examples),[8] there is one example in which the verb follows *kan* that could be considered as an auxiliary.

>   [17] For never sith that I was born,
>   Ne no man elles me beforn,
>   Mette, I trowe stedfastly,
>   So wonderful a drem as I
>   The tenthe day now of Decembre,
>   The which, as *I kan* now *remembre*,
>   I wol yow tellen everydel. (*HF* 59-65)

Along with the meaning of *kan*, the verb shows the Ex's active process of recalling to mind his dream, as cited by

---
[8] There is no example with the 1st-person plural Ex found in Chaucer or in Gower.

the *MED* (s.v. *remembren*, v. 1a. (c)). The idea of the Ex's active process can explain the personal construction in [18].

> [18] A ful gret savour and a swote
> Me toucheth in myn herte rote,
> As helpe me God, whan *I remembre*
> Of the fasoun of every membre. (*Rom* 1025-28)

Here, the narrator is offering a great compliment on the beauty of the lady called "Beaute" with a detailed description of her appearance. Also in this case, the process of remembering *the fasoun of every membre* is agreeable to the Ex and the activeness of the Ex can be seen.

There is another example with the Ex *me* in *Boece*.

> [19] But I wolde that thou woldest answere to this: Remembrestow that thow art a man?"
> *Boece.* "Whi schulde *I* nat *remembren* that?" quod I.
> (*Bo* 1 pr6.54-58)

Answering the question in the previous line, this sentence is a negative interrogative, which implies a strong affirmative. That means that the focus[9] of utterance is placed on the Ex's act of remembering.

Next, there is one example in which the verb co-occurs with a non-finite clause.

> [20] Allas, Lyno, whi art thow so unkynde?
> Why ne *haddest thow remembred* in thy mynde
> To taken hire, and lad hire forth with the? (*LGW* 2716-18)

In this case the verb with a non-finite clause refers "to necessary actions and whether they are done or not" (Carter and McCarthy 2006: 516) as in Present-day Eng-

---

[9] The term "focus" refers to "the centre ... of their [= speakers'] communicative interest" (Crystal 2003: 183).

lish (PDE). The sentence is also a negative interrogative. Therefore, the personal use means the emphasis on the Ex.

Finally, there are two examples with the 2nd-person singular Ex in an *if*-clause. Unlike [15] or [16], however, they are a usual conditional clause, not conveying the speaker's politeness towards the addressee, as shown in [21].

> [21] And *yif thou remembrest* wel the kende, the maneris, and the desserte of thilke Fortune, thou shalt wel knowe that, as in hir, thow nevere ne haddest ne hast ylost any fair thyng. (*Bo* 2 pr1.21-25)

So far, Section 1 has analysed the data and suggested the interpretations of impersonal and personal examples based on the premise of the mental attitude and politeness of the Ex.

2. *Thinken/Thenken*

In Chaucer's time there are two morphologically-similar verbs: *thinken* and *thenken*. The former usually has the impersonal use, meaning "To seem, to appear" (*OED*, s.v. *think*, v.¹), and the latter means "To conceive in the mind, exercise the mind; To call to mind, take into consideration; To be of opinion, deem, judge, etc." (*OED*, s.v. *think*, v.²) in the personal use. However, "in ME., owing to the fact that both *þync-* and *þenc-* gave ME. *þink-*, and both *þúht* and *þóht* appeared in ME. as *þouȝt, thought*, they became confused and finally fell together" (*OED*, s.v. *think*, v.¹). Therefore, this chapter deals with both verbs, although they are under different headings in glossaries and concordances of Chaucer's works.

As for the data on Chaucer, this chapter uses Benson's concordance, which cites all examples of the verbs according to their uses.[10] In contrast, for those of Gower and Langland it is necessary to classify the examples into the two uses because examples in the two uses are mixed under one heading of their concordances. Since this section follows the same criteria for the classification as the previous section, even if they are categorised into either use in the concordances, this section does not classify some examples into either use. Therefore, as a matter of convenience (and in order to avoid confusion), the word *think* is used for the two verbs. Thus, the number of examples in each use is: 175 in the impersonal use and 162 in the personal use in Chaucer; 135 in the impersonal use and 200 in the personal use in Gower; 38 in the impersonal use and 18 in the personal use in Langland.

2.1. Syntactic and Prosodic Features of *Think*

This section discusses the syntactic and prosodic features of the impersonal and personal uses in *think*. As said above, unlike the other verbs dealt with in this book, all examples of *think* are already grouped into the two uses in Benson's concordance. Its meanings in the two uses, therefore, are also dealt with in relation to those features.

2.1.1. Complement Types

Firstly, the complement types in which *think* appears are considered. As in PDE, the verb often takes an NC and an adjectival or nominal phrase which adds information

---

[10] This classification is based on the case of the Ex, resulting in an incoherent situation in which the verb in the examples with almost the same complement can be classified differently.
    [a]   This Phebus gan aweyward for to wryen,
          And *thoughte* his sorweful herte brast atwo. (*MancT* 262-63)
    [b] Hir *thoughte* hir cursed herte brast atwo. (*MLT* 697)
Examples [a], in which *thought* is juxtaposed with the personal verb *gan + for to wryen*, and [b] are classified as personal and impersonal respectively. All of these kinds of expressions, except [a], have a dative Ex and are classified as impersonal.

about the NC, and, apart from the Ex, it sometimes takes the adjectival phrase only. For instance, in [22] the verb *thynketh* co-occurs with the adjective *best*.

[22]   "I seye this: be ye redy with good herte
       To al my lust, and that I frely may,
       As *me best thynketh*, do yow laughe or smerte,
       And nevere ye to grucche it, nyght ne day?   (*ClT* 351-54)

In this case, an NC may be omitted, but these kinds of examples are classified into the IC type. The data are tabulated according to the complement types listed below.

Table 5. Frequency of *Think* According to Complement Type

Complement	Chaucer		Gower		Langland	
	I	P	I	P	I	P
IC	52 (50)	27 (26)	31	18	26	1
NC (NP)	29 (27)	26 (22)	23	26	8	7
NC (PP)		17 (15)	3	15		1
SC (non-finite)	7 (7)	22 (11)	8	95		9
SC (finite)	87 (81)	70 (64)	70	46	4	

This table shows that the impersonal use is more frequent in the examples with an IC while the personal use is more frequent in those with an NC (PP) or SC (non-finite). The first point may have relevance to the clause types and the grammatical persons of the Ex, and will be treated later.

As for the second point, when the verb takes an SC (non-finite), the verb often conveys the Ex's intention, decision, or plan to do something, as in [23].

[23] But for to tellen forth in special
     Of this kynges sone of which I tolde,
     And leten other thing collateral,
     Of hym *thenke I* my tale forth *to holde*,
     Both of his joie and of his cares colde;   (*Tr* 1.260-64)

However, when the impersonal construction appears with an SC (non-finite), the examples almost always take a phrase adding information about the action expressed by the SC as well. In this case, the verb shows the Ex's perception or understanding of the action, as in [24].

[24] "But tel me now, syn that *the thynketh so light*
To changen so in love ay to and fro,
Whi hastow nat don bisily thi myght
To chaungen hire that doth the al thi wo?   (*Tr* 4.484-87)

Although the personal use is dominant in examples with an NC (PP), there are a few examples of the impersonal construction in Gower. In this case the verb co-occurs with an adjectival or nominal phrase which adds information about the (pro)noun in the PP (*MED*, s.v. *thinken*, v.(1) 9.).

[25] So that *him thenketh of a day
A thousand yer*, til he mai se
The visage of Penolope,   (*CA* 4.220-22)

In [25], for instance, the verb takes the PP *of a day* and the nominal phrase *A thousand yer* which adds information about *a day*.

When the verb takes an NC (NP), it often takes an adjectival or nominal phrase which adds information about the NP, as in [26].

[26] Ye knowe ek that in forme of speche is chaunge
Withinne a thousand yeer, and wordes tho
That hadden pris, now *wonder nyce and straunge
Us thinketh hem*, and yet thei spake hem so,
And spedde as wel in love as men now do;   (*Tr* 2.22-26)

In this case, the verb conveys the Ex's perception of the NP, and the impersonal use demonstrates its overwhelming lead: 89 per cent in Chaucer, 90 per cent in Gower, and 100 per cent in Langland.

In contrast, with an NC (NP) only, the personal use is dominant: 81 per cent in Chaucer, 83 per cent in Gower, and 54 per cent in Langland. The examples include those in which the verb is juxtaposed with another verb. Many of the impersonal examples have the NC which can, strictly speaking, be a predicative NP which adds information about the implied complement, like *wonder* in [27].

[27]   Whan I had red thys tale wel
And overloked hyr everydel,
Me thoghte wonder yf hit were so,
For I had never herd speke or tho
Of noo goddes that koude make
Men to slepe, ne for to wake,
For I ne knew never god but oon.   (*BD* 231-37)

There are two examples with *this* as an NC which refers to the following clause, as in [28].

[28] *Me thynketh this*, sith that Troilus is here,
It were good, if that ye wolde assente,
She tolde hireself hym al this er she wente. (*Tr* 2.1629-31)

In connection with the complement types, the types of moods in an SC (finite) have also been examined. Both the indicative and subjunctive moods appear in both the impersonal and personal examples. Therefore, the types are not a key factor in the choice of either construction.

2.1.2. Clause Types

Next, let us look at clause types. Before the classification, I will refer to examples without a conjunction which are separated from another clause by commas or dashes,[11] as

---

[11] Punctuation is put in by the editors of the contemporary editions and not by the authors. However, as long as this research is based on those editions, I will follow the editors.

in [29], or which are inserted between quoted internal speeches, as in [30].

[29] And by the same resoun, *thynketh me*,
   I sholde to the knotte condescende,
   And maken of hir walkyng soone an ende.   (*SqT* 406-08)

[30]   When I had seen al this syghte
   In this noble temple thus,
   "A, Lord," *thoughte I*, "that madest us,
   Yet sawgh I never such noblesse
   Of ymages, ne such richesse,
   As I saugh graven in this chirche;   (*HF* 468-73)

These kinds of examples are classified as "parenthetical".

Table 6 indicates that the impersonal use is dominant in *as*- and parenthetical clauses in all the three poets. There are 12 personal examples in Chaucer's parentheticals, with all of them as in [30].

Table 6. Frequency of *Think* According to Clause Type

Clause	Chaucer I	Chaucer P	Gower I	Gower P	Langland I	Langland P
al(thogh)	1 (1)	1 (1)				
as	35 (32)	4 (2)	24	7	13	
for	12 (11)	8 (8)	8	11		
for whi	1 (1)					
if	3 (3)	3 (1)	1	2		1
lest	1 (1)	1 (1)				
main	69 (65)	97 (87)	64	107	11	9
parenthetical	16 (16)	12 (12)	5	1	12	
relative	13 (11)	8 (7)	3	22		4
syn	1 (1)					
that	18 (18)	15 (9)	18	15	1	
ther as / wher(as)	2 (2)		3	3		
tho(u)gh			2		1	
whan	2 (2)	6 (4)	3	13		1
what(as evere)		6 (5)	4	6		2
wheither / whider	1 (1)					1
wherefore		1 (1)				
wherof				12		
whil				1		

Chapter 4   Verbs of Remembering and Thinking   93

In more detail, a correlation between those clauses and the complement types the verbs take there is noted.

Table 7. Complement Types in *As*- and Parenthetical Clauses

	Complement	Chaucer I	Chaucer P	Gower I	Gower P	Langland I
as-clause	IC	34	1	16	5	13
	NC (NP)	1		1		
	NC (PP)			1		1
	SC (non-finite)		1	1	1	
	SC (finite)		1	6		
parentheticals	IC	14	12	5	1	10
	NC (NP)					2

Table 7 shows the close correlation between the two clauses and the IC type. A couple of typical examples in Chaucer are [29] and [31].

[31] And over the gate, with lettres large iwroughte,
There were vers iwriten, *as me thoughte*,
On eyther half, of ful gret difference,
Of which I shal yow seyn the pleyn sentence: (*PF* 123-26)

The function of the clauses will be discussed in Section 2.2.

2.1.3. Word Order and Rhyme

How influential are word order and the demands of rhyme in the choice between the impersonal and personal uses? Firstly, Table 8 shows the frequency of word order in which *think* appears.

Table 8. Frequency of *Think* According to Word Order

Word Order	Chaucer I	Chaucer P	Gower I	Gower P	Langland I	Langland P
EV	26 (25)	12 (11)	23	17	23	1
it VE	6 (6)		1			
V *to* E	1 (0)					
VE	17 (17)	15 (15)	1			
CEV					1	
ECV	1 (1)		1		2	
EVC	1 (1)		5			
EVX	90 (84)	90 (70)	70	160	2	2
EXV		3 (3)		1		2
it VEX			1			
VEX	2 (2)	18 (18)		5		1
XEV	1 (1)	20 (17)	4	12	7	12
XVE	1 (1)	1 (1)		1		
CEVX	1 (1)		1			
CEXV					2	
CVEX	1 (1)		1			
ECVX	1 (1)					
EVCX	3 (3)		1			
EVXC	11 (10)	3 (3)	7	2		
EXVC			2			
it VECX	1 (1)		4			
it VEXC			2			
VEXC			1			
X *it* VEC			2			
X *to* ECV	1 (1)					
XCEV				1	1	
XECV			1			
XEVC	6 (6)		3			
XVEC	4 (3)		4			

NB The letter "C" indicates an adjectival or nominal phrase which adds information about the X.

This table gives an indication of Chaucer's peculiar use of the "VE" order. This order appears both in the personal and impersonal uses, but when rhyme is taken into consideration, the personal examples, 12 of which are like [30] above, can be ignored. All the 17 examples of the impersonal use appear in an *as-* or parenthetical clause. Ten of them have the Ex in rhyme position, nine of them having the 1st-person singular Ex *me*, as in [29].[12] This is

---

[12] There are examples in which *me thinketh/thought* seems to be used

a rhyme-clause as Masui points out (1964: 184). The same is equally true of the "*it* VE" order.

Table 8 also shows the dominance of either use in the "EV", "VEX", "XEV", "EVXC", "XEVC", and "XVEC" orders. In the "EV" order, not the Ex yet the verb sometimes exists in rhyme position: 12 out of 36 examples in Chaucer's verse and 11 out of 40 examples in Gower. This type includes [31] above. That fact, however, does not seem to have anything to do with the choice between the two constructions.

In the "XEV" order, the X is usually an NC (NP) or SC (non-finite), with which the personal use tends to be dominant as seen in Table 5. In the "VEX" order, Gower always has an SC (non-finite), while Chaucer has an SC (finite) as well. The other orders, which contain a C, show that the verb *think* means the Ex's perception or understanding of the X, and the verb is commonly used in the impersonal. In this way, the correlation between these orders and the two uses is dependent on the complement types and the verb meanings.

2.1.4. Grammatical Persons of Experiencer

Finally, I investigate the grammatical persons of the Ex. Table 9 shows the frequency of the three verbs in each grammatical person of the Ex.

---

for alliteration in *Piers Plowman*. In many of them the verb appears in parentheticals as shown below:
   And as thei wente by the weye, of Dowel carped,
   Thei mette with a mynstral, as *me* tho thoughte.   (*PPl* 13.221-22)
According to Burrow and Turville-Petre, "One very characteristic feature of Langland's verse is the alliteration of an unstressed syllable before a non-alliterating stressed syllable" (1996: 61).

96   Part I   Synchronic Variation in Chaucer's Text

Table 9. Frequency of *Think* According to Grammatical Person of Ex

Person of Ex	Chaucer I	Chaucer P	Gower I	Gower P	Langland I	Langland P
1st	92 (89)	47 (42)	52	82	34	7
2nd	8 (7)	17 (10)	4	3	0	1
3rd	75 (69)	98 (86)	79	115	4	10

This table shows that in Chaucer and Langland the impersonal use is more frequent with a 1st-person Ex and the personal with a 2nd- or 3rd-person Ex. This is the similar tendency as that discussed in Section 1.1.3 above; that is to say, the person hierarchy. In Gower, to the contrary, the personal use is more frequent with a 1st-person Ex. According to Table 10, an SC (non-finite) more frequently co-occurs with a 1st-person Ex in Gower, while an IC does in Chaucer and Langland.

Table 10. Complement Types with 1st-person Ex

Complement	Chaucer I	Chaucer P	Gower I	Gower P	Langland I	Langland P
IC	34	7	17	5	21	
NC (NP)	15	5	3	8	8	4
NC (PP)		9		6	1	1
SC (non-finite)		10		57		3
SC (finite)	43	16	32	6	4	

Thus, the complement types are more associated with the impersonal and personal uses, and furthermore with the meanings of the verb, than the grammatical persons of the Ex.

In association with the grammatical persons of the Ex, there is an interesting example found in Chaucer.

> [32]   "Madame," quod he, "how *thynke ye* herby?"
> "How that *me thynketh*?" quod she. "So God me speede,
> I seye a cherl hath doon a cherles dede.   (*SumT* 2204-06)

In [32] *think* is used personally with the 2nd-person Ex *ye* and impersonally with the 1st-person Ex *me*. This may be explained by the person hierarchy, but as for line 2204, according to Manly and Rickert (1940: VI 231), the earliest manuscript, the Hengwrt, has the dative *yow*, while about 40 per cent of the later manuscripts, including the Ellesmere, have the nominative *ye*. Concerning editions, Skeat (1919) adopts *yow*, but F. N. Robinson (1957) and Benson (2008) adopt the Ellesmere model. When the meanings of the verb are taken into consideration, each form can reflect the Ex's mental attitude towards the story the speaker told. Benson has no comment on why he chose *ye*, but following his edition, I can interpret this passage as follows: after telling "an odious meschief" (l. 2190) he has received, the speaker really wants the listener to sympathise keenly with him.[13]

So far Section 2.1 has explained that in addition to rhyme, the complement types and the clause types are closely related to the personal and impersonal constructions.

2.2. Pragmatic Aspect of Parenthetical *Think*

This section considers a pragmatic aspect of parenthetical *think*, especially with a 1st-person singular Ex. As seen in Tables 6 and 7, the verb is sometimes used parenthetically: with(out) a conjunction *as* and with an IC and sometimes a pronominal adverb *so*. These phrases are used in the present tense, as in [29] and [33] and in the past tense, as in [31] and [34].

> [33] Wher shal I seye to yow welcom or no,
>   That alderfirst me broughte unto servyse
>   Of love — allas! — that endeth in swich wise?
>
>   "Endeth than love in wo? Ye, or men lieth,
>   And alle worldly blisse, *as thynketh me*.   (*Tr* 4.831-35)

---

[13] Ohno (2013) discusses this passage from a cognitive perspective.

[34]   "And whan I had my tale y-doo,
       God wot, she acounted nat a stree
       Of al my tale, *so thoghte me*. (*BD* 1236-38)

During the process of the confusion of *thinken* and *thenken* and the impersonal-to-personal transition, there occurred "the gradual specialization of impersonal THINK in the first person towards the end of Middle English period" (Palander-Collin 1999: 160), ending up with the form *methinks* which is still contained in contemporary dictionaries. According to Palander-Collin's research of the *Helsinki Corpus*, however, the specialisation can be seen in the fifteenth century, as Table 11 shows.

Table 11. Frequencies of 1st Person Singular as Compared to Other Persons with Different Uses of *Think* in Middle English (excerpt from Palander-Collin (1999: 161-62))

		IMPERSONAL		PERSONAL			
		opinion		opinion		'have in mind'	
1350-1420	1sg.	14	(21%)	2	(11%)	15	(23%)
	oth.	53	(79%)	17	(89%)	49	(77%)
	Total	67	(100%)	19	(100%)	64	(100%)
1420-1500	1sg.	50	(72%)	4	(12%)	8	(14%)
	oth.	19	(28%)	30	(88%)	51	(86%)
	Total	69	(100%)	34	(100%)	59	(100%)

This phenomenon has been dealt with by many scholars, often in terms of grammaticalisation. According to Hopper and Traugott, grammaticalisation "is usually thought of as that subset of linguistic changes whereby a lexical item or construction in certain uses takes on grammatical characteristics, or through which a grammatical item becomes more grammatical" (2003: 2). A grammaticalised form is then called a pragmatic marker, which "is defined as a phonologically short item that is not syntactically connected to the rest of the clause (i.e., is parenthetical), and has little or no referential meaning but serves pragmatic or procedural purposes" (Brinton 2008: 1). Recently, Brinton says, "Following Quirk *et al.* (1972: 778) in *A Grammar*

Chapter 4 Verbs of Remembering and Thinking

of Contemporary English, I will refer to these clausal pragmatic markers [= "parenthetical items of a clausal nature, such as *I mean, I see*, or *you know*" (1-2)] as 'comment clauses'" (2008: 2). She classifies clausal pragmatic markers[14] as follows (2008: 2):

(a) first-person pronoun + present-tense verb/adjective: *I think, I suppose, I guess, I reckon, I fear, I hope, I hear, I feel, I understand, I admit, I see, I'm sure, I'm convinced, I'm afraid*;
(b) second-person pronoun + present-tense verb/adjective: *you know, you see*;
(c) third-person pronoun + present-tense verb/adjective: *it seems, they say, they allege, one hears*;
(d) conjunction + first-/second-/third-person pronoun + present-tense verb/adjective: *as I'm told, as I understand (it), as you know, so it seems, as everybody knows*;
(e) imperative verb: *look, say, listen, say, mind you, mark you*; and
(f) nominal relative clause: what's more, *what's more {surprising, annoying, strange*, etc.}, *what annoys me*.

Although she says, "Unlike non-clausal pragmatic markers, comment clauses ... arise primarily in the EModE and LModE periods" (2008: 2), Chaucer, Gower, and Langland have clauses which belong to categories (a) and (d). This section, therefore, will deal with parenthetical *think* both from the viewpoint of the personal and impersonal uses and from the viewpoint of comment clauses.

---

[14] According to Brinton (2008: 246-53), there are several studies of syntactic origin of clausal pragmatic markers, and Akimoto (2010: 16) summarised them as below.
   A. Matrix clause hypothesis
   B. Parenthetical analysis
   C. Other syntactic sources
      (a) Imperative matrix clause
      (b) Adverb/relative clause
      (c) Interrogative clause or tags
According to them, neither of them is conclusive (Brinton 2008: 246-53 and Akimoto 2010: 16-17).

2.2.1. Types of Parentheticals

As seen in 2.1.2 above, the personal use, found in Chaucer and Gower, has the limited variation of form and use: usually *tho(u)ght(e) I* inserted between quoted internal speeches, as in [30], and the only one example of *I thenke* found in Gower.

> [35] Forthi, if it you bothe liste,
> My doghter Thaise be youre leve
> *I thenke* schal with you beleve
> As for a time; and thus I preie,   (*CA* 8.1294-97)

It can be said that those clauses are inserted into the middle of another clause. However, according to Brinton's classification, the [30] type is not a clausal pragmatic marker, although it may be parenthetical, and therefore the type is excluded from the subsequent research.

The impersonal use has a wider variation in word order, tense, conjunction, co-occurring adverb, and position. In addition to Ex + *think* ([29]), types with a conjunction *as* ([31] and [33]) and with a pronominal adverb *so* ([34]), one more type is observed, as in [36] and [37].

> [36] "Hooste," quod I, "ne beth nat yvele apayd,
> For oother tale certes kan I noon,
> But of a rym I lerned longe agoon."
> "Ye, that is good," quod he; "now shul we heere
> Som deyntee thyng, *me thynketh by his cheere.*"
>   (*Thop* 707-11)

> [37] Ac on a May morwenynge on Malverne Hilles
> Me bifel a ferly, *of Fairye me thoghte.*   (*PPl* P.5-6)

In [36] *by his cheere* shows the speaker's criterion in saying *deyntee*, and in [37] *of Fairye* is additional information to the aforementioned *a ferly*. However, when considering Brinton's definition of a comment clause above, this section excludes this type, confining to the types illustrated by [29], [31], [33], [34], and [35].

2.2.2. Positions of Parentheticals

Palander-Collin, dealing with a few corpora such as the *Helsinki Corpus*, "looked at different sentence structures with METHINKS (METHOUGHT) and I THINK (I THOUGHT)" (1999: 165). She pays attention to the positions of Ex + *think* in a sentence and concludes that "towards Early Modern English METHINKS (METHOUGHT) started to behave more and more like adverbials" (1999: 166), showing Table 12.

Table 12. Possible Sentence Structures with *Methinks* (*Methought*) [=I] and *I Think* (*I Thought*) [=P] in *Helsinki Corpus*. (excerpt from Palander-Collin (1999: 165))

	medial		final		AS-clause	
	I	P	I	P	I	P
M4 (1420-1500)	6	0	2	0	4	0
E1 (1500-1570)	5	2	1	1	0	1
E2 (1570-1640)	1	9	3	0	0	1
E3 (1640-1710)	6	16	2	4	0	3

In her wake, this section will focus on the positions of parenthetical *think*. In this case, since "In initial position, the status of such forms [= *I think* or *you know*] is syntactically indeterminate between matrix clauses (with *that* deleted) and true parentheticals" (Brinton 2008: 12), the medial and final positions will be treated. In [29], [31], and [35] a parenthetical appears in the medial position, and in [33] and [34] it appears in the final position.

Table 13 shows the similar tendency as the M4 period of Table 12.[15]

---

[15] There is no need to go into further consideration of the extent of grammaticalisation, which would carry us far away from the purpose of this paper. For further information of this topic, see Y. Nakao (2010).

Table 13. Positions of Parenthetic *Think* + 1st-Person Singular Ex

Tense		medial		final	*as*-clause	
		I	P	I	I	P
Chaucer	Present	3		1 (1)	10	
	Past	2		2 (1)	10	
Gower	Present	3	1		2	1
	Past	1			6	
Langland	Present	5			8	
	Past	1		1	5	

NB   The figures in brackets itemise the number of example with *so*.

The parentheticals appear both in present and past tense forms. As for this, Palander-Collin states (1999: 166):

> The existence of separate present and past tense forms seems to provide the first counter-evidence against the adverbial nature of METHINKS (METHOUGHT). But because the origins of the phrase are in any case verbal, it should not perhaps be so surprising that initially this sort of dichotomy remains.

According to her, the numbers of METHINKS (in the present tense) and METHOUGHT (in the past tense) are 29 and 21 in the M4 period of the *Helsinki Corpus*. In the data on Chaucer and his contemporaries, the parenthetical impersonal *think*, excluding the examples in an *as*-clause, occurs 13 and 7 times in the present and past tenses respectively.

2.2.3. Function of Parenthetical *Think* in Chaucer

Let us look more closely at the function of parenthetical *think* in Chaucer. There are seven types according to conjunction, tense, and the person of the Ex, and the frequency of each type is tabulated below.

Table 14. Types of Parenthetical *Think*

Conj.	Tense	Person of Ex	Type	Chaucer I	Gower I	P	Langland I
-	pres.	1st	(i)	4	3	1	5
	past	1st	(ii)	4	1		2
		others	(iii)	4	1		1
as	pres.	1st	(iv)	10	2	1	8
		others	(v)	3			
	past	1st	(vi)	10	6		5
		others	(vii)	10	2	1	

Before proceeding to the main theme of this section, Types (iii), (v), and (vii) are looked at briefly. They have a 2nd- or 3rd-person Ex, which means that the speaker is talking about another person's point of view or perception of the proposition stated near the clause. Examples with a 3rd-person Ex occur in narrative as in [38] and [40].

[38] Therwith, whan he was war and gan biholde
How shet was every wyndow of the place,
As frost, *hym thoughte*, his herte gan to colde;
(*Tr* 5.533-35)

[39] Lordynges, this question, thanne, wol I aske now,
Which was the mooste fre, *as thynketh yow*?
Now telleth me, er that ye ferther wende.
I kan namoore; my tale is at an ende. (*FranT* 1621-24)

[40] Thus twies in his slepyng dremed hee;
And atte thridde tyme yet his felawe
Cam, *as hym thoughte*, and seide, "I am now slawe.
(*NPT* 3012-14)

Citation [39] is the only example with the 2nd-person Ex. After telling a story about "*gentillesse* and troth" (Benson 2008: 895), the Franklin, the narrator, is asking the other pilgrims a question. The answer may vary, and so he adds *as thynketh yow* to demand their impressions.

Then, let us look at the types with the 1st-person singular Ex. Firstly, the types without the conjunction *as* are dealt with. Type (i) has such examples as below:

[41] I sey nat that she ne had knowynge
What harm was, or elles she
Had koud no good, *so thinketh me*. (*BD* 996-98)

[42]   The knotte why that every tale is toold,
If it be taried til that lust be coold
Of hem that han it after herkned yoore,
The savour passeth ever lenger the moore,
For fulsomnesse of his prolixitee;
And by the same resoun, *thynketh me*,
I sholde to the knotte condescende,
And maken of hir walkyng soone an ende. (*SqT* 401-08)

To Type (ii) belong the following examples:

[43]   "And whan I had my tale y-doo,
God wot, she acounted nat a stree
Of al my tale, *so thoghte me*. (*BD* 1236-38)

[44] So fair it was that, trusteth wel,
It semede a place espirituel,
For certys, as at my devys,
Ther is no place in paradys
So good inne for to dwelle or be
As in that gardyn, *thoughte me*. (*Rom* 649-54)

For many scholars, these kinds of parentheticals seem to express evidentiality: "the speaker's or writer's point of view, opinion, attitude or subjective truth" (Palander-Collin 1999: 26). Quotations [41] and [43] are spoken by the same speaker, who is talking about his deceased love. The pronominal adverb *so* refers to a proposition whose truth is not ascertained by the speaker.[16] By using the parentheticals with the adverb, he tries to offer his interpretation of the situations whatever the facts. In example [42], following a common saying (Benson 2008: 894

---

[16] See Yasui et al (1983: 561-63).

Chapter 4   Verbs of Remembering and Thinking   105

and 1036; Whiting 1968: P408), the narrator is saying that it is right time to come down to the main point of his story. Here the parenthetical *thynketh me* helps to add the individuality of his judgement.

In [44], like in [43], the parenthetical is used to express the narrator's perception, but it is noteworthy that it is used in describing the things in the narrator's dream. It seems to imply his subtle uncertainty about them. Researching the impersonal use in the writings of the anchorite, Julian of Norwich, Yoshikawa says as follows (2008: 146):

> her [= Julian's] use of the impersonal 'me thought' intimates that she is not fully confident in her understanding of this dream because it was supernaturally shown to her; it lies beyond human understanding.

Although it is not as religious as Julian's writing, [44] is in the allegorical dream poetry, *The Romaunt of the Rose*. This point is expounded in Chapter 5.

Next, the types with *as* is treated. Type (iv) includes the following:

[45] Poverte a spectacle is, *as thynketh me*,
   Thurgh which he may his verray freendes see.
                                          (*WBT* 1203-04)

[46] Wher shal I seye to yow welcom or no,
   That alderfirst me broughte unto servyse
   Of love — allas! — that endeth in swich wise?

   "Endeth than love in wo? Ye, or men lieth,
   And alle worldly blisse, *as thynketh me*.   (*Tr* 4.831-35)

To Type (vi) belong the examples below:

[47] He koude rooste, and sethe, and broille, and frye,
   Maken mortreux, and wel bake a pye.

> But greet harm was it, *as it thoughte me*,
> That on his shyne a mormal hadde he. (*GP* 383-86)

[48] And over the gate, with lettres large iwroughte,
There were vers iwriten, *as me thoughte*,
On eyther half, of ful gret difference,
Of which I shal yow seyn the pleyn sentence: (*PF* 123-26)

In [45] the parenthetical is used when the speaker creates a metaphor[17] which may sound quirky and needs a detailed description. Citation [46] is from Criseyde's speech, who is devastated to know that she has to leave Troilus. The passage adjacent to the parenthetical is incomprehensible under normal circumstances, although it is a sign of her desperation. In these ways, these types of parentheticals are often used to introduce rather erratic ideas. At the same time, as in [46], they may be uttered in order to make the speakers themselves accept the ideas.

In the past tense, parentheticals seem to function as those in Type (ii) do. In [47] *as it thoughte me* shows the narrator's personal feeling, and in [48] *as me thoughte* is used when the narrator describes the things in his dream.

Thus, although different in form, Types (i) and (ii) and Types (iv) and (vi) seem similar in function. They show the speakers' individual perception or judgement and their uncertainty about the proposition stated before.

3. Summary

As for *remembren*, an imaginable cause of the impersonal use is a calque on an Old French expression which Chaucer introduced when translating *Boece*. The use is utilised for rhyme in his verse, but at the same time the use can express the Ex's mental attitude. The impersonal and per-

---

[17] The *OED* cites this as the first example of the figurative use of *spectacle* (s.v. *spectacle*, n.¹ 6. c.). For this idea, see Benson's note (2008: 874).

sonal constructions have a closer relation to a 1st-person Ex and to a 2nd- or 3rd-person Ex, respectively. This "person hierarchy" attests that the impersonal and personal uses show mental attitudes of the Ex.

As for *thinken/thenken*, although the "person hierarchy" can be observed, the complement types are more associated with the impersonal and personal uses, and furthermore with the meanings of the verb. At the same time, the impersonal use is dominant in *as-* and parenthetical clauses. The analysis of these clauses with the 1st-person Ex *me* has found a tangible sign of their use as comment clauses in the medial and final positions, although they have some variations in word order, tense, conjunction and co-occurring adverb. They show the speakers' individual perception or judgement and their uncertainty about the proposition stated before.

Chapter 5

Verbs of Dreaming[1]

There are two verbs that refer to dreams in Chaucer's works: *meten* and *dremen*. *Meten* had existed since the Old English period and *dremen* appeared in the thirteenth century. After their coexistence, the former disappeared in the middle of the seventeenth century (*OED*, s.v. *mete*, v.[2] and *dream*, v.[2]). Concerning Chaucer's works, van der Gaaf observes that "The two verbs are quite synonymous, and are used indiscriminately" (1904: 77). However, it is worth noting that no occurrence of *dremen* appears in *The Book of the Duchess*, while the verbs appear equally in the other works, as Table 1 below shows. In the poem, which deals with the death of a duchess, *dremen* may be avoided, because the word may remind the audience or readers of the other word *dream* which means "joy, pleasure, gladness, mirth, rejoicing" (*OED*, s.v. *dream*, n.[1]), although they are generally thought to be different words.

Table 1. Frequency of *Meten* and *Dremen* in Chaucer's Works

Work	meten	dremen
Rom	2	2
BD	9	0
HF	7	5
PF	6	2
Bo	0	2
Tr	8	5
LGW	2	0
CT	13	6
Ven	0	1

These two verbs had been used impersonally, but after the emergence of the personal use in the fourteenth century, the impersonal use began to disappear around 1400 (van

---

[1] This chapter is based on Ohno (1999) and (2007b).

der Gaaf 1904: 75 and T. Nakao 1972: 297). Chaucer and his contemporaries each have their own use of *meten* and *dremen*. In Chaucer's works, composed in the midst of the transition, the two verbs are used both personally and impersonally. Also in Langland's *Piers Plowman* (*PPl*) they are used both personally and impersonally, but only personally in Gower's *Confessio Amantis* (*CA*). Considering the diachronic aspect of the transition, this may be because "Gower is more advanced" as van der Gaaf (1904: 76) says. However, there may be another way to understand the choice of a particular use in Chaucer's works.

The two verbs are often used especially in Chaucer's dream poems, whose framework of narrative is different from that of poems which came before him, such as *King Horn* and *Havelok the Dane* and of his contemporaries' works such as *PPl* and *CA*. The narrator of Chaucer's early poems "uses self-conscious presentation as a means to establish a new form of narrative" while earlier poets "adopt the perspective of an omniscient narrator" and his contemporaries "achieve a remarkable perspectival art by the manipulation of viewpoint" (Edwards 1989: 46-47). Chaucer also often uses dreams as a means to begin the stories, as Masui (1976: 83-84) points out. Such a narrative technique may be reflected in the use of *meten* and *dremen* within his works, and if so, the use requires close attention.

Many syntactic studies have been devoted to the transition from the impersonal to the personal construction,[2] and several scholars point out the semantic difference between the personal and impersonal uses. For instance, Fischer and van der Leek argue that in the personal use "the animate experiencer is nominative subject and therefore the initiator of the 'action'" whereas in the imperson-

---

[2] Some leading scholars are van der Gaaf, Elmer, Fischer and van der Leek, and Ogura.

al use "the experiencer, bearing dative or accusative case, is only passively related to what is expressed in the verb" (1983: 351). However, the impersonal and personal uses of a particular verb, especially of *meten* or *dremen*, have not been closely investigated from the combined view of syntax and semantics.

This chapter, dealing mainly with Chaucer's examples and with others' listed below for comparison, will analyse the syntactic and prosodic features of the verbs in the impersonal and personal uses (Section 1), and prove that the semantic and furthermore pragmatic functions are correlated with those syntactic features, and finally endure reasonable interpretations of the two uses (Section 2). The data for this study come from (1) "all the undoubtedly Chaucerian works in the Riverside Chaucer" (Benson 1993: ix), (2) *PPl*, (3) *CA*, (4) *Matter of England* and *Breton Lays* in French and Hale (1964), and (5) the examples dated 1300-1399 in the *MED* (s.v. *meten* and *dremen*) and the *OED*. The data (1)-(3) are mainly examined, (4) and (5) used as reference.

Before initiating the main issue, let us review the consensus on what the personal use is and what the impersonal use is in the case of the dream verbs. An example like [1], which has a nominative Ex, is classified as personal:

[1] ... "This nyght thrie,
To goode mot it turne, of yow *I mette*." (*Tr* 2.89-90)

An example like [2], which has an oblique Ex, is classified as impersonal:

[2] "O Seinte Marie, benedicite!
What eyleth this love at me
To bynde me so soore?
Me dremed al this nyght, pardee,
An elf-queene shal my lemman be
And slepe under my goore. (*Thop* 784-89)

Examples like [3], where the case of the Ex is obscure, and [4], where the verb is in a non-finite form, are not classified as personal or impersonal.

>[3] *The lovere met* he hath his lady wonne.   (*PF* 105)

>[4] Or yf that spirites have the myght
>To make folk to *dreme* a-nyght;   (*HF* 41-42)

However, examples like [5] and [6] are classified as personal: in [5] the Ex *no man elles* is compared with the nominative *I*, and in [6] the Ex *many wightes* is followed by the verb in the plural form.

>[5] Ne *no man elles* me beforn,
>*Mette*, I trowe stedfastly,
>So wonderful a drem as *I*   (*HF* 60-62)

>[6] For this trowe I, and say for me,
>That dremes signifiaunce be
>Of good and harm to *many wightes*
>*That dremen* in her slep a-nyghtes
>Ful many thynges covertly
>That fallen after al openly.   (*Rom* 15-20)

The use of such an example as [7], where an auxiliary occurs, is decided by the case of the Ex.

>[7] I hope, ywis, to rede so som day
>That *I shal mete* som thyng for to fare
>The bet, and thus to rede I nyl nat spare.   (*PF* 697-99)

As Denison says, in Old English "an auxiliary + impersonal verbal group behaves exactly like a finite impersonal, its argument structure and case assignment being entirely determined by the impersonal verb" (1990b: 145). He points out the same phenomenon in Chaucer (1990b: 163), adducing the following example:

[8] *Hym wolde thynke* it were a disparage
   To his estaat ... (*ClT* 908-09).

There is still disagreement in interpretation about a few examples like [9] and [10]. Benson (2008: 1241) considers [9] impersonal and Davis et al (s.v. *dremed*) consider both [9] and [10] impersonal.

[9]   "O Seinte Marie, benedicite!
   What eyleth this love at me
      To bynde me so soore?
   Me dremed al this nyght, pardee,
   An elf-queene shal my lemman be
      And slepe under my goore. (*Thop* 784-89)

[10]   That it was May me thoughte tho —
   It is fyve yer or more ago —
   That it was May, thus *dremed me*,
   In tyme of love and jolite,
   That al thing gynneth waxen gay,
   For ther is neither busk nor hay
   In May that it nyl shrouded ben
   And it with newe leves wren. (*Rom* 49-56)

The *MED* (s.v. *dremen*, v.(2) 1(c)), however, observes that the two examples take a reflexive construction with the oblique pronoun *me* used for a reflexive and so *dremen* is used personally. In [11] the pronoun *Hym* denotes *That oon of hem* in the previous line and this sentence seems to take a reflexive construction, although it is not clear whether *That oon of hem* is the nominative subject.

[11] That oon of hem, in slepyng as he lay,
   Hym mette a wonder dreem agayn the day. (*NPT* 3077-78)

Such an example of *meten*, however, cannot be found elsewhere in Chaucer and as far as all the data are concerned, there is one more example of this kind in the A-text of *PPl*, example [12], which is cited in the *OED* (s.v. *marvellous*, adj. a.). However, the pronoun *I* in the example is omitted in Schmidt's edition (1997: 126), which is based on the B-text.

[12] Þe Meruiloste Meetynge Mette *I* me þenne
(*PPl* (A) IX 59 (*OED*))

Resolution of this issue is beyond this chapter, so I will follow the views of Benson and Davis et al. The pronoun *Hym* in [11] can be considered not a reflexive but a resumptive pronoun of the Ex *That oon of hem*, and so the example can be classified as impersonal. Kerkhof states that "Pronouns of the third person, both singular and plural, often serve to resume a subject preceding in the shape of a noun" (1982: 235), quoting the following example:

[13] The oon of you, al be hym looth or lief,
    He moot go pipen in an yvy leef; (*KnT* 1837-38)

1. Syntactic and Prosodic Aspects

This section investigates the syntactic and prosodic features of the personal and impersonal uses of *meten* and *dremen*.

1.1. Complement Types and Word Order

The verbs take various sentence structures: with an implied (IC), nominal (NC), or sentential complement (SC). Tables 2-7 show the frequency of the verbs in each structure in the works examined in this chapter.

Chapter 5 Verbs of Dreaming

Table 2. Complement Types and Word Order in Chaucer

Complement		Word Order	meten I	meten P	?	dremen I	dremen P	?
IC		EV	4	1			1	
		VE				1	3	
NC	(NP)	EVX	3	3 (1)			3	
		EXV		1				
		XEV	1	7	13 (1)		1	6
		XVE						
	(PP)	EVX		1			5	
		XEV		1			1	
SC (finite)		EVX	8	3		1	1	
		VEX		1				

NB The brackets itemise the number of the examples in prose. The symbol "?" indicates "Not Classified".

Table 3. Complement Types and Word Order in Langland

Complement		Word Order	meten I	meten P	?	dremen I	dremen P	?
IC		EV	1			1		
NC	(NP)	EVX	1					
		XVE	2		1			1
	(PP)	XEV				1		
SC (finite)		EVX	1	1				

Table 4. Complement Types and Word Order in Gower

Complement	Word Order	meten P	?	dremen P	?
IC	EV	3			
NC (NP)	EVX	1	2	1	3
	XEV	5		2	
SC (finite)	EVX	4		3	

Table 5. Complement Types and Word Order in *Matter of England* and *Breton Lays*

Complement	Word Order	meten P	?	dremen I
NC (NP)	XEV	1	1	
	XVE			2

116   Part I   Synchronic Variation in Chaucer's Text

Table 6. Complement Types and Word Order in *OED* and *MED* (dated 1300-1349) (except the examples tabulated in the tables above)

Complement		Word Order	*meten* I	*meten* P	*meten* ?	*dremen* I	*dremen* P	*dremen* ?
IC		EV	3	2			1	
NC	(NP)	EVX	4	1				
		EXV						
		XEV	2	4	8			2
	(PP)	EVX		1			1	
		XEV					1	
SC (finite)		EVX	4	2				

Table 7. Complement Types and Word Order in *OED* and *MED* (dated 1350-1399) (except the examples tabulated in the tables above)

Complement		Word Order	*meten* I	*meten* P	*meten* ?	*dremen* I	*dremen* P	*dremen* ?
IC		EV					1	
		VE	1					
NC	(NP)	EVX		2			1	
		EXV			5			5
		XEV		2			3	
		XVE refl.		1				
	(PP)	EVX		1				
SC (finite)		EVX		1			2	

Referring to the diachronic change of the uses, Tables 6 and 7 show a slight decrease of the impersonal use from the first to the last half of the fourteenth century.

From Table 2 it is clear that in Chaucer's works the impersonal use is more frequent with an IC as in [14] and with an SC (finite) as in [15].

> [14] And, as *me mette*, they sate among
>   Upon my chambre roof wythoute,   (*BD* 298-99)
>
> [15]   But as I slepte, *me mette* I was
>   Withyn a temple ymad of glas,   (*HF* 119-20)

Conversely, the personal use is greater with an NC, especially with an NC (PP) as in [16].

[16] And eek I seyde *I mette* of hym al nyght, (*WBT* 577)

The personal use of *meten* and *dremen* can be found also in the structure beginning with an NP, which is a relative pronoun.

[17] "This man gan fallen in suspecioun,
Remembrynge on his dremes that *he mette*, (*NPT* 3032-33)

This tendency is also shown by the examples from the *OED* and the *MED* (Tables 6 and 7). However, I cannot find such a tendency in Langland (Table 3); the impersonal use predominates in all the three structures. In Gower the personal use predominates. From the variety outlined above, it is obvious that different writers have different perspectives towards the personal and impersonal uses.

1.2. Grammatical Persons of Experiencer

There is one additional point worth noting in the syntactic features: the grammatical persons of the Ex. This section deals with Chaucer, Langland, and Gower.

Firstly, Table 8, showing the frequency of *meten* and *dremen* by the person of the Ex, indicates that those examples with the 1st-person singular Ex have a clear tendency towards the impersonal use and those with a 2nd- or 3rd-person Ex to the personal.

Table 8. Grammatical Persons of the Ex in Chaucer

Person of Ex	Complement	*meten* I	*meten* P	*dremen* I	*dremen* P
1st (singular)	IC	4	1	1	
	NC	3	6		1
	SC	7	2	1	
2nd	NC		1		2
3rd	IC				4
	NC	1	6		7
	SC	1	2		1

Next, as Table 9 shows, all the six examples of the impersonal use in Langland have the 1st-person Ex, *me*, regardless of which complement type they take.

Table 9. Grammatical Persons of the Ex in Langland

Person of Ex	Complement	*meten* I	*meten* P	*dremen* I	*dremen* P
1st (singular)	IC	1			
	NC	3		1	
	SC	1	1		
3rd	IC				1

Finally, Table 10 displays Gower, who is said to be "more advanced" (van der Gaaf 1904: 46), uses the verbs personally with the 1st-person singular Ex as well as a 2nd- or 3rd-person Ex.

Table 10. Grammatical Persons of the Ex in Gower

Person of Ex	Complement	*meten* P	*dremen* P
1st (singular)	IC	1	
	NC	1	1
	SC	2	2
2nd	NC	1	
3rd	IC	2	
	NC	4	2
	SC	2	1

Concerning all the data dealt with in this chapter, 75 per cent of the examples of the impersonal use have the 1st-person singular Ex and 69 per cent of the examples of the personal use a 2nd- or 3rd-person Ex.

An important point to note in Table 8, is that the three examples with a 2nd-person Ex, [18]-[20], are in the personal use, though they have very few occurrences.

[18] "Certes also *ye men*, that ben erthliche beestes, *dremen* alwey your bygynnynge, (*Bo* 3 pr3.1-2)

[19] Certes this dreem, which *ye han met* to-nyght,
Cometh of the greete superfluytee
Of youre rede colera, pardee, (*NPT* 2926-28)

[20] "Peraunter, ther *thow dremest* of this boor, (*Tr* 5.1282)

This may be so because the examples have an NC, which has a marked trend towards the personal use, as seen before. Contrarily, the examples can also be explained from the viewpoints of the meaning and function of the verbs. In [18] the verb *dremen* denotes an active process of thinking: "to imagine". In [19] and [20] the addressee's action of dreaming expressed by the verbs in question, is repeated after the details of his dream have been described and the focus[3] of utterance seems to be placed on the action.

1.3. Clause Types

One more point of syntactic features must be clarified: clause types in which the two verbs appear. Table 11 reveals that an *as*-clause has only the impersonal use, as in [21].

---

[3] The term "focus" refers to "the centre ... of their [= speakers'] communicative interest" (Crystal 2003: 183).

120   Part I   Synchronic Variation in Chaucer's Text

Table 11. Frequency of Clause Types and Grammatical Persons of Ex in Chaucer and Langland

	Clause	Chaucer I	Chaucer P	Langland I	Langland P
meten	main	10 (3)	7 (2)	4	1 (1)
	as	3		1	
	parenthetical	1			
	but		1		
	for-why		1		
	relative	1	6		
	that	1	3		
dremen	main	1	8 (1)	1	1
	relative		4		
	that	1	3		

NB   The figures in brackets itemises the number of main clauses following a subordinate clause.

All the four examples have the 1st-person Ex, which is closely associated with the impersonal use.

> [21] In suche wordes gan to pleyne
> Dydo of hir grete peyne,
> As *me mette* redely —
> Non other auctour alegge I.   (*HF* 311-14)

The table also reveals that in Chaucer, as stated in Section 1.1 above, a relative clause almost always has the personal use, even with the 1st-person Ex, as in [22].

> [22] O Thought, that wrot al *that I mette*,
> And in the tresorye hyt shette
> Of my brayn, now shal men se
> Yf any vertu in the be
> To tellen al my drem aryght.   (*HF* 523-27)

The relative clause specifies the dreamer, and the focus of utterance may be placed on the act of dreaming, the verb being used in the personal use. That is worth noting and will be dealt with in Section 2.

1.4. Rhyme

Finally, let us consider the aspect of rhyme in Chaucer. From Table 12 it is clear that Exs are scarcely utilised for rhyme although the verbs may sometimes be.

Table 12. Frequency of Ex or Verb in Rhyme

		Chaucer I	Chaucer P	Gower P
dremen	Ex in Rhyme	1 / 2	1 / 14	0 / 6
	Verb in Rhyme	0 / 2	1 / 14	0 / 6
meten	Ex in Rhyme	0 / 16	0 / 18	0 / 13
	Verb in Rhyme	1 / 16	7 / 18	8 / 13

NB The figures after the slash denote the total number of examples classified into either use.

The two examples in which the Ex is in rhyme position are quoted below:

[23]   That it was May me thoughte tho —
         It is fyve yer or more ago —
         That it was May, thus *dremed me*,
         In tyme of love and jolite,
         That al thing gynneth waxen gay,   (*Rom* 49-53)

[24] Hym thoughte his dreem nas but a vanitee.
     Thus twies in his slepyng *dremed hee*;
     And atte thridde tyme yet his felawe
     Cam, as hym thoughte, and seide, "I am now slawe.
                                          (*NPT* 3011-14)

In [23] the Ex *me* rhymes with *jolite* in the following line, and in [24] the Ex *hee* with *vanitee* in the preceding line.

So far, I have seen that in Chaucer the personal and impersonal uses of *meten* and *dremen* are largely concerned with the syntactic features of the verbs. The impersonal use is associated with an IC or SC, the 1st-person singular Ex, and an *as*-clause, while the personal use with an NC and a relative clause. Now it is necessary to examine how closely those features are linked with the function and meaning. In the next section the personal and impersonal uses of the verbs are investigated from semantic and pragmatic points of view.

2. Semantic and Pragmatic Aspects

This section discusses the relation between the sentence structures of *meten* and *dremen* and their meaning and function in Chaucer's works. It proves that the semantic and pragmatic function can give interpretations peculiar to the impersonal and personal uses.

2.1. Complement Type 1: IC

Concerning the type with an IC, both the personal and impersonal uses have five examples in Chaucer's works, as Table 2 indicates above. All the examples of the impersonal use have the 1st-person singular Ex and function parenthetically outside the proposition in which a dream is described. They are found only in Chaucer's works.

[25] And, *as me mette*, they sate among
　　　Upon my chambre roof wythoute,　(*BD* 298-99)

[26]　That it was May me thoughte tho —
　　　It is fyve yer or more ago —
　　　That it was May, *thus dremed me*,
　　　In tyme of love and jolite,
　　　That al thing gynneth waxen gay,
　　　For ther is neither busk nor hay
　　　In May that it nyl shrouded ben
　　　And it with newe leves wren.　(*Rom* 49-56)

Some examples, as in [26], have a pronominal adverb *thus* that refers to the proposition describing a dream. Like *so*, whose function is explained by Yasui et al (1983: 561-63), *thus* refers to a proposition whose truth is not ascertained by the speaker. As a result, the verb indicates a spontaneous and passive process of thinking. In addition, it can be suggested that when the 1st-person Ex plus *meten* or *dremen* is used parenthetically, it is syntactically free and somewhat grammaticalised,[4] expressing the speakers' mental attitude towards the propositional content, i.e. towards the details of their own dream, rather than describing the cognitive act of dreaming. Specifically, the 1st-person parentheticals very likely function as pragmatic markers expressing epistemic modality. The parentheticals without *thus*, as in [25], become more epistemic and the focus of utterance is placed on the propositional content more clearly.[5]

This opinion is inspired by the pragmatic studies on verbs such as *gessen*, *trowen*, *witen*, *semen* and *thinken* by Palander-Collin and Brinton. Especially, Brinton argues that such phrases as *I gesse* are "not merely metrical tags ... or a convenient rhyme" (1996: 263) but, as epistemic parentheticals, express the speakers' attitude towards what they are speaking of. Although the verbs in her study are in the present tense and *meten* and *dremen* treated here are in the past tense, it is reasonable to say that *meten* and *dremen* may have attained some epistemic force but not as much as the verbs Brinton deals with.

---

[4] Brinton summarises the definitions of the term "grammaticalisation", as follows (1996: 51):
 grammaticalization is the development of fully grammatical forms (function words, clitics, and inflections), as well as of "more grammatical" forms such as derivational affixes, from independent lexical items (see Hopper—Traugott 1993: 4-6). Another view of grammaticalization, however, argues that grammatical markers develop from the fixing of discourse functions.
 Here in this chapter, the term "grammaticalised" is used in the latter sense.

[5] Concerning the syntactic development of the 1st-person epistemic parentheticals, Brinton (1996: 252) states that the example with a pronominal adverb *so* belongs to Stage II and the example with a conjunction *as* to Stage III. This means the latter is more advanced in the process of grammaticalisation.

All the parentheticals in Chaucer's works are in the impersonal use with the 1st-person singular Ex. As far as my corpus is concerned, there is no 2nd-person parenthetical. This may be natural because it is not likely that the speaker reports to the addressee what the addressee dreamt, although the speaker may repeat the addressee's dream after it has been told. As Palmer says, it is "not normal to tell others what they are doing" (1986: 222). Only one 3rd-person parenthetical is found in Gower, who uses the verbs only personally, as shown in [27].

> [27] And with that priente, *as he tho mette*,
> Upon the queenes wombe he sette
> A Seal, and goth him forth his weie.   (*CA* 6.2149-51)

It is natural that the speakers should use more epistemic expressions when telling what they have experienced in their sleep, than when repeating others' dreams. As to the narrator of Chaucer's early poems, Edwards suggests (1989: 47):

> he uses self-conscious presentation as a means to establish a new form of narrative, one based on a sense of poetic indeterminacy. The poems are constituted within the dreamer's imagination and memory and enacted through an authorial voice with a wide range of tones. ... the narrator's presentation of himself reminds us, as Clemen observes, that we are given "impressions, not facts" (116). The narrator speaks "as me thoght," as he has seen and now remembers.

It should be noted that *meten* and *dremen* with a 1st-person Ex co-occur with the impersonal use of *thinken*, which was dealt with in Section 2 of Chapter 4. *Me thought* is often used parenthetically in *PPl* as well as in Chaucer's works as examples [28] and [29] show.

> [28]   That it was May *me thoughte tho* —
> It is fyve yer or more ago —

That it was May, *thus dremed me*,
In tyme of love and jolite,
That al thing gynneth waxen gay,
For ther is neither busk nor hay
In May that it nyl shrouded ben
And it with newe leves wren.   (*Rom* 49-56)

[29] The merveillouseste metels *mette me* thanne
That ever [wight dremed] in world, as I wene.
A muche man, *as me thoughte*, lik to myselve,
Cam and called me by my kynde name.   (*PPl* 8.68-71)

From these examples, it is clear that these three verbs share some similarities in their semantic and pragmatic aspects, as seen in Section 2 of Chapter 4.

Among the examples of the personal use, the following is worth noting.

[30] That after tymes of the yer, by kynde,
Men dreme, and that th'effect goth by the moone.
(*Tr* 5.376-77)

[31] 'For youres is alle that ever ther ys
For evermore, myn herte swete!
And never to false yow, but *I mete*,
I nyl, as wys God helpe me soo!'   (*BD* 1232-35)

In these citations, the verbs *dremen* and *meten* are not used in a parenthetical and do not refer to the dream the Ex actually dreamt, either. The verbs, in the present tense, indicate the human cognitive act of dreaming. Thus, it is safe to say that the verbs do not bear epistemic modality which may be connected with the impersonal use.

2.2. Complement Type 2: NC

Regarding Type 2, the personal use has 23 examples compared to four examples of the impersonal in Chaucer's works. Several examples of the personal use have *dremen* denoting an active mental act: "to imagine."

[32] But natheles, yet gan she hym biseche,
Although with hym to gon it was no fere,
For to ben war of *goosissh poeples* speche,
That dremen thynges whiche as nevere were, (*Tr* 3.582-85)

In the other examples, especially the examples where *meten* and *dremen* are in a relative clause introduced by the NP, as in example [33], the clause specifies the dreamer and the focus of utterance is placed on the act of dreaming, as seen in Section 1.3 above.

[33] O Thought, that wrot *al that I mette*,
And in the tresorye hyt shette
Of my brayn, now shal men se
Yf any vertu in the be
To tellen al my drem aryght. (*HF* 523-27)

As seen in Table 11, in Chaucer and Langland, almost all the examples in a relative clause are in the personal use, which can be explained by the restrictive feature of the clause.

At least as far as Chaucer's works are concerned, when Type 2 occurs, the dream is often detailed in the neighbouring passages of the story. For instance, [33] is included in the *Proem* (ll. 509-28), which is followed by the detailed description of the dream. It seems that in this structure, the focus of utterance is placed on the action expressed by the verbs concerned, rather than on the details of the dream. For another instance, [34] has *meten* with an NP in line 3078 and is followed by *hym thought* with an SC describing the man's dream.

[34] But herkneth! To that o man fil a greet mervaille:
That oon of hem, in slepyng as he lay,
Hym mette a wonder dreem agayn the day.
Hym thoughte a man stood by his beddes syde,

And hym comanded that he sholde abyde,
And seyde hym thus: 'If thou tomorwe wende,
Thow shalt be dreynt; my tale is at an ende.'
(*NPT* 3076-82)

There are some examples where *meten* and *dremen*, in the present or future tense, indicate a cognitive act of dreaming. They are used personally.

[35] I hope, ywis, to rede so som day
That *I shal mete* som thyng for to fare
The bet, and thus to rede I nyl nat spare. (*PF* 697-99)

[36] *Men dreme* alday of owles and of apes,
And of many a maze therwithal;
Men dreme of thyng that nevere was ne shal.
(*NPT* 3092-94)

Three of four examples of the impersonal have the 1st-person singular Ex, which helps to make the expression more epistemic than a 2nd- or 3rd-person Ex, as [37] shows, although the examples used personally with the 1st-person Ex, prevail in number as is seen in [35] and Table 8.

[37] Yet shoulde he fayle to rekene even
The wondres *me mette* in my sweven. (*BD* 441-42)

2.3. Complement Type 3: SC

Finally, Type 3 has nine examples of the impersonal use and seven of the personal in Chaucer's works. As to the impersonal use, in eight examples, the verbs concerned are used with the 1st-person Ex *me* in order to describe the speaker's own dream.

[38] *Me dremed* al this nyght, pardee,
An elf-queene shal my lemman be
And slepe under my goore. (*Thop* 787-89)

[39] *Me mette* how I lay in the medewe thoo,
To seen this flour that I so love and drede;
And from afer com walkyng in the mede
The god of Love, and in his hand a quene,
And she was clad in real habit grene.
. . .
Therwith *me thoghte* his face shoon so bryghte
That wel unnethes myghte I him beholde;
And in his hand *me thoghte* I saugh him holde
Twoo firy dartes as the gledes rede,
And aungelyke hys wynges saugh I sprede.
(*LGW* F210-14, 232-36)

As in Type 1 ([28] and [29]), this structure also co-occurs with *me thought* ([39]) and the focus of utterance seems to be placed on the clause relating the dream, and the verbs concerned are likely to function like epistemic markers outside the clause.

As seen in Table 8 above, three examples of the personal use have a 3rd-person Ex. One example, which is in lines 3139-40 in [40], is a negative interrogative.

[40] Lo Cresus, which that was of Lyde kyng,
Mette he nat that he sat upon a tree,
Which signified he sholde anhanged bee?
Lo heere Andromacha, Ectores wyf,
That day that Ector sholde lese his lyf,
She dremed on the same nyght biforn
How that the lyf of Ector sholde be lorn,
If thilke day he wente into bataille. (*NPT* 3138-45)

In this case the negative interrogative, which implies a strong affirmative, shows that the focus of utterance is placed on the Ex's act of dreaming as well as on the details of the dream. It is safe to say that the case is true also in lines 3143-45. These two examples, therefore, are used where the speaker exemplifies the idea that people previously dream what will happen in the future.

3. Summary

Different writers make different choices between the personal and impersonal uses of *meten* and *dremen* even if they are contemporary. In Chaucer's works, from the viewpoint of syntax, the personal use predominates when the verbs take an NC, especially a relative pronoun, or a 2nd- or 3rd-person Ex. To the contrary, the impersonal use predominates when the verbs take an IC in parentheticals, an SC or the 1st-person Ex. From semantic and pragmatic points of view, when the details of a dream are described, the impersonal use shows the Ex's epistemic modality towards the content of the dream. By contrast, the personal use frequently occurs when the focus of utterance seems to be placed on the act of dreaming expressed by the verbs in question, with the dream detailed elsewhere in the story. The personal use always appears when *dremen* means "to imagine".

From all the findings, I can conclude the following. When the focus of utterance is placed on the proposition in which the details of a dream are described, the verbs concerned tend to be used epistemically with the 1st-person singular Ex in parentheticals or in the Ex + V + SC (finite) structure, showing the speaker's uncertainty about the detail. As a result, the subjecthood of the Ex is restrained or put in the background, and the verbs become impersonal. In this case, the Exs dreamt not of their own will but involuntarily. Contrarily, when the focus of utterance is placed on the proposition in which the act of dreaming is described, or when *dremen* denotes an active and volitional process of thinking, the subjecthood of the Ex is brought forward and the verbs frequently become personal, especially in the Ex + V + NC structure. In this way, in Chaucer's works the personal and impersonal uses of *meten* and *dremen* allow their distinctive interpretations.

Summary of Part I[1]

Thus far, Part I has involved surveys examining 17 verbs which utilise the impersonal use. Now given are summaries of their frequency in the personal and impersonal uses by the complement type and the person of the Ex.

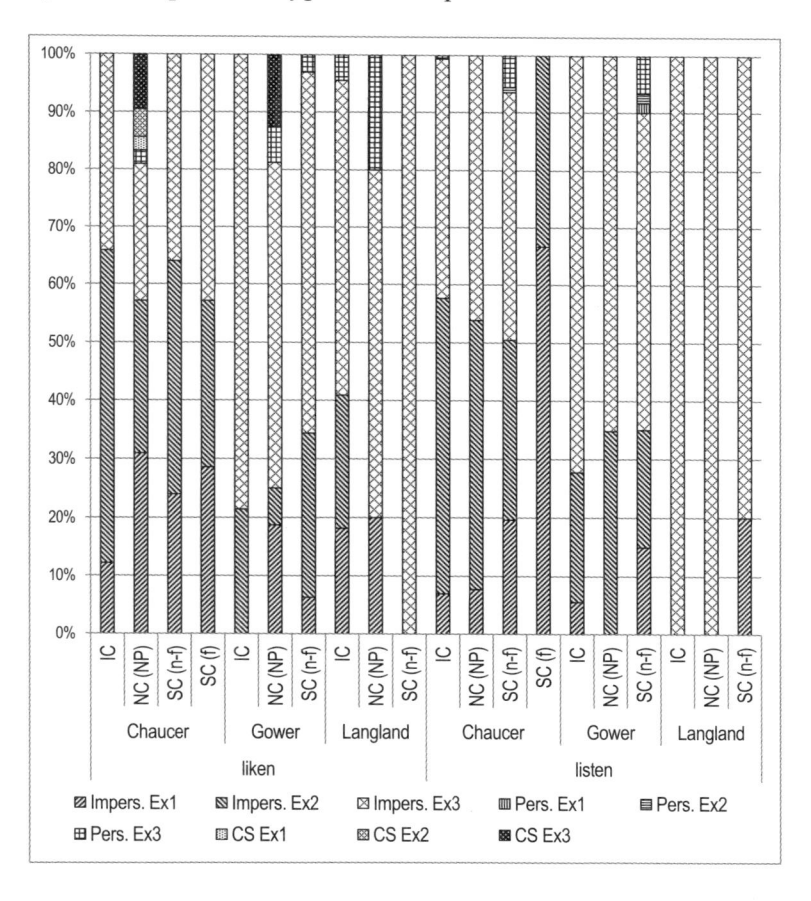

[1] This summary is also based on Ohno (2010).

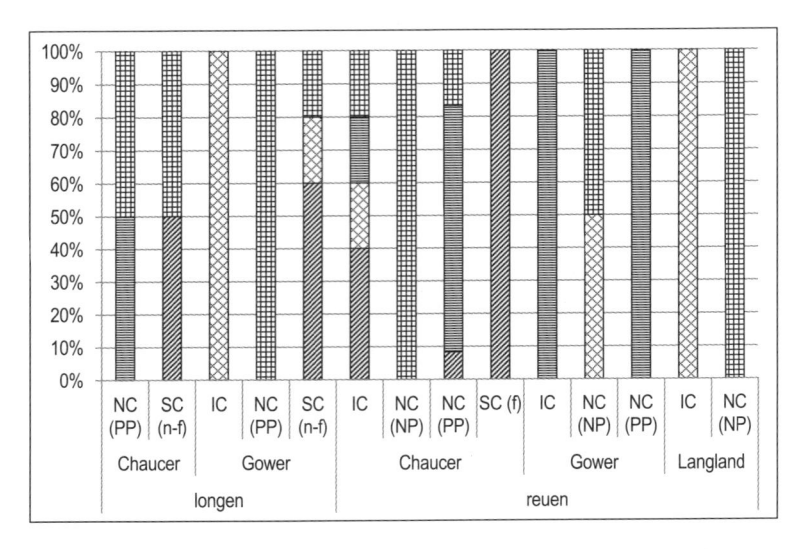

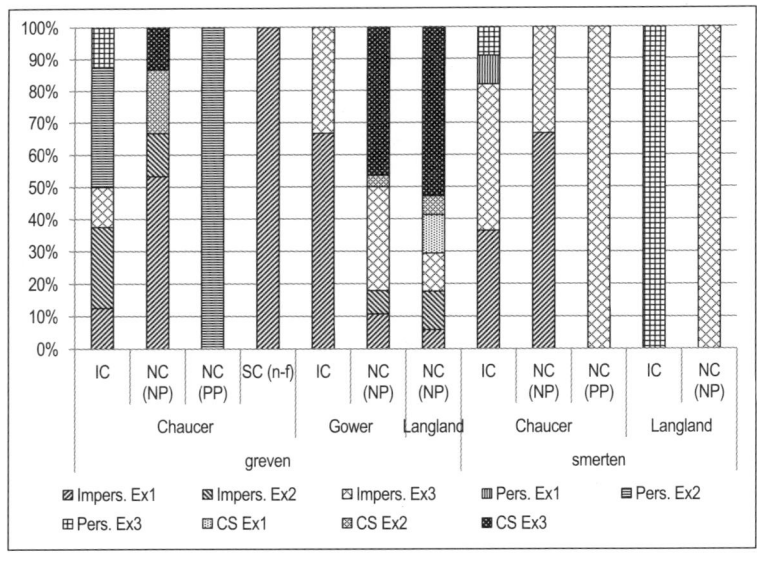

132   Part I   Synchronic Variation in Chaucer's Text

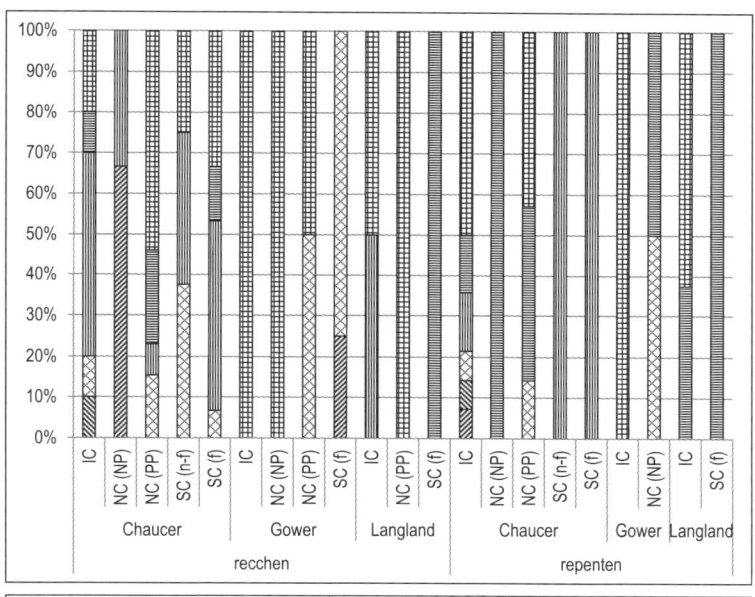

Summary of Part I 133

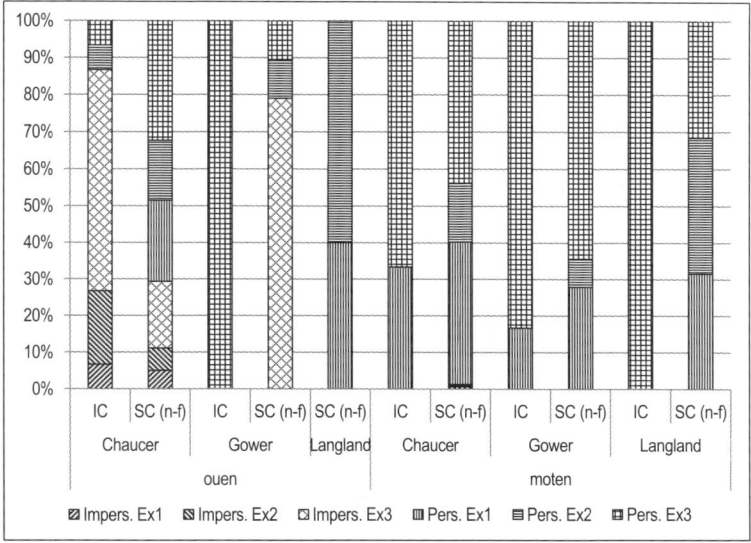

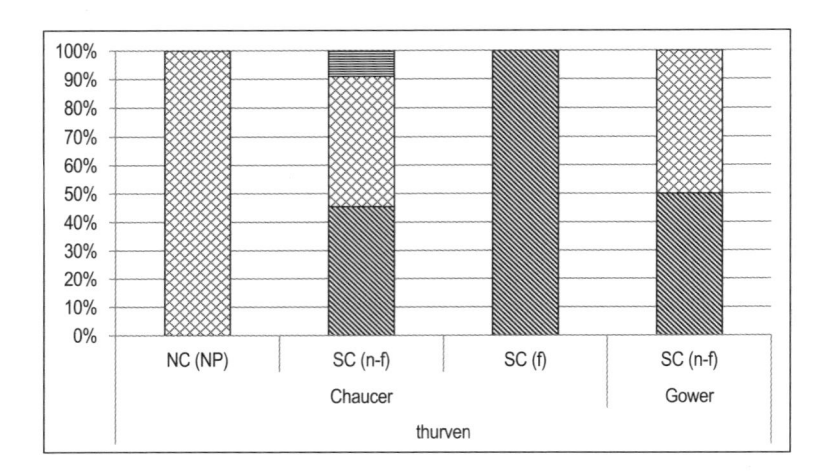

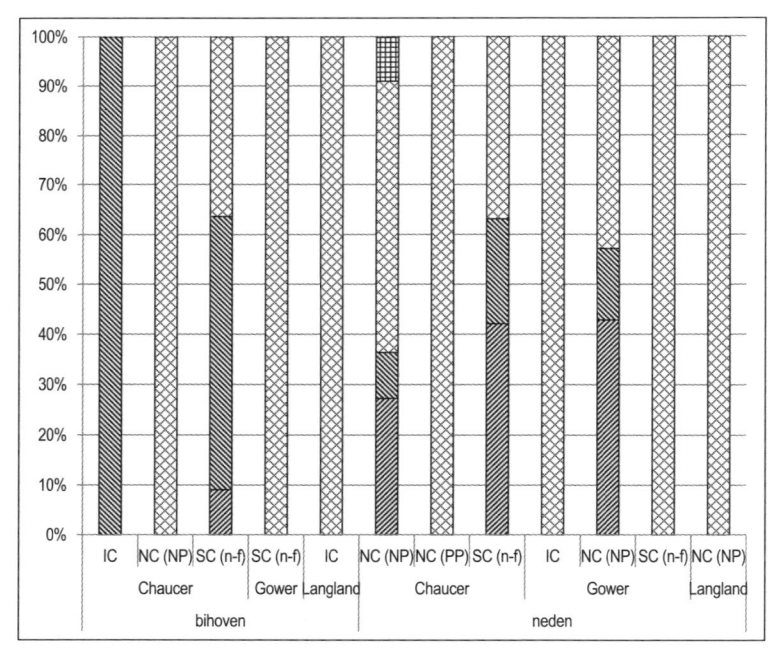

134   Part I   Synchronic Variation in Chaucer's Text

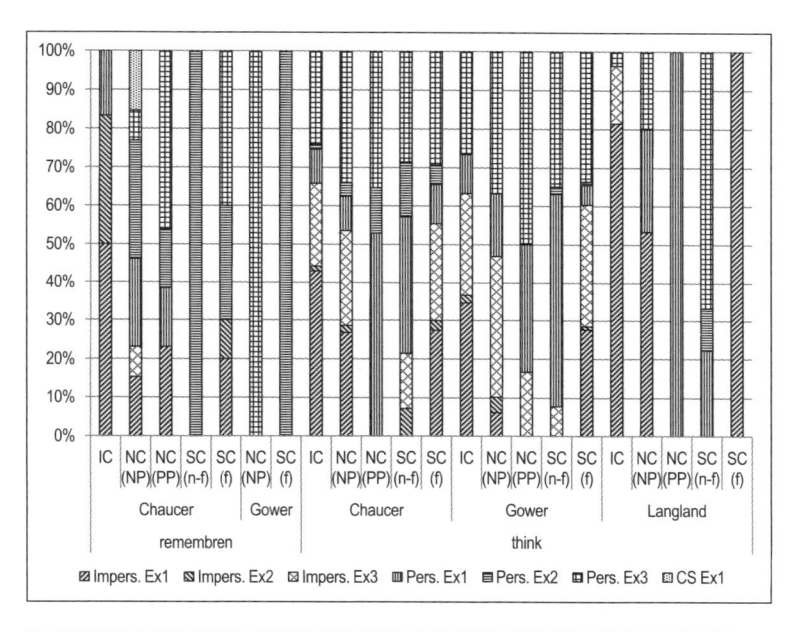

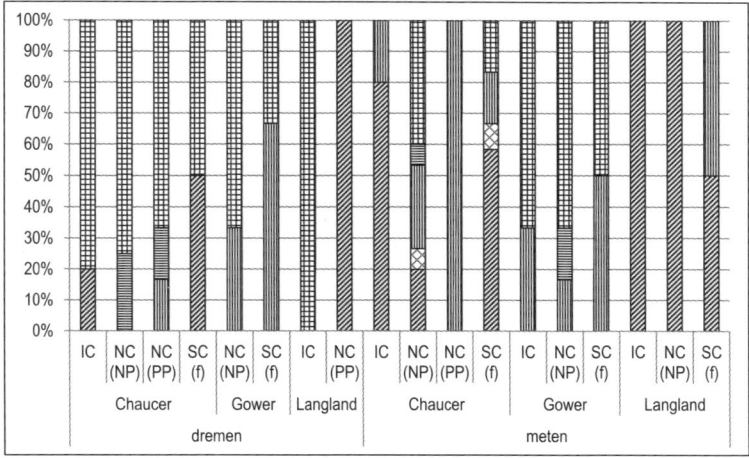

Figure 1. Frequency of Verbs by Syntactic Feature
NB The "n-f" and "f" denote "non-finite" and "finite" clauses respectively.

136   Part I   Synchronic Variation in Chaucer's Text

The figure brings out the following:

(1) As for the impersonal and personal uses, *liken, listen, greven, dremen, repenten, moten, thurven, bihoven,* and *neden* are used almost always in either one use or the other, while some of the other verbs have both uses almost as frequently. Concerning the ratio of the uses, Chaucer uses *meten, dremen, ouen, recchen, think,* and *remembren* differently from Gower or Langland.

(2) As for the complement type, Type I (i.e. with an IC) is dominantly in the impersonal use, while the personal use is prominent in Type II (i.e. with an NC). Concerning Type III (i.e. with an SC), verbs with a non-finite clause are likely to appear in the personal construction, while those with a finite one tend to occur in the impersonal construction, except for *remembren.*

(3) As for the grammatical person of the Ex, *liken* and *listen* show the tendency to appear in the impersonal use with a 1st-person Ex, especially *me*, while they tend to be in the personal use with a 2nd- or 3rd-person Ex. This tendency is also found in Chaucer's *dremen, meten, think, remembren,* and *greven*, while it has no application to *ouen, recchen,* and *repenten*, which tend to occur in the impersonal use with a 3rd-person Ex.

(4) Personal *liken* and *listen* with a 3rd-person Ex co-occur with an NP or non-finite clause. Additionally, in the case of *think*, for instance, the complement types occurring in the impersonal construction frequently have a 2nd- or 3rd-person Ex, while those occurring in the personal use frequently have a 1st-person Ex.

These facts, especially (4), show that not only the person of the Ex, but also the complement type is a determinant in choosing either construction.

Next, it is also necessary to look at the word order involving a verb in question. Figure 2 shows the frequency of the major orders.

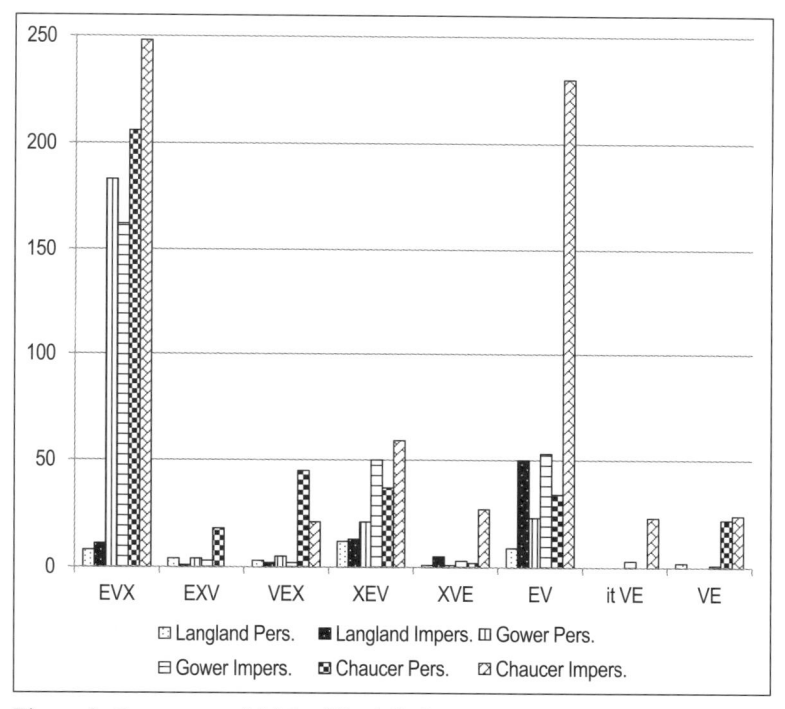

Figure 2. Frequency of Major Word Orders
NB   The letters "E" and "X" represent "Ex" and "complement" respectively.

This figure shows the following:

(1) the impersonal construction appears prominently in "EV" order.

(2) the impersonal construction with "*it* VE" and "XVE" orders is peculiar to Chaucer.

The fact (2) is associated with the positions of the Ex and the verb in one line, that is to say, rhyme. Table 1 indicates that in Chaucer *think*, *liken*, and *remembren* frequently appear with the Ex in rhyme position. These examples constantly reoccur in Chaucer's verse.

Table 1. Ex in Rhyme

		Impersonal		Personal	
		Ex in rhyme	Total no. in verse	Ex in rhyme	Total no. in verse
liken	Ch	22 (18)	77	1 (1)	1
	Gw	0	58	0	2
listen	Ch	1 (0)	283	0	7
	Gw	0	95	0	6
dremen	Ch	1 (1)	2	1 (1)	14
	Gw	0	0	0	6
greven	Ch	1 (1)	14	0	5
	Gw	0	17	0	0
think	Ch	16 (16)	165	1 (1)	139
	Gw	1 (1)	135	0	200
remembren	Ch	4 (4)	5	0	7
	Gw	0	0	1 (1)	2

NB   The brackets itemise the number of personal pronouns. "Ch" and "Gw" stand for Chaucer and Gower respectively.

This fact is further related to the impersonal construction in an *as-* or *if-*clause. The complement types and the grammatical persons of the Ex in those clauses are tabulated in Table 2. This table shows that impersonal *liken*, *listen* and *ouen* in an *as-*clause are characteristic in Chaucer, as pointed out by Masui (1964), who calls this kind of clause "a rhyme clause".

Table 2. Complement Types and Grammatical Persons of Ex in *As-* or *If*-clause

Verb	Clause	Chaucer	Gower	Langland
liken	as	freq. with IC; esp. with 2nd-pers. Ex	freq. with 3rd-pers. Ex; with IC or non-finite clause	freq. with IC; esp. with 3rd-pers. Ex
liken	if	freq. with 2nd-pers. Ex and IC or non-finite clause	freq. with 2nd-pers. Ex; esp. with non-finite clause	freq. with IC; esp. with 2nd- or 3rd-pers. Ex
listen	as	freq. with IC; esp. with 2nd-pers. Ex	freq. with IC; esp. with 3rd-pers. Ex	only with 3rd-pers. Ex and IC
listen	if	freq. with IC; esp. with 2nd-pers. Ex	freq. with 2nd-pers. Ex; esp. with non-finite clause	freq. with 3rd-pers. Ex and IC or non-finite clause
ouen thinken	as	freq. with IC; esp. with 1st-pers. Ex	with 1st- or 3rd-pers. Ex and IC or clause	only with 1st-pers. Ex and IC
ouen	as	freq. with IC; esp. with 3rd-pers. Ex	-	-

Finally, adding the result of the semantic and pragmatic examinations to the previous examples, it can be said that the choice between the impersonal and personal constructions seems to depend on the degree of the Ex's involvement with the action or state expressed by the verb and in some cases on the focus of utterance in a sentence.

Thus, while either use is often utilised for prosodic purposes such as rhyme, there are many examples where both uses seem to appear for other purposes. Therefore, it is difficult to draw a clear boundary line as Allen, Fischer and van der Leek, etc. although their theory is valuable. As far as this Part is concerned, however, at least in Chaucer there are many examples in which either construction, superficially assigned for the above-said factors, can allow nuanced interpretations of the Ex or the speaker when examined from a pragmatic or semantic frame of reference.

Part II

Diachronic Variation in Chaucer's Manuscripts

Part II directs attention to a diachronic aspect, expanding the idea of Part I. It investigates how the degree of the Ex's involvement in the action or feelings expressed by the verbs, the narrator's way of speaking, and the focus of utterance, affect the choice between the impersonal and personal uses. Using the manuscripts of *The Canterbury Tales*, Chapter 6 clarifies an overall picture of the fluctuation between the two uses, and Chapter 7, as a case study, carefully analyses some examples which show the considerable change from the impersonal to the personal use in the manuscripts and try to show what this change can mean.

Chapter 6

Tendencies of Variation

The aim of this chapter is to obtain an overall grasp of the fluctuation between the impersonal and personal uses found in the manuscripts (MSS) of Chaucer's works. We tend to get chronological information about the impersonal construction from books on the history of the English language. For example, Hogg and Denison (2006: 112-13) summarise the diachronic change of the construction according to the period as follows.

Table 1. Diachronic Change of Impersonal Construction

Changes in:	*subject*: subjectless/impersonal
Old English	common
Middle English	subject position becomes obligatorily filled
Modern English	extinct (some lexicalised expressions)

However, the division[1] among the three periods is broad, and the process of the change is not expounded.

It may be common and convenient to base a diachronic research on corpora such as the *Helsinki Corpus*, but it is not to be overlooked that a corpus consists of extracts from many different texts of various genres. Therefore, I think it much more useful to treat the MSS of the same work, which can show the scribes' usage of or linguistic instinct for a certain word in the same context.

Among Chaucer's works, I choose *The Canterbury Tales* (*CT*) as my data, because "there are eighty-four extant

---

[1] The division is slightly different according to a scholar. For instance, Hogg and Denison (2006: 2-3) says, "From c.1100 to around the end of the fifteenth century is called the Middle English (ME) period, and from c.1500 to the present day is called Modern English (ModE)." Laing and Lass (2006: 418) defines early ME as "all written English from about 1150 to 1325", and according to T. Nakao (1972), the ME period is from about 1150 to about 1500.

manuscripts ... including Caxton's two editions" (Ono 1969: 51), which will suffice for my statistic research. Although the author's original manuscript does not exist, the earliest MS, the Hengwrt, is thought to have been produced while Chaucer was alive. The dates of the MSS range from about 1400 to about 1500, with the peak in the middle of the period, as shown in Table 2.

Table 2. Approximate Dates of Copying of 84 MSS

Date	MS
Beginning of 15c	Hg El
c. 1400	Ad^4 Me
c. 1410-20	Cp
1422-36	Ps
c. 1425	Ll^2 Pw He
1st quarter of 15c	Dd Ha^4 La
2nd quarter of 15c	Ad^2 Ad^3 Bo^2 Ds^2 En^1 En^2 Gg Hk Hl^4 Ii Kk Lc Ld^1 Ln Ph^3 Pl Ry^2 Sl^1
Middle of 15c	Ar Ds Ha^2 Ha^3 Ht Mc Mg Mm Ox Ra^1 Ra^3 St Tc^1
1457	Np
1461-83	To
c. 1475	Si
1476	Gl
1478	Cx^1
3rd quarter of 15c	Bo^1 Bw Ch Cn Dl Do En^3 Fi Ha^1 Ha^5 Hl^1 Hl^2 Ll^1 Ne Nl Ph^1 Ph^2 Ph^4 Py Ra^2 Ry^1 Se
1483-85	Ma
1484	Cx^2
1490	Ct
4th quarter of 15c	Ad^1 Hl^3 Hn Ld^2 Pp Ra^4 Sl^2 Sl^3 Tc^2 Tc^3
End of 15c	Ee

NB   This table is made up based on Pearsall (1994: 321-25).

Concerning the regional dialects the MSS mainly use, Manly and Rickert (1940: I 550) comment as follows. Among 83 MSS, 53 are East Midland, West Midland forms are found in 11 MSS, "West Midland forms in combination with a large number of Northern ones occur" in seven, and "Northern features appear in considerable numbers" in the other two.[2]

---

[2] Mosser (1996) and Seymour (1997) give more detailed descriptions of some (but not all) of the MSS.

The MSS often have different readings from their exemplars, and "Sometimes variant readings result from errors of the scribe, but sometimes they may have been substituted for the original and reveal the scribe's usage or fluctuation of usage" (Ono 1969: 51). Horobin, analysing different spellings of certain words, has the same opinion, saying (2003: 72):

> It appears from this analysis that scribes did preserve spellings which are characteristic of Type III London English, the language which stands at the head of the textual tradition. However the influence of this variety was evidently complex. It appears that scribes were more likely to preserve such forms where they were reinforced by the practice of their own or other contiguous dialects. Where a form was not supported by local use scribes were unlikely to preserve it.

The dates of the MSS range from about 1400 to about 1500, and their analysis can disclose the details of the transition from the impersonal to the personal use. The information about the variants is from Manly and Rickert.

1. Brief Sketch of Transition by Previous Studies

There are some descriptive researches of the impersonal construction, commencing with van der Gaaf (1904). Among them is Elmer, who does a diachronic survey of several verbs by the type of complement they take. His survey generally reports that when they take a nominal complement (NC) such as a NP and PP, the verbs begin to take the personal use in the thirteenth century, as well as in the fourteenth century when taking a sentential complement (SC) such as finite and non-finite clauses. It also reports that the impersonal use disappeared around the seventeenth century. Similarly, T. Nakao (1972: 298) observes that most of the impersonal verbs in the ME period started the transition to the personal use in the first half of the fourteenth century, finishing the transition by the end of the ME period, although some verbs like *think*, *liken*, *listen*, and *repenten* retained the impersonal use until the beginning of the sixteenth century. These two scholars offer more ample information than Hogg and Denison, yet still could not reveal details such as the ordering of superiority of the two uses within one century.

Concerning Chaucer, Tani surveys the fluctuation between the two uses in *Troilus and Criseyde* and concludes as follows (1995c: 29):

> Variant readings ... show a hidden force working on the impersonal construction. In spite of the many possible variations, almost all the changes found in our corpus are restricted to the variants showing the change from type A [= the impersonal use] to type D [= the personal use].

A larger number of the MSS will enable this chapter to gain a more detailed understanding of the fluctuation.

2. Ordering of Superiority of Two Uses in Chaucer's Texts

Let us look at the ordering found in Chaucer's texts, which Part I showed discretely in each chapter. Thus far in this book, I have used Benson's edition, which comments about the editing of *CT* as follows (2008: 1120):

> For our textual presentation, we adopt the same eclectic (and perhaps not completely consistent) procedures used in Robinson's second edition. The text of the Tales remains based, as was Robinson's, on El. However, in the light of Manly and Rickert's elaborate demonstration, one can no longer, as Robinson recognized, follow El for every lection. In response to Manly and Rickert, Robinson emended into his El text a substantial number of readings from other copies, particularly Hg.

As seen above, the Hengwrt is the earliest MS (earlier than the Ellesmere by about 10 years), and concerning the

Chapter 6 Tendencies of Variation

verbs dealt with in this book there are some different readings found between the Hengwrt and Benson's edition[3] as follows.

Table 3. Different Readings between Benson and Hengwrt MS

Verb	Tale and Line	Benson	Hengwrt
thenken	SumT 2204	ye	yow
thinken	MerT 1964	hire	omitted
thinken	Thop 954	yow	ye
behoven	ParsT 630	the (article)	I*
moten	Mel 1855	ye	yow
ouen	Mel 1248	yow	ye
ouen	Mel 1298[4]	yow	ye
listen	MerT 2173	yow	ye
smerten	GP 230	hym	he

NB Concerning the reading marked with an asterisk, the line is not recorded in the Hengwrt, and therefore the reading is the Ellesmere's.

It is important to reflect these variant readings in my survey, for this chapter discusses the fluctuation of the uses between the Hengwrt (or the Ellesmere, concerning the examples not contained in the Hengwrt) and the later MSS. Including the readings, Table 4 shows the ordering of the superiority of the two uses in Chaucer.

---

[3] All the variants in all the manuscripts are recorded in Manly and Rickert.

[4] T. Nakao (1972: 299) cites this from F. N. Robinson's edition as an example of the blending of the impersonal and personal uses. However, this does not deny his opinion, because there is one more example of the blending found in *ouen*, which is attested by the Hg manuscript.

And whan she saugh hir tyme, she sente for thise adversaries to come unto hire into a pryvee place and shewed wisely unto hem the grete goodes that comen of pees and the grete harmes and perils that been in werre, and seyde to hem in a goodly manere hou that *hem oughten* have greet repentaunce of the injurie and wrong that they hadden doon to Melibee hir lord, and unto hire, and to hire doghter. (*Mel* 1728-32)

148   Part II   Diachronic Variation in Chaucer's Manuscripts

Table 4. Frequency of Uses in Each Verb in *CT*

Verb	Impersonal Use	Personal Use	Cause Subject	Not Classified
listen	126 (298)	4 (9)		17 (41)
liken	48 (106)	0 (1)	2 (7)	6 (18)
longen	1 (1)	1 (4)		1 (4)
greven	9 (16)	2 (5)	4 (5)	5 (14)
recchen	3 (10)	18 (39)		7 (19)
repenten	3 (4)	16 (24)		11 (14)
reuen	3 (5)	5 (15)		8 (28)
smerten	3 (12)	2 (3)		3 (14)
dremen	1 (2)	5 (15)		0 (6)
meten	4 (16)	7 (18)		2 (13)
bihoven	6 (15)	1 (1)		7 (28)
neden	13 (30)	1 (1)		37 (71)
ouen	24 (40)	23 (73)		39 (83)
moten	3 (5)	156 (313)		72 (154)
thurven	5 (12)			1 (3)
remembren	2 (14)	12 (27)	1 (2)	11 (25)
think	69 (174)	57 (161)		32 (107)

NB   The brackets show the total numbers of examples in Chaucer's entire works.

As seen in Part I, in Chaucer's time, the impersonal use is dominantly found in *listen, liken, greven, smerten, bihoven, neden,* and *thurven*.

3. Overall Picture of Variation in Manuscripts

Before conducting a statistical survey it should be noted that this kind of variation may be caused by the confusion between the letters *þ* and *y*[5] as speculated from [3] below. Moreover, this chapter will not treat the effect of the confusion separately from the variation. What is also to be noted is the replacement of the nominative pronoun *ye* by the oblique form *you*. About the nominative use of *you*, the *OED* comments that "In early use sometimes app. for emphasis, as opposed to *ye* unemphatic; but often beside *ye* as a mere alternative" (s.v. *you*, pers. pron. 2. a.). In agreement with the dictionary, Nevalainen states that Figure 1 "indicates that nothing much happens in the re-

---

[5] See Sisam (1921: 275).

placement process in the fifteenth century: the change is still in its incipient stage, the incoming form having a frequency below 10 percent of the cases" (2006: 562-63). According to her, this figure includes the impersonal structures, and if she counts the impersonal *you* as subject, the numerical numbers in the figure will become smaller. Therefore, it can be said that the replacement hardly happened in the fifteenth century.

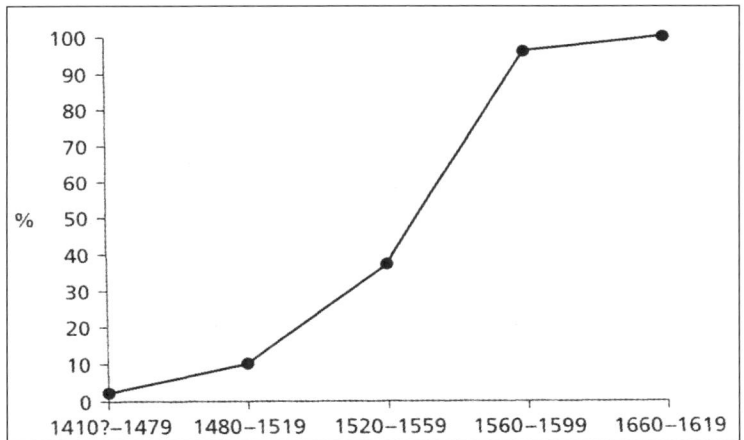

Figure 1. Replacement of Subject *Ye* by *You*. (originally in Nevalainen and Raumolin-Brunberg (2003: 60). Quoted in Nevalainen (2006: 563).)

As in Part I, the attention will be paid to the complement types which the verbs in question take, as well as to the grammatical persons of the Ex. In [1] the verb *neden* takes the nominal complement (NC) *no gyde*, and in [2] the verb *thinken* takes the sentential complement (SC (finite)) *this is weel ysayd*.

[1] John knew the wey — *hem nedede no gyde* —
And at the mille the sak adoun he layth.   (*RvT* 4020-21)

[2] And if *yow thynketh this is weel ysayd*,
   Seyeth youre avys, and holdeth you apayd.   (*KnT* 1867-68)

3.1. Statistical Data of Variation

One example of the variant readings is shown in [3]:

[3]   ... "Sire, ther is namoore to seyne,
   But, whan *yow list* to ryden anywhere,
   Ye mooten trille a pyn, stant in his ere,
   Which I shal yow telle bitwix us two.   (*SqT* 314-17)
                  yow] *þow* (15 MSS); *ye* (11 MSS)

Here, in the second line, the verb *list* has the dative Ex *yow*. This passage is recorded by 52 MSS, among which 15 have *þow* and 11 have *ye* instead of *yow*. That means that 50 per cent of the MSS have the variant reading for the personal use. This rate, which indicates the degree of variation in one example, is called "the rate of variation" (RtV).

In addition to the rate of variation, the term "the range of variation" (RnV) is used to refer to the degree of variation in one verb, i.e. how many examples in one verb witness a variant reading.

The statistical data[6] about the variation are tabulated below. For example, the table of *listen* shows the following. There are 126 impersonal examples and 78 of them have at least one variant reading, the range of variation being 61.9 per cent.

---

[6] *Longen* is excluded from the survey because of a serious lack of examples in *CT*, as Table 4 shows.

Table 5. Variation from Impersonal to Personal Use (I-P Variation)

	No. of Original Examples	No. of Examples with Variant	RnV	Avg. RtV
listen	126	78	61.9	20.8
liken	48	19	39.6	7.9
greven	9	1	11.1	60.8
reuen	3	1	33.3	1.8
smerten	3	2	66.7	34.0
recchen	3	1	33.3	47.5
repenten	3	3	100	11.9
bihoven	6	3	50.0	4.0
moten	3	3	100	55.4
neden	13	8	61.5	7.6
ouen	24	18	75.0	22.3
thurven	5	5	100	17.0
remembren	2	2	100	19.6
think	69	29	42.0	11.8
dremen	1	1	100	2.0
meten	4	4	100	28.0
TOTAL	324	179	55.4	18.0

Table 6. Variation from Personal to Impersonal Use (P-I Variation)

	No. of Original Examples	No. of Examples with Variant	RnV	Avg. RtV
listen	4	1	25.0	77.1
liken	0	0	0	0
greven	2	0	0	0
reuen	5	1	20.0	29.5
smerten	2	0	0	0
recchen	18	0	0	0
repenten	16	1	6.3	7.3
bihoven	0	0	0	0
moten	156	31	19.9	4.4
neden	1	0	0	0
ouen	23	10	43.5	10.0
thurven	1	1	100	36.7
remembren	12	1	8.3	1.8
think	58	9	15.5	6.9
dremen	5	0	0	0
meten	7	1	14.3	2.0
TOTAL	309	56	18.1	8.1

As a whole, about 55 per cent of the impersonal examples have the personal reading, and about 18 per cent of the personal examples have the opposite reading in the MSS. In addition, the average rate of the I-P variation is twice as

152   Part II   Diachronic Variation in Chaucer's Manuscripts

much as that of the P-I variation.

In order to understand the tables better, let us look at Figures 2 and 3, which indicate the RnV and the average RtV of each verb in a scatter plot.

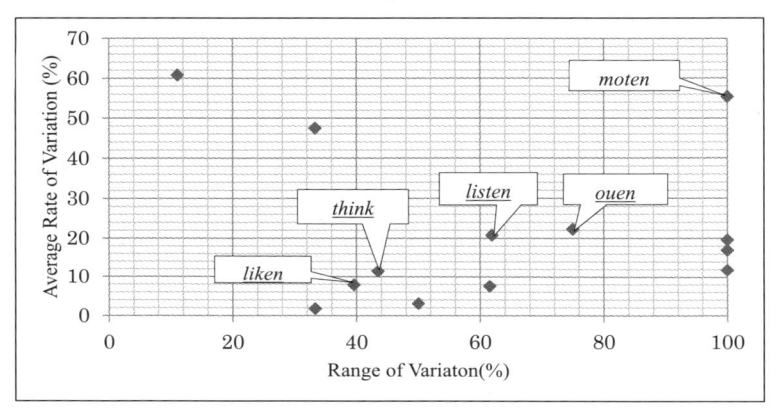

Figure 2. RnV and Avg. RtV of I-P Variation

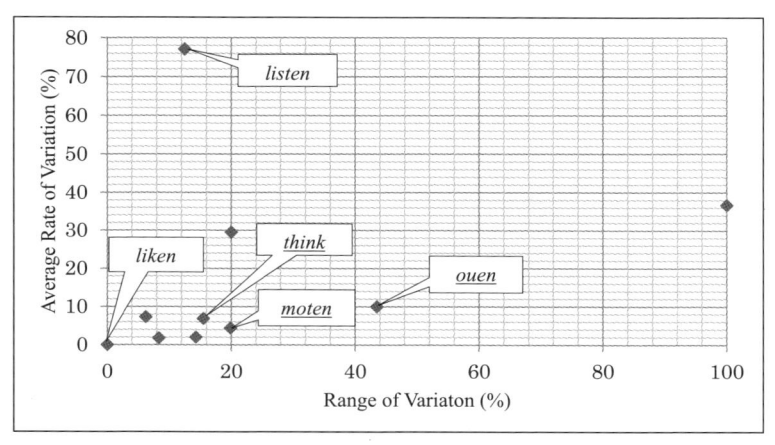

Figure 3. RnV and Avg. RtV of P-I Variation

Tagged are the verbs which originally have more than 20

examples in either the impersonal or personal use. The underlined ones have more than 20 examples in the use in question; in other words, they are statistically-useful to some extent.

These figures clearly show that the I-P variation is observed in more than 40 per cent of examples of the verbs. To the contrary, the P-I variation occurs in less than half the examples in each verb, and the rate of variation is lower. As for an individual verb, *ouen* is unique in that it has more than 20 examples in each use and shows a wider range of variation in both the ways.

3.2. Syntactic Aspects of Variation

Let us consider the variation from the syntactic aspects: the grammatical persons of the Ex and the complement types. Tables 7 and 8 summarise their relationship with the range of variation.

Table 7. Range of I-P Variation According to Grammatical Person of Ex and Complement Type

Person of Ex	RnV	Compl.	RnV
1st	27.7	IC	51.1
2nd	83.9	NC	39.3
3rd	52.4	SC	63.0

Table 8. Range of P-I Variation According to Grammatical Person of Ex and Complement Type

Person of Ex	RnV	Compl.	RnV
1st	15.5	IC	6.1
2nd	35.3	NC	6.7
3rd	13.8	SC	21.6

Firstly, concerning the grammatical persons of the Ex, the tables indicate that the I-P variation is dominant in all the types. The variation is particularly noticeable with a 2nd-person Ex, while it is minor with a 1st-person Ex. This tendency is synchronically observed in Chaucer's *liken, listen*, and *remembren*, as seen in Part I.

Next, let us examine the complement types. In all types, perceptible variation towards the personal use can be observed. Among them, more considerable variation is seen in the examples with an SC, which, however, shows much greater variation towards the impersonal use. The diachronic fact seen in Section 1 that examples with an SC appeared in the personal use later than those with an NP may have something to do with this phenomenon.

A closer investigation of each verb, including which verb affects this overall picture, will be conducted later in Section 4.

3.3. Other Types of Variation

In addition to the two types of variation discussed above, there are a number of examples in which the "Not Classified" has a personal or impersonal reading. One example is [4]:

> [4] eke whan he is in heele of body and wol nat faste whan other folk faste, withouten cause resonable; eke whan he slepeth moore than *nedeth*, or whan he comth by thilke enchesoun to late to chirche, or to othere werkes of charite;
> (*ParsT* 374)
> *nedeth*] *hym n.* (3 MSS); *he n.* (2 MSS)

Here the Ex is added before the verb *nedeth* in the two ways. The table below shows the frequency of the examples.

Table 9. Frequency of Variation from "Not Classified" to Personal or Impersonal Use

Verb	To Personal Use	To Impersonal Use
listen	3	
liken		2
reuen	1	
recchen	1	
repenten	1	
moten	8	1
neden	5	7
ouen	8	
think	2	2

This table can be parallel to the overall inclination seen above.[7]

3.4. Dative Experiencer in Rhyme

As seen in Part I, there are some examples in which a dative pronominal Ex is placed in rhyme position. There are 14 examples of this kind (eight in *thinken*, five in *liken*, and one in *remembren*) in *CT*, and three of them have the variant reading towards the personal use.[8]

[5] But — Lord Crist! — whan that *it remembreth me*
Upon my yowthe, and on my jolitee,
It tikleth me aboute myn herte roote. (*WBT* 469-71)
                                         it] *I* (10 MSS)

[6] Lordynges, this question, thanne, wol I aske now,
Which was the mooste fre, *as thynketh yow*?
                       (*FranT* 1621-22)   *yow*] *ye nowe* (1 MS)

---

[7] The "Not Classified" includes the following type of examples:
 Who sorweth now but woful Palamoun,
 That *moot* namoore goon agayn to fighte? (*KnT* 2652-53)
                             That] *Thei* (9 MSS); *He* (2 MSS)
This kind of data may give a false colour to the tendency of variation, because this kind of examples may be often considered as the personal use. However, this book employs this kind of classification for purposes of accuracy, partly because the word order is not necessarily a decisive factor in determining the use of a verb.

[8] This work contains no example with the nominative pronominal Ex in rhyme position.

[7] The knotte why that every tale is toold,
If it be taried til that lust be coold
Of hem that han it after herkned yoore,
The savour passeth ever lenger the moore,
For fulsomnesse of his prolixitee;
And by the same resoun, *thynketh me*,
I sholde to the knotte condescende,
And maken of hir walkyng soone an ende.   (*SqT* 401-08)
  me] *he* (1 MS)

In [5] the impersonal *it* is replaced by *I* and the original Ex *me* is regarded as the reflexive pronoun. In [6], even after the Ex *yow* is replaced, rhyme is kept by adding a new rhyme word *nowe*. In [7], the grammatical person is changed as well to protect rhyme, and this may cause some change in the context. Thus, the necessity of rhyme is absolute.

3.5. Manuscripts with I-P Variants

There is a difference in the number of I-P variants among the MSS. The top 10 MSS which include more variants are: Nl, Ii, Cx^1, Tc^2, Ne, He, Ph^3, En^3, To, and Ry^1. Among them, according to Table 2, He was produced in about 1425 and Ii and Ph^3 in the second quarter of the fifteenth century. This shows that the variation appeared in the early period of the century.

Concerning manuscript groups, Ii, Cx^1, Tc^2, Ne, and He belong to P. Robinson's fundamental witness group AB (1997: 81), and the four except Ii compose Manly and Rickert's constant group b. However, all the MSS in all of P. Robinson's fundamental witness groups record personal variants, although they differ in the number of variants. Within the group b, later MSS contain more personal variants, which may show a diachronic influence of the transition from the impersonal to the personal use.

Concerning the regional dialects, Ph^3 and Ry^1 among the 10 MSS have West Midland forms and the others are

"East Midland in language" (Manly and Rickert 1940: I 550). When all MSS are considered from a viewpoint of dialects, there does not appear to be any specific property among them. Thus, the scribes' usage seems to be more reflected in the variation.

4. Syntactic Analysis of Individual Verb

This section, using more detailed information than that found in Tables 4 to 8, makes a closer analysis of the variation in each verb.

4.1. *Liken* and *Listen*

Liken and *listen* almost always appear in the impersonal use in *CT*, and especially, all the examples are impersonal when the Ex is in the 1st person. As for their variation, let us look at Tables 10 and 11.

Table 10. Variation of *Listen*
(I-P: Maximum RtV = 77.6; Average RtV = 20.8) (P-I: RtV = 77.1)

Person of Ex	Total No. of Examples (Total)	No. of Examples Including Variant Reading (Variant)	RnV (%)
1st	20 / 0	4 / 0	20.0 / 0
2nd	50 / 1	49 / 1	98.0 / 100
3rd	56 / 3	25 / 0	44.6 / 0
Complement (Compl.)	Total	Variant	RnV (%)
Implied (IC)	72 / 1	44 / 1	61.1 / 100
NC	9 / 0	6 / 0	66.7 / 0
SC	45 / 0	28 / 0	62.2 / 0

NB The data of the two types of variation is presented in one table. For example, there are 56 impersonal examples with the 3rd-person Ex, and 25 of them have at least one variant reading, the range of the I-P variation being 44.6 per cent. In contrast, there are three personal examples with the 3rd-person Ex, and none of them have a variant reading, the range of the P-I variation being 0 per cent.

Table 11. Variation of *Liken*
(I-P: Max. RtV = 22.9; Avg. RtV = 7.9)

Ex	Total	Variant	RnV (%)
1st	8 / 0	2 / 0	22.2 / 0
2nd	22 / 0	11 / 0	50.0 / 0
3rd	19 / 0	6 / 0	31.6 / 0
Compl.	Total	Variant	RnV (%)
IC	22 / 0	9 / 0	40.9 / 0
NC	15 / 0	5 / 0	33.3 / 0
SC	11 / 0	5 / 0	45.5 / 0

NB   One example has two Exs in the 1st and 3rd persons, counted twice.

Concerning the I-P variation, the RnV is lowest with a 1st-person Ex and highest with a 2nd-person Ex, as a whole. In *listen*, the examples with a 2nd-person Ex have the highest RnV (98.0 per cent) and the highest Avg. RtV (28.0). The RnV in each complement type seems almost the same (approximately 60), but when the examples are narrowed down to those with a 2nd-person Ex, all the examples except one have the variation. Even a parenthetical "*as/if + the/you + leste*" clause, as in [8], frequently experiences the variation, and this is partly because it is not subject to the restriction of rhyme, as seen in Chapter 1. *Liken* has a similar tendency to *listen*, although the numerical values are smaller. Here are a few examples with a higher RtV.

[8] Love, *if thee list*, for I love and ay shal;
    And soothly, leeve brother, this is al.
                    (*KnT* 1183-84) (RtV = 77.6)

[9] If he be povre, she helpeth hym to swynke;
    She kepeth his good, and wasteth never a deel;
    Al that hire housbonde lust, *hire liketh* weel;
    She seith nat ones "nay," whan he seith "ye."
                    (*MerT* 1342-45) (RtV = 22.9)

Quotation [9] is the example of *liken* with the highest RtV.

4.2. *Greven, Recchen, Repenten, Reuen*, and *Smerten*

Next, the verbs of grieving and regretting are evaluated. In Chaucer's texts, as seen in Chapter 2, they have different characteristics. *Grenven* and *reuen* have more impersonal examples with a 1st-person Ex, while in *recchen* the impersonal use remains in the examples with a 3rd-person Ex.

Concerning the I-P variation, although the RtV in each verb is high, the RnV is totally low, except in *repenten*. Below are the statistical data of each verb. An example with the highest RtV and comments are given to some verbs.

Firstly, *greven* has one example where personal variants are recorded: [10].

Table 12. Variation of *Greven*
(I-P: RtV = 60.8)

Ex	Total	Variant	RnV (%)
1st	6 / 0	0 / 0	0 / 0
2nd	3 / 2	1 / 0	33.3 / 0
Compl.	Total	Variant	RnV (%)
IC	2 / 2	1 / 0	50.0 / 0
NC	7 / 0	0 / 0	0 / 0

[10] "To yow, my lord, sire Apius so deere,
　　　Sheweth youre povre servant Claudius
　　　How that a knyght, called Virginius,
　　　Agayns the lawe, agayn al equitee,
　　　Holdeth, expres agayn the wyl of me,
　　　My servant, which that is my thral by right,
　　　Which fro myn hous was stole upon a nyght,
　　　Whil that she was ful yong; this wol I preeve
　　　By witnesse, lord, so that it nat *yow greeve*.
　　　　　　　　　(*PhyT* 178-86) (RtV = 60.8)

In [10] most of the variant readings add the nominative pronoun *ye* and preserve *yow*, i.e. they change the impersonal use to the reflexive use. The variation does not seem to considerably change the function of the person referred by the pronoun as an Ex, as Ogura pronounces:

> in active sentences the emphasis is put on the subject that performs the action, while in 'impersonal', reflexive, and '*be + past ptc*' sentences the focus is on the person to whom the action is directed. (1991: 87)

Next, in *smerten*, the two examples with an IC have the I-P variation.

Table 13. Variation of *Smerten*
(I-P: Max. RtV = 65.9; Avg. RtV = 34.0)

Ex	Total	Variant	RnV (%)
1st	1 / 1	1 / 0	100 / 0
3rd	2 / 1	1 / 0	33.3 / 0
Compl.	Total	Variant	RnV (%)
IC	2 / 2	2 / 0	100 / 0
NC	1 / 0	0 / 0	0 / 0

The variation with a high RtV, in [11], may be partly due to the juxtaposed verb *gamen* because the impersonal use of *gamen* seems rare in the fifteenth century. The *OED* quotes two impersonal examples of the verb from the works dated at the beginning of the thirteenth century (s.v. *game*, v. †2. †b.), and to them the *MED* (s.v. *gāmen* (v.) (b)) adds [11] as the latest quotation.

> [11] God loved he best with al his hoole herte
>   At alle tymes, thogh *him* gamed or *smerte*,
>   And thanne his neighebor right as hymselve.
>   (*GP* 533-35) (RtV = 65.9)

Then, concerning *recchen*, quotation [12] is one example with a 3rd-person Ex, in which the impersonal often remains.

Table 14. Variation of *Recchen*
(I-P: RtV = 47.5)

Ex	Total	Variant	RnV (%)
1st	2 / 8	0 / 0	0 / 0
2nd	0 / 1	0 / 0	0 / 0
3rd	1 / 9	1 / 0	100 / 0
Compl.	Total	Variant	RnV (%)
IC	1 / 5	1 / 0	100 / 0
NC	2 / 3	0 / 0	0 / 0
SC	0 / 10	0 / 0	0 / 0

[12]   Save this, she preyede hym that, if he myghte,
       Hir litel sone he wolde in erthe grave
       His tendre lymes, delicaat to sighte,
       Fro foweles and fro beestes for to save.
       But she noon answere of hym myghte have.
       He wente his wey, as *hym* no thyng ne *roghte*,
       But to Boloigne he tendrely it broghte.
                        (*ClT* 680-86) (RtV = 47.5)

Although it can be safe to say that even this kind of example may experience the I-P variation with a high rate of occurrence, this is the only example in *CT*, and the variation of the other examples is not able to be traced.

Next, all the impersonal examples of *repenten* experience the I-P variation, but the Avg. RtV is not so high (approximately 12 per cent).

Table 15. Variation of *Repenten*
(I-P: Max. RtV = 18.5; Avg. RtV = 11.9) (P-I: RtV = 7.3)

Ex	Total	Variant	RnV (%)
1st	1 / 1	1 / 0	100 / 0
2nd	1 / 5	1 / 1	100 / 20.0
3rd	1 / 10	1 / 0	100 / 0
Compl.	Total	Variant	RnV (%)
IC	3 / 9	3 / 0	100 / 0
NC	0 / 6	0 / 1	0 / 16.7
SC	0 / 1	0 / 0	0 / 0

What is common among the three impersonal examples is that at least in one of the later MSS the impersonal use is changed into the reflexive use, like *greven* above.

162   Part II   Diachronic Variation in Chaucer's Manuscripts

> [13]   What sholde I seye but, at the monthes ende,
> This joly clerk, Jankyn, that was so hende,
> Hath wedded me with greet solempnytee,
> And to hym yaf I al the lond and fee
> That evere was me yeven therbifoore.
> But afterward *repented me* ful soore;
> He nolde suffre nothyng of my list.
>
>   (*WBT* 627-33) (RtV = 16.7)

In [13], for instance, many of the later MSS add the nominative Ex *I* before the verb, the dative Ex *me* reconsidered as the reflexive pronoun.

Finally, *reuen* is dealt with. However, my findings are indecisive in reference to the variation of the verb because of the small number of occurrences.

Table 16. Variation of *Reuen*
(I-P: RtV = 1.8; P-I: RtV = 29.5)

Ex	Total	Variant	RnV (%)
1st	3 / 0	1 / 0	33.3 / 0
2nd	0 / 4	0 / 0	0 / 0
3rd	0 / 1	0 / 1	0 / 100
Compl.	Total	Variant	RnV (%)
IC	1 / 2	0 / 1	0 / 50.0
NC	1 / 3	1 / 0	100 / 0
SC	1 / 0	0 / 0	0 / 0

Concerning the P-I variation as a whole, both the RnV and the RtV are extremely low.

> [14] And wher my colour was bothe fressh and reed,
> Now is it wan and of a leden hewe —
> Whoso it useth, soore shal *he rewe*! —
> And of my swynk yet blered is myn ye.
>
>   (*CYT* 727-30) (RtV = 29.5)

Quotation [14], where *he* has the variant reading *hym*, is formally included in the P-I variation. However, *he* is originally a resumptive pronoun referring *Whoso it useth*, and by changing it to *hym*, many later MSS seem to con-

Chapter 6   Tendencies of Variation   163

sider that construction as reflexive. Then, I conclude that no P-I variation occurs in [14].

As far as the verbs of grieving and regretting are concerned, with some variant readings towards the reflexive use, the function of the Ex does not seem to be profoundly affected by the variation.

4.3. *Bihoven, Moten, Neden, Ouen,* and *Thurven*

Thirdly, the verbs of obligation and necessity are discussed. As for the frequency in Chaucer's text, the impersonal use is overwhelming in *bihoven, neden,* and *thurven*; the personal use is so in *moten*; the personal use is rather frequent in *ouen*, as seen in Chapter 3.

On the whole, the I-P variation is frequently observed. This may be because of auxiliarisation of the verbs. As in the previous section, the statistical data of each verb is tabulated, to which are added a few examples and comments.

Firstly, in *bihoven*, although the total number of examples is extremely limited, the variation occurs in the examples with a 2nd- or 3rd-person Ex with the low Avg. RtV.

Table 17. Variation of *Bihoven*
(I-P: Max. RtV = 5.8; Avg. RtV = 3.3)

Ex	Total	Variant	RnV (%)
1st	1 / 0	0 / 0	0 / 0
2nd	1 / 0	1 / 0	100 / 0
3rd	4 / 0	2 / 0	50.0 / 0
Compl.	Total	Variant	RnV (%)
NC	3 / 0	1 / 0	33.3 / 0
SC	3 / 0	2 / 0	66.7 / 0

Next, all the examples of *thurven* have the variation, although with the different Avg. RtVs.

164   Part II   Diachronic Variation in Chaucer's Manuscripts

Table 18. Variation of *Thurven*
(I-P: Max. RtV = 40.7; Avg. RtV = 17.0) (P-I: RtV = 36.7)

Ex	Total	Variant	RnV (%)
2nd	4 / 1	4 / 1	100 / 100
3rd	1 / 0	1 / 0	100 / 0
Compl.	Total	Variant	RnV (%)
SC	5 / 1	5 / 1	100 / 100

The example with the highest RtV is [15].

[15] He is to greet a nygard that wolde werne
A man to lighte a candle at his lanterne;
He shal have never the lasse light, pardee.
Have thou ynogh, *thee thar* nat pleyne thee.
(*WBT* 333-36) (RtV = 40.7)

However, the types of the grammatical person of the Ex and of the complement are too limited to conduce to convincing results.

It is noteworthy that a single MS has both the I-P and P-I variations about the same verb. For example, seven MSS record the variant reading towards the personal use in [15] and that towards the impersonal use in [16].

[16] And al be it so that youre emprise be establissed and ordeyned by greet multitude of folk, yet *thar ye* nat accomplice thilke ordinaunce but yow like.
(*Mel* 1068) (RtV = 36.7)

This may mean that a single MS shows no coherent attitude about the use of the same verb because of several causes mentioned at the beginning of this chapter. This phenomenon will not be peculiar to this verb.

Next, let us look at *neden*.

Table 19. Variation of *Neden*
(I-P: Max. RtV = 31.3; Avg. RtV = 7.6)

Ex	Total	Variant	RnV (%)
1st	2 / 0	1 / 0	50.0 / 0
2nd	3 / 0	2 / 0	66.7 / 0
3rd	8 / 1	5 / 0	62.5 / 0
Compl.	Total	Variant	RnV (%)
NC	5 / 1	4 / 0	80.0 / 0
SC	8 / 0	4 / 0	50.0 / 0

The two examples of the highest Avg. RtV in *neden* are [17] and [18].

[17]   This mayde, of which I wol this tale expresse,
So kepte hirself *hir neded* no maistresse,
(*PhyT* 105-06) (RtV = 31.3)

[18] Ful sooty was hire bour and eek hir halle,
In which she eet ful many a sklendre meel.
Of poynaunt sauce *hir neded* never a deel.
No deyntee morsel passed thurgh hir throte;
Hir diete was accordant to hir cote.
(*NPT* 2832-36) (RtV = 14.3)

These quotations have a 3rd-person Ex and an NC in common. The Avg. RtV of the examples with a 3rd-person Ex (10.3) is higher than that of those with a 1st- or 2nd-person Ex (2.0 and 3.6 respectively), and that of the examples with an NC (12.4) is higher than that of those with an SC (2.8). When the fact that the only example of the verb in the personal use in Chaucer's texts (*ParsT* 700) has the same syntactic features is taken into consideration, either (not necessarily both) of them may be associated with the personal use.

In addition, *ouen* also has a high RnV of 75.0 per cent in the I-P variation, as seen in Table 5 above. When the Avg. RtV is considered, there is no crucial difference among the complement types.

Table 20. Variation of *Ouen*
(I-P: Max. RtV = 68.3; Avg. RtV = 22.3)
(P-I: Max. RtV = 26.9; Avg. RtV = 10.0)

Ex	Total	Variant	RnV (%)
1st	4 / 8	4 / 4	100 / 50.0
2nd	3 / 7	3 / 5	100 / 71.4
3rd	17 / 8	11 / 1	64.7 / 12.5
Compl.	Total	Variant	RnV (%)
IC	7 / 1	4 / 0	57.1 / 0
SC	17 / 22	14 / 9	82.4 / 40.9

However, the variation is least active with a 3rd-person Ex in terms of both the RnV and the Avg. RtV, although the example with the highest RtV (*ClT* 1120; RtV = 68.3) has a 3rd-person Ex. This tendency is similar to the fact observed in Chapter 3 that the impersonal use is most frequent with a 3rd-person Ex. From observing this, I have concluded that with the root meaning, the impersonal use seems dominant when the addresser's involvement in the obligation is slighter. The conclusion can be fortified by the finding of this section.

Concerning the P-I variation of *ouen*, there is no conspicuous characteristic.

Finally, *moten* occurs predominantly in the personal use in Chaucer's texts with only five examples of the impersonal use. Three examples of them are in *CT*, as in Table 4. The three examples have a 1st- or 2nd-person Ex, and all of them witness the I-P variation with a high Avg. RtV.

Table 21. Variation of *Moten*
(I-P: Max. RtV = 93.8; Avg. RtV = 55.4)
(P-I: Max. RtV = 12.2; Avg. RtV = 4.4)

Ex	Total	Variant	RnV (%)
1st	1 / 67	1 / 9	100 / 13.4
2nd	2 / 24	2 / 9	100 / 37.5
3rd	0 / 65	0 / 13	0 / 20.0
Compl.	Total	Variant	RnV (%)
IC	0 / 3	0 / 0	0 / 0
SC	3 / 153	3 / 31	100 / 20.3

The example with the highest RtV is [19], where the

Hengwrt reads *yow* and most of the later MSS, including the Ellesmere, read *ye* as shown in Benson's edition.

[19] And therfore, if ye wole that men do yow obeisance, *ye moste* deemen moore curteisly; (*Mel* 1855) (RtV = 93.8)

This verb also has many examples with the P-I variation, but the Avg. RtV is too small to be noted.

4.4. *Remembren* and *Think*

As seen in Chapter 4, the impersonal construction of *remembren* is typical of Chaucer, who frequently uses the construction with a 1st-person Ex. Table 22 indicates that both of the two impersonal examples in *CT* have the variant readings towards the personal use with the Avg. RtV same as that of all the verbs treated in this chapter.

Table 22. Variation of *Remembren*
(I-P: Max. RtV = 20.9; Avg. RtV = 19.6) (P-I: RtV = 1.8)

Ex	Total	Variant	RnV (%)
1st	2 / 3	2 / 0	100 / 0
2nd	0 / 1	0 / 0	0 / 0
3rd	0 / 8	0 / 1	0 / 12.5
Compl.	Total	Variant	RnV (%)
NC	2 / 10	2 / 0	100 / 0
SC	0 / 2	0 / 1	0 / 50.0

By contrast, the P-I variation occurs in one example (*FranT* 1123), but only one MS has the variant reading.

Next, in Chaucer's texts, *think* frequently appears impersonally with a 1st-person Ex and with an IC or SC (finite), often in an *as*-clause or parenthetical, as seen in Chapter 4.

It is worth noting that the I-P variation is not active with a 1st-person Ex in terms of both the RnV (7.1) and the Avg. RtV (4.3).

Table 23. Variation of *Think*
(I-P: Max. RtV = 50.9; Avg. RtV = 11.8)
(P-I: Max. RtV = 34.1; Avg. RtV = 6.9)

Ex	Total	Variant	RnV (%)
1st	28 / 13	2 / 3	7.1 / 23.1
2nd	4 / 4	4 / 1	100 / 25.0
3rd	37 / 41	23 / 5	62.2 / 12.2
Compl.	Total	Variant	RnV (%)
IC	21 / 7	7 / 0	33.3 / 0
NC	10 / 13	2 / 1	20.0 / 7.7
SC	38 / 38	21 / 8	55.3 / 21.1

As mentioned in Chapter 4, Palander-Collin observes "the gradual specialization of impersonal THINK in the first person towards the end of Middle English period" (1999: 160), showing the table below. These two facts are consistent with each other.

Table 24. Frequencies of First Person Singular as Compared to Other Persons with Different Uses of THINK in Middle English (excerpt from Palander-Collin (1999: 161-62))

		IMPERSONAL		PERSONAL			
		opinion		opinion		'have in mind'	
1350-1420	1sg.	14	(21%)	2	(11%)	15	(23%)
	oth.	53	(79%)	17	(89%)	49	(77%)
	Total	67	(100%)	19	(100%)	64	(100%)
1420-1500	1sg.	50	(72%)	4	(12%)	8	(14%)
	oth.	19	(28%)	30	(88%)	51	(86%)
	Total	69	(100%)	34	(100%)	59	(100%)

Furthermore, one of two examples showing the variation with a 1st-person Ex, [20], has *he* as the variant of *me*, which may collapse the context.

[20] And by the same resoun, *thynketh me*,
　　I sholde to the knotte condescende,
　　And maken of hir walkyng soone an ende.　(*SqT* 406-08)
　　　　　　　　　　　　　　　　　　　　　　me] *he* (1 MS)

The situation concerning a 1st-person Ex is easy to understand, because most of the impersonal examples with the Ex have the Ex in rhyme position, which prevents the variation.

Let us focus on the clause types. As a whole, there are three impersonal examples in a parenthetical as in [20], and in one more example (*PhyT* 134) the variation is recorded, although the RtV is 2.0. There are 16 impersonal examples with an IC in an *as*-clause, and four of them have the variation with the Avg. RtV of 9.7. However, the four do not include the examples with a 1st-person Ex. The other clauses do not show a close relationship with the variation.

The example with the highest RtV (50.9) is line 965 in [21], in which the verb takes the 3rd-person Ex *hir*. *Hir* in line 967 also has the rather high RtV of 20.4.

> [21] But nathelees, *hir thoughte* that she dyde
> That she so longe sholde a conseil hyde;
> *Hir thoughte* it swal so soore aboute hir herte
> That nedely som word hire moste asterte; (*WBT* 965-68)

The P-I variation also has more relevance to a 1st-person Ex, but the Avg. RtV is basically low.

4.5. *Dremen* and *Meten*

Finally, the verbs of dreaming are examined. As seen in Chapter 5, Gower uses them only personally, while Chaucer and Langland share the impersonal use frequently in *meten* and rarely in *dremen*. In *CT*, there is only one example of *dremen* in the impersonal use and four of *meten*, and all the examples have personal variants.

The only example of *dremen* is [22], which is quoted in Chapter 5 as [38].

> [22] *Me dremed* al this nyght, pardee,
> An elf-queene shal my lemman be
> And slepe under my goore. (*Thop* 787-89)

Chapter 5 states that in the citation the dative Ex is appropriate to describe the speaker's own dream. Although this *me* has the variant reading *I*, it is recorded in only one MS.

Table 25. Variation of *Dremen*
(I-P: RtV = 2.0)

Ex	Total	Variant	RnV (%)
1st	1 / 1	1 / 0	100 / 0
3rd	0 / 4	0 / 0	0 / 0
Compl.	Total	Variant	RnV (%)
IC	0 / 1	0 / 0	0 / 0
NC	0 / 3	0 / 0	0 / 0
SC	1 / 1	1 / 0	100 / 0

In *meten*, however, all the impersonal examples witness personal variants, and the Avg. RtV is rather high (28.0) as in [23] and [24], although three of four examples have the 1st-person singular Ex.

Table 26. Variation of *Meten*
(I-P: Max. RtV = 33.3; Avg. RtV = 28.0) (P-I: RtV = 2.0)

Ex	Total	Variant	RnV (%)
1st	3 / 1	3 / 0	100 / 0
2nd	0 / 1	0 / 0	0 / 0
3rd	1 / 5	1 / 1	100 / 20.0
Compl.	Total	Variant	RnV (%)
NC	1 / 6	1 / 1	100 / 16.7
SC	3 / 1	3 / 0	100 / 0

[23] But herkneth! To that o man fil a greet mervaille:
 That oon of hem, in slepyng as he lay,
 Hym mette a wonder dreem agayn the day.
  (*NPT* 3076-78) (RtV = 33.3)

[24] My mouth hath icched al this longe day;
 That is a signe of kissyng atte leeste.
 Al nyght *me mette* eek I was at a feeste.
 Therfore I wol go slepe an houre or tweye,
 And al the nyght thanne wol I wake and pleye."
  (*MilT* 3682-86) (RtV = 31.9)

The P-I variation of the verbs of dreaming is low in terms of the RnV and the RtV and does not deserve special mention.

5. Summary

As far as all the verbs treated in this chapter are concerned, I can say that the tendency of the I-P variation can dovetail with the findings of Part I, although some influence of personalisation or auxiliarisation cannot be avoided.

Furthermore, this chapter has found a distinguishing feature of *listen*. Allen, examining Shakespeare's *please* with an IC in an adverbial clause,[9] finds an honorific example of "*if it please* + 2nd-person Ex" in Shakespeare (1995b: 286). Unlike *please, like,* and *will*, however, *if you list* does not have this kind of use in early Modern English, as Chen points out (1998: 30). No example of this kind is found in Chaucer's *listen*, either. That means that "*if* + 2nd-person Ex + *list*", which frequently has a variant reading towards the personal use, has gained a higher "degree of control" (Allen 1995b: 286).

Finally, I have found that even a single MS has the fluctuation between the impersonal and personal uses in its variant readings; because of this I draw the conclusion that the context (as well as the confusion between *y* and *þ*) may be instrumental in the variation.

---

[9] Allen calls this type of clause "UNPROP clause".

Chapter 7

Explanations for Variation: Case Studies[1]

Chapter 6 presented an overview of the fluctuation between the impersonal and personal uses found in the manuscripts of *The Canterbury Tales*. This view can fortify the conclusion about the two uses presented in Part I. In accord with the results of the previous chapters, Chapter 7 focuses on the examples which have variant readings with higher rates of frequency. Additionally, it attempts to give them contextual and syntactic explanations of what interpretations these variant readings can make possible. Therefore, this chapter avoids the simple comment that these variants are attributed to automatic replacement influenced by the transition from the impersonal to the personal use.

In my corpus, there are 34 examples in the impersonal use which witness variants in the personal use (the I-P variation) at rates of more than 33.3 per cent, and four examples in the personal use which witness variants in the impersonal use (the P-I variation). Therefore, this chapter mainly discusses the I-P variation. The number of examples in each verb is as follows.

---

[1] This chapter is based on Ohno (2001) and (2007c).

Table 1. Number of Examples of I-P Variation at Higher Rates of Frequency

Verb	No. of Examples
listen	19 (0/19/0)
ouen	5 (2/2/1)
thinken	3 (0/1/2)
moten	2 (0/2/0)
greven	1 (0/1/0)
meten	1 (0/0/1)
recchen	1 (0/0/1)
smerten	1 (0/0/1)
thurven	1 (0/1/0)

NB   The brackets itemise the number of examples with a 1st-/2nd-/3rd-person Ex respectively.

The table shows the high frequency in the examples with a 2nd-person Ex, which may raise the possibility that the scribes may have regarded the letter *þ* as *y* unidirectionally. However, 18 out of 25 examples of this kind have originally the Ex *yow*, which will remove the possibility. As for the other syntactic aspects, I cannot say there is any tendency, mostly because of the prominence of *listen* in the data.

1. Examination of Examples

Among the nine verbs, this chapter proposes the above-mentioned explanations for the variation in *listen*, *thinken*, *ouen*, *recchen*, and *thurven*.

1.1. *Listen*

The I-P variation in *listen* is only recorded in the examples with a 2nd-person Ex. It is also noteworthy that 12 of 19 examples have the verb in an *if*-clause. There is no salient feature concerning the complement types: 10 examples have an IC, seven a non-finite clause, and the other two an NP *what*.

As mentioned at the end of Chapter 6, conditional clauses with *listen* + a 2nd-person Ex do not function as mere "expressions of deference" (Chen 1998: 28). The fact that the variation is very frequently found there may mean that the addressers confirm the intentions of the addressee(s).

[1] We stryve as dide the houndes for the boon;
 They foughte al day, and yet hir part was noon.
 Ther cam a kyte, whil that they were so wrothe,
 And baar awey the boon bitwixe hem bothe.
 And therfore, at the kynges court, my brother,
 Ech man for hymself ther is noon oother.
 Love, *if thee list*, for I love and ay shal;   (77.6)[2]
 And soothly, leeve brother, this is al.
 Heere in this prisoun moote we endure,
 And everich of us take his aventure."   (*KnT* 1177-86)

Quotation [1], for example, is from the speech of Arcite to Palamon in *The Knight's Tale* (*KnT*). They fall in love with one and the same lady Emelya. Although they are imprisoned now, they are rivalling for her on the assumption of their release. Here in the citation, *if thee list* in line 1183, with the 2nd-person singular Ex, is not an expression of politeness but rather a kind of provocation or challenge to his rival in love. Thus, this *thee* may well have the variant readings in the personal use.

To quote another example of *listen* in a conditional clause:

[2]   ... "Sire, ther is namoore to seyne,
 But, whan *yow list* to ryden anywhere,   (50.0)
 Ye mooten trille a pyn, stant in his ere,
 Which I shal yow telle bitwix us two.
 Ye moote nempne hym to what place also,
 Or to what contree, that *yow list* to ryde.   (28.8)
 And whan ye come ther as *yow list* abyde,   (51.9)
 Bidde hym descende, and trille another pyn,
 For therin lith th'effect of al the gyn,
 And he wol doun descende and doon youre wille,

---

[2] The figures in the brackets show the rate of variation (RtV).

> And in that place he wol abyde stille.
> Though al the world the contrarie hadde yswore,
> He shal nat thennes been ydrawe ne ybore.
> Or, *if yow liste* bidde hym thennes goon, (39.2)
> Trille this pyn, and he wol vanysshe anoon
> Out of the sighte of every maner wight,
> And come agayn, be it by day or nyght,
> Whan that *yow list* to clepen hym ageyn (14.0)
> In swich a gyse as I shal to yow seyn
> Bitwixe yow and me, and that ful soone.
> Ride whan *yow list*; ther is namoore to doone." (16.0)
>   (*SqT* 314-34)

Quotation [2] is a speech of a knight who came to Cambyuskan's palace as an envoy of his king in *The Squire's Tale*. He has a gift with him, which is a magical steed made of brass. Here he is explaining elaborately how to handle the horse. *Listen* is repeated five times in adverbial clauses including an *if*-clause, and in every case the knight pays deep regard to the intentions of Cambyuskan, who is the owner and driver of the horse. The I-P variation can be found in the examples.

This phenomenon that the addresser confirms the intentions of the addressee(s), can be connected with the politeness of the addresser, in this case the knight, towards the addressee, King Cambyuskan. Leech (1983: 132) formulates six maxims of the politeness principles, and among them the action of emphasising the intentions of the addressee here corresponds to the maxim: (I) TACT MAXIM (in impositives and commissives) (b) Maximize benefit to *other*.

Let us look at one more example of *listen*.

> [3]   Yow loveres axe I now this questioun:
> Who hath the worse, Arcite or Palamoun?
> That oon may seen his lady day by day,
> But in prison he moot dwelle alway;

> That oother wher hym list may ride or go,
> But seen his lady shal he nevere mo.
> Now demeth as *yow liste*, ye that kan,   (36.7)
> For I wol telle forth as I bigan.   (*KnT* 1347-54)

Back in *KnT*, the Knight asks a question "Who hath the worse, Arcite or Palamoun?" (l. 1348) of the pilgrims he is travelling with, at the end of the first part. By encouraging their unrestricted and independent thinking, he keeps them in suspense and makes his tale and their pilgrimage more enjoyable.[3]

1.2. *Ouen*

Concerning *ouen*, this chapter provides two examples; one is [4] from *The Clerk's Tale* (*ClT*).

> [4]   Thise ladyes, whan that they hir tyme say,
> Han taken hire and into chambre gon,
> And strepen hire out of hire rude array,
> And in a clooth of gold that brighte shoon,
> With a coroune of many a riche stoon
> Upon hire heed, they into halle hire broghte,
> And ther she was honured as *hire oghte*.   (68.3)
> (*ClT* 1114-20)

The 3rd-person singular pronouns refer to Grisilde, who, after receiving baptisms of fire from her husband Walter, is told the delightful truth. Quotation [4] narrates how she comes back to her chamber and recovers her position as

---

[3] The anti-example is *Mel* 2173, where the Hengwrt reads *ye* but the later MSS, including the Ellesmere, read *yow* with the RtV of 77.1 per cent.
   Thre thynges, certes, shal ye wynne therby:
   First, love of Crist, and to youreself honour,
   And al myn heritage, toun and tour;
   I yeve it yow, maketh chartres as *yow* leste;   (*MerT* 2170-73)
This passage is from Januarie's speech to his young wife May. He is asking her to be true to him in exchange for his heritage. Contextually speaking, the *as*-clause in line 2173 should portray May's freedom.

marquise. Regarding the impersonal use here, Chapter 3 explained that the statement is based on the social status or standing of the Ex. With the findings in the chapter taken into consideration, it can be said that the personal readings of *as hire oghte* show the narrator's involvement in the story, who compassionately thinks that no other person can be the marquise.

The other is [5]. This is also from *ClT*.

> [5] For sith a womman was so pacient
> Unto a mortal man, wel moore *us oghte* (60.7)
> Receyven al in gree that God us sent;
> For greet skile is he preeve that he wroghte. (*ClT* 1149-52)

After telling the story of Grisilde, the Clerk is addressing the moral to the pilgrims. As seen in Chapter 3, a 1st-person Ex is associated more with the personal use of *ouen*, showing the addressers' deeper involvement in their own obligation. The high RtV in this example coincides with the tendency.

1.3. Thurven

Thurven also witnesses the I-P variation.

> [6] Have thou ynogh, what *thar thee* recche or care (20.0)
> How myrily that othere folkes fare?
> For, certeyn, olde dotard, by youre leve,
> Ye shul have queynte right ynogh at eve.
> He is to greet a nygard that wolde werne
> A man to lighte a candle at his lanterne;
> He shal have never the lasse light, pardee.
> Have thou ynogh, *thee thar* nat pleyne thee. (40.7)
> (*WBT* 329-36)

Citation [6] is from *The Wife of Bath's Tale*. The Wife of Bath is calling bad names to her husband, who always chides her and tries to control her. She hates his behaviour because she puts strong emphasis on women's freedom from, and sovereignty over their husbands. Chapter 3, which mainly discusses *ouen*, has concluded that the personal use appears dominant when statements or their grounds about the agents' obligation are more subjective. This idea can also be applied to the I-P variation in [6]. It can also be said that *thee thar* in line 336, appearing after the repetition of the conditional clause in line 329, conveys her intense and more subjective emotion.

This verb also has the P-I variation: [7].

> [7] And al be it so that youre emprise be establissed and ordeyned by greet multitude of folk, yet *thar ye* nat accomplice thilke ordinaunce but yow like.
> (*Mel* 1068) (RtV = 36.7)

This is Prudence's speech in *The Tale of Melibee*, in which she is remonstrating with her husband Melibeus impetuously not to get his revenge on the adversaries who injured his wife and daughter, citing Seneca's words. The results of Chapter 3 can make the following interpretation possible: her opinion is thought to be based on sententious and objective grounds. However, although her personal use of *ouen* and *moten* has the P-I variation, the occurrences are not high (around 10 per cent).

1.4. *Recchen*

ClT has one example of the impersonal *recchen* whose personal variants are recorded in the later MSS.

> [8]   Save this, she preyede hym that, if he myghte,
>   Hir litel sone he wolde in erthe grave
>   His tendre lymes, delicaat to sighte,
>   Fro fowles and fro beestes for to save.
>   But she noon answere of hym myghte have.
>   He wente his wey, as *hym* no thyng ne *roghte*,   (47.5)
>   But to Boloigne he tendrely it broghte.   (*ClT* 680-86)

In [8], following her husband's order that their second child should be killed as was their first child, Grisilde allows his "confidential servant" (Benson's note on *privee man* (2008: 144)) to take him away. She then prays to the servant that the child will not be roughly buried. However, the servant does not listen to her.

As mentioned in Chapter 2, the impersonal use can show the uninvolvement of the Ex with the action expressed by the verb, and the *as*-clause in line 685 helps to show the servant's indifference to her prayer. The replacement of the impersonal use with the personal use may illustrate the subjecthood of the servant, suggesting an interpretation that he rejects her prayer intentionally.

1.5. *Think*

There is an interesting example of the I-P variation in *think*, [9], which is from *The Summoner's Tale*.

[9]   The lady of the hous ay stille sat
       Til she had herd what the frere sayde.
       "Ey, Goddes mooder," quod she, "Blisful mayde!
       Is ther oght elles? Telle me feithfully."
          "Madame," quod he, "how *thynke ye* herby?" (39.5)
          "How that *me thynketh*?" quod she. "So God me speede, (0)
       I seye a cherl hath doon a cherles dede.
       What shold I seye? God lat hym nevere thee!
       His sike heed is ful of vanytee;
       I holde hym in a manere frenesye."   (*SumT* 2200-09)

As mentioned in Section 2.1.4 of Chapter 4, line 2204 has *yow* in the Hengwrt MS and Skeat's edition, but *ye* in about 40 per cent of MSS including the Ellesmere and in Benson's edition. None of the three editors, including F. N. Robinson, makes any comment about their choice.

The pronoun *he* in [9] refers to a friar who solicited an ailing peasant for a contribution hypocritically and was endowed with his wind. The friar, in his wrath, visited the lord of the peasant, and told the "odious meschief" (l. 2190) to him and his wife. He relentlessly asked them to hand a punishment to the peasant.

In the case of the Hengwrt, the friar's speech in line 2204 can show his deference (or feigned politeness) to the wife, and in the case of the Ellesmere, his speech can show his urgency, as he desires her decided opinion favourable to him.[4]

Contrarily, the wife's words in line 2203 show her imperturbability, which can be reflected in the impersonal use in line 2205 in all MSS. Her comments in line 2206-09 are also merely her general impressions about the peasant and show that she does not deal with the friar seriously.

2. Summary

The I-P variations with high rates of frequency occurred within 100 years after Chaucer's death. In addition, some occurred between the Hengwrt and Ellesmere MSS, which were produced by the same scribe, Adam Pinkhurst.[5] Horobin, surveying morphological differences between the two MSS, suggests that those differences "are representative of ongoing changes in the London dialect during this period, and also of differences in editorial policy between these two very different witnesses to Chaucer's text" (2003: 58). He points out that the Ellesmere attempts "to regularise the inconsistencies found in Hg" often with "the sociolinguistic phenomenon of hypercorrection" (2003: 58). His findings may explain the variations found between the two MSS, and they may be further applied for the variations found in many of the later MSS.

By contrast, when considered semantically and pragmatically, the examples with the I-P variation with a higher rate of frequency can give different interpretations

---

[4] Ohno (2013) discusses this passage from a cognitive perspective.
[5] See Mooney and Takamiya.

from those in the Hengwrt MS and from those with lower occurrences in later MSS. In particular, considering the frequent variation in the examples of *listen* with a 2nd-person Ex, can lead to a subsequent different evolution of *listen* and *liken*[6] based on their semantic difference.

---

[6] Similarly, Loureiro-Porto points out a factor which "may have caused a different evolution of *need* and *behove*": "the increasing non-volitionality of the experiencer of *behove*, which develops nuances of appropriateness rather than of necessity and survives as a verb meaning 'be appropriate, be incumbent'" (2010: 696).

Conclusion

Within this book I have examined the choice between the impersonal and personal uses in Chaucer in comparison with his contemporary poets. From a diachronic viewpoint, the use gradually changes into the personal use, and we are apt to make a sweeping generalisation that the transition went quite uniformly. However, in Chaucer's time the extent of the transition varies depending on the verb. For instance, the impersonal use remains stronger in the verbs of sorrow, pleasure, and dream, where the Ex's function as a recipient is more emphasised. I have also observed that different verbs have different relationships between the two uses and the grammatical persons of the Ex: the impersonal use is frequently found with a 1st-person (especially singular) Ex in verbs such as *liken*, *thinken*, *dremen*, etc., while the use is frequent with a 3rd-person Ex in verbs of obligation.

We are also inclined to decide prematurely, that the two constructions were used interchangeably at a certain point in the middle of the transition. It may be true that the choice of either use is affected by the demands of rhyme, the juxtaposition of a verb with another personal verb, the shared subject, etc., which shows that the two uses accept some overlap between them. However, even the contemporary poets used some verbs differently as seen in the case of the dream verbs. My research from the semantic and pragmatic viewpoints has exploited the possibility that two uses retain exclusive meanings and functions in those days, which make their peculiar interpretations of the context.

In Part I, in more depth, using abundant and detailed data, my investigations have illustrated that the two uses are closely connected with the degree of Ex's involvement with the mental activities expressed by the verbs, utilising the arguments of the previous studies, some of which seem intuitive. They have also highlighted the syntactic, semantic, and pragmatic environments favourable for each of the impersonal and personal uses. Thus, they have enabled a deeper understanding of the context, focusing on the feelings of the characters and the narrators.

Furthermore, in Part II, I have examined the linguistic feeling or sensitivity of the scribes in the fifteenth century, when the transition was going further. They do not run counter to the transition, but add more personal readings suitable to their ways of expression at that time, which coincides with the idea acquired as the result of Part I. Here is also detected the nonuniformity of the variation according to the verb. For instance, verbs such as *liken*, *greven*, *reuen*, etc. are not active in the variation, while *listen* with a 2nd-person Ex is fairly active. In *think*, the variation is scarcely witnessed in the examples with a 1st-person Ex.

Finally, all of my surveys have increased awareness of the interpersonal or pragmatic aspect of the two uses, especially between the addressers and the addressees. Using the two constructions, the addressers often seem to humble themselves or discipline themselves and to have a regard for the addressees. It is well exemplified by the phenomena that the ratios of the two uses vary according to the grammatical person of the Ex in Chaucer's text, and that the impersonal *listen* used in an *if*-clause witnesses the wide and dense variation towards the personal use in the later manuscripts.

Thus, this book has also tried to show that the choice of either construction can be one characteristic of Chaucer's language. I hope this book will help to obtain or update the information about the language in the age of Chaucer and his scribes. I also hope that it can be contributory to advancing some studies which presents briefly what the impersonal construction is, without mentioning "how Chaucer exploited the variety available to him in his writing" (Horobin 2007: ix).

Bibliography

Primary Sources

Benson, Larry D., ed. (2008) *The Riverside Chaucer*. 3rd ed. Oxford: Oxford UP.
French, Walter Hoyt and Charles Brockway Hale, eds. (1964) *Middle English Metrical Romances*. 2 vols. New York: Russell & Russell.
Hofland, Knut et al, eds. (1999) *The Helsinki Corpus of English Texts: Diachronic Part. ICAME Collection of English Language Corpora*. 2nd ed. CD-ROM. Bergen: The HIT Centre, U of Bergen.
Macaulay, G. C., ed. (1900) *The English Works of John Gower*. 2 vols. London: Oxford UP.
Schmidt, A. V. C., ed. (1995) *William Langland: The Vision of Piers Plowman: A Critical Edition of the B-Text Based on Trinity College Cambridge MS B. 15. 17*. 2nd ed. London: J. M. Dent.

Secondary Sources

Akimoto, Minoji, ed. (2010) *Comment Clause no Shiteki Kenkyu: Sono Kinou to Hattatsu*. Tokyo: Eichosha Phoenix.
Allen, Cynthia L. (1986) "Reconsidering the History of *Like*." *Journal of Linguistics*, 22, 375-409.
Allen, Cynthia L. (1995a) *Case Marking and Reanalysis*. Oxford: Oxford UP.
Allen, Cynthia L. (1995b) "On Doing as You Please." *Historical Pragmatics: Pragmatic Developments in the History of English*. Ed. Andreas H. Jucker. Amsterdam: John Benjamins. 275-308.
Allen, Cynthia L. (1997) "The Development of an 'Impersonal' Verb in Middle English: The Case of *Behoove*." *Studies in Middle English Linguistics*. Ed. Jacek Fisiak. Berlin: Walter de Gruyter. 1-22.
Baugh, A. C., ed. (1963) *Chaucer's Major Poetry*. New Jersey: Prentice-Hall.
Benson, Larry D., ed. (1993) *A Glossarial Concordance to the Riverside Chaucer*. Vol. I. New York: Garland.
Brinton, Laurel J. (1996) *Pragmatic Markers in English: Grammaticalization and Discourse Functions*. Berlin: Mouton.

Brinton, Laurel J. (2008) *The Comment Clause in English.* Cambridge: Cambridge UP.
Brook, G. L. (1958) *A History of the English Language.* London: André Deutsch.
Brown, Penelope and Stephen C. Levinson. (1987) *Politeness: Some Universals in Language Usage.* Reissued. Cambridge: Cambridge UP.
Burnley, David. (1983) *A Guide to Chaucer's Language.* London: Macmillan.
Burrow, J. A. and Thorlac Turville-Petre. (1996) *A Book of Middle English.* 2nd ed. Oxford: Blackwell.
Cannon, Christopher. (1998) *The Making of Chaucer's English.* Cambridge: Cambridge UP.
Carter, Ronald and Michael McCarthy. (2006) *Cambridge Grammar of English.* Cambridge: Cambridge UP.
Chen, Guohua. (1998) "The Degrammaticalization of Addressee-Satisfaction Conditionals in Early Modern English." *Advances in English Historical Linguistics.* Ed. Jacek Fisiak and Marcin Krygier. Berlin: Mouton. 23-32.
Clemen, Wolfgang. (1963) *Chaucer's Early Poetry.* Trans. C. A. M. Sym. London: Methuen.
Coates, Jennifer. (1983) *The Semantics of the Modal Auxiliaries.* London: Croom Helm.
Cooper, Helen. (1996) *Oxford Guides to Chaucer:* The Canterbury Tales. 2nd ed. Oxford: Oxford UP.
Cowen, Janet and George Kane. (1995) *The Legend of Good Women.* Michigan: Colleagues P.
Crystal, David. (2003) *A Dictionary of Linguistics and Phonetics.* 5th ed. Oxford: Blackwell.
Davis, Norman et al, eds. (1979) *A Chaucer Glossary.* Oxford: Clarendon.
Denison, David. (1990a) "The Old English Impersonals Revived." *Papers from the 5th International Conference on English Historical Linguistics: Cambridge, 6-9 April 1987.* Ed. Law S. Adamson et al. Amsterdam/ Philadelphia: John Benjamins. 111-40.
Denison, David. (1990b) "Auxiliary + Impersonal in Old English." *Folia Linguistica Historica*, 9 (1), 131-66.
Denison, David. (1993) *English Historical Syntax: Verbal Constructions.* London: Longman.

Donaldson, E. T., ed. (1975, 1984) *Chaucer's Poetry.* 2nd ed. New York: Wiley. Rpt. Harper Collins.
Edwards, Robert R. (1989) *The Dream of Chaucer: Representation and Reflection in the Early Narratives.* Durham: Duke UP.
Elliott, Ralph W. V. (1969) "Chaucer's Reading." *Chaucer's Mind and Art.* Ed. A. C. Cawley. London: Oliver and Boyd. 46-68.
Elliott, Ralph W. V. (1974) *Chaucer's English.* London: André Deutsch.
Elmer, Willy. (1981) *Diachronic Grammar: The History of Old and Middle English Subjectless Constructions.* Tübingen: Niemeyer.
Fischer, Olga. (1992) "Syntax." *The Cambridge History of the English Language.* Vol. II. *1066-1476.* Ed. Norman Blake. Cambridge: Cambridge UP. 207-408.
Fischer, Olga C. M. and Frederike C. van der Leek. (1983) "The Demise of the Old English Impersonal Construction." *Journal of Linguistics,* 19, 337-68.
Fisher, John H., ed. (1989) *The Complete Poetry and Prose of Geoffrey Chaucer.* 2nd ed. Fort Worth: Harcourt Brace College Publishers.
Gray, Douglas, ed. (2003) *The Oxford Companion to Chaucer.* Oxford: Oxford UP.
Higuchi, Masayuki. (1990) "Impersonal Constructions in Chaucer's English." *Kotoba to Bungaku to Bunka to.* Ed. Masachiyo Amano et al. Tokyo: Eichosha Shinsha. 205-20.
Hogg, Richard and David Denison, eds. (2006) *A History of the English Language.* Cambridge: Cambridge UP.
Hopper, Paul J. (1991) "On Some Principles of Grammaticization." *Approaches to Grammaticalization.* Vol. 1. Ed. Elizabeth Closs Traugott and Bernd Heine. Amsterdam and Philadelphia: John Benjamins. 17-35.
Hopper, Paul J. and Elizabeth Closs Traugott. (2003) *Grammaticalization.* 2nd ed. Cambridge: Cambridge UP.
Horn, Laurence R. and Gregory Ward, eds. (2006) *The Handbook of Pragmatics.* Malden: Blackwell.
Horobin, Simon. (2003) *The Language of the Chaucer Tradition.* Cambridge: D. S. Brewer.
Horobin, Simon. (2007) *Chaucer's Language.* Basingstoke: Palgrave Macmillan.
Ikegami, Yoshihiko. (1985) "Gengo Riron no Tachiba kara: Eigo ni Okeru 'Agentivity' no Hyougen wo Megutte." *The Methods of*

English Historical Linguistics. Ed. Yoshio Terasawa and Akio Oizumi. Tokyo: Nan'un-do. 33-62.

Jespersen, Otto. (1927, 1983) *A Modern English Grammar on Historical Principles.* Part III. London: George Allen & Unwin. Rpt. Tokyo: Meicho Fukyu Kai.

Jimura, Akiyuki. (1983) "Chaucer's Use of Impersonal Constructions in *Troilus and Criseyde*: by aventure yfalle." *Bulletin of Otani Women's University*, 18, 14-27.

Jimura, Akiyuki. (2005) *Studies in Chaucer's Words and His Narratives.* Hiroshima: Keisuisha.

Kerkhof, J. (1982) *Studies in the Language of Geoffrey Chaucer.* 2nd, revised and enlarged ed. Leiden: E. J. Brill.

Kim, Hyeree. (1999) "A Lexical Approach to the History of the Quasi-Impersonal Subject 'It'." *English Studies*, 80, 318-42.

Kopytko, Roman. (1993) *Polite Discourse in Shakespeare's English.* Poznań: Adam Mickiewicz UP.

Kurath, Hans et al, eds. (1952-2001) *Middle English Dictionary.* Ann Arbor: The U of Michigan P. [*MED*]

Laing, Margaret and Roger Lass. (2006) "Early Middle English Dialectology: Problems and Prospects." *The Handbook of the History of English.* Ed. Ans van Kemenade and Bettelou Los. Malden: Blackwell. 417-51.

Leech, Geoffrey. (1983) *Principles of Pragmatics.* New York: Longman.

Levinson, Stephen C. (1983) *Pragmatics.* Cambridge: Cambridge UP.

Loureiro-Porto, Lucía. (2010) "A Review of Early English Impersonals: Evidence from Necessity Verbs." *English Studies*, 91, 674-99.

Mair, Christian. (1988) "The Transition from the Impersonal to the Personal Use of the Verb *Like* in Late Middle English and Early Modern English: Some Previously Neglected Determinants of Variation." *Historical English: on the Occasion of Karl Brunner's 100th Birthday.* Ed. Manfred Markus. Institut für Anglistik, Universität Innsbruck. 210-18.

Manly, John M. and Edith Rickert. (1940) *The Text of The Canterbury Tales: Studied on the Basis of All Known Manuscripts.* 8 vols. Chicago: The U of Chicago P.

Masui, Michio. (1962) *Studies in Chaucer.* Tokyo: Kenkyusha.

Masui, Michio. (1964) *The Structure of Chaucer's Rime Words: An Exploration into the Poetic Language of Chaucer.* Tokyo: Kenkyusha.

Masui, Michio. (1976) *Chaucer no Sekai*. Tokyo: Iwanami.
Matsushita, Tomonori, ed. (1998) *A Glossarial Concordance to William Langland's* The Vision of Piers Plowman: *The B-Text*. Vol. I. Tokyo: Yushodo.
McCawley, Noriko A. (1976) "From OE/ME 'Impersonal' to 'Personal' Constructions: What Is a 'Subject-less' S?" *Papers from the Parasession on Diachronic Syntax*. Ed. Sanford B. Steever et al. Chicago: Chicago Linguistic Society. 192-204.
McMillan, Ann, trans. (1987) *The Legend of Good Women by Geoffrey Chaucer*. Houston: Rice UP.
Minnis, A. J. (1995) *Oxford Guide to Chaucer: The Shorter Poems*. Oxford: Clarendon.
Miura, Ayumi. (2007) "The Impersonal Verb *Remembren* in Chaucer Revisited." *Language and Information Sciences*, 5, 213-28.
Mooney, Linne R. (2006) "Chaucer's Scribe." *Speculum*, 81, 97-138.
Mosser, D. W. (1996) "Witness Descriptions." *The Wife of Bath's Prologue on CD-ROM*. Ed. P. M. W. Robinson. Cambridge: Cambridge UP.
Mustanoja, Tauno F. (1960) *A Middle English Syntax*. Part I. *Parts of Speech*. Helsinki: Société Néophilologique.
Nagashima, Daisuke. (1985) "Ikegami Yoshihiko shi no Kasetsu ni Kansuru 2, 3 no Gimon." *The Methods of English Historical Linguistics*. Ed. Yoshio Terasawa and Akio Oizumi. Tokyo: Nan'un-do. 63-65.
Nakano, Hirozo. (1993) *Eigo Houjodoushi no Imiron*. Tokyo: Eichosha.
Nakao, Toshio. (1972) *History of English II*. Tokyo: Taishukan.
Nakao, Yoshiyuki. (1999) "Chaucer no *Moot/Moste* no Imiron: Gaiteki Youin no Mibunkasei." *Gengo Kenkyu no Chouryu*. Ed. Toshiaki Inada et al. Tokyo: Kaitakusha. 231-46.
Nakao, Yoshiyuki. (2002) "The Semantics of Chaucer's *Moot/Moste* and *Shal/Sholde*: Conditional Elements and Degrees of Their Quantifiability." *English Corpus Linguistics in Japan*. Ed. Toshio Saito et al. Amsterdam: Rodopi. 235-47.
Nakao, Yoshiyuki. (2010) "Chaucer no Comment Clause." *Comment Clause no Shiteki Kenkyu: Sono Kinou to Hattatsu*. Ed. Minoji Akimoto. Tokyo: Eichosha Phoenix. 51-80.
Nakau, Minoru. (1994) *Principles of Cognitive Semantics*. Tokyo: Taishukan.

Nevalainen, Terttu. (2006) "Historical Sociolinguistics and Language Change." *The Handbook of the History of English*. Ed. Ans van Kemenade and Bettelou Los. Oxford: Blackwell. 558-88.

Nevalainen, Terttu and Helena Raumolin-Brunberg. (2003) *Historical Sociolinguistics: Language Change in Tudor and Stuart England*. Harlow: Pearson Education Limited.

Ogura, Michiko. (1986) *Old English 'Impersonal' Verbs and Expressions*. Copenhagen: Rosenkilde and Bagger.

Ogura, Michiko. (1990) "What Has Happened to 'Impersonal' Constructions?" *Neuphilologische Mitteilungen*, 91, 31-55.

Ogura, Michiko. (1991) "*Displese Yow* and *Displeses Yow*: OE and ME Verbs Used Both 'Impersonally' and Reflexively." *Poetica*, 34, 75-87.

Ogura, Michiko. (1996) *Verbs in Medieval English: Differences in Verbs Choice in Verse and Prose*. Berlin: Mouton.

Ogura, Michiko. (2003) "'Reflexive' and 'Impersonal' Constructions in Medieval English." *Anglia*, 121, 535-56.

Ohno, Hideshi. (1995) "The Use of *Liken* in Chaucer." *ERA*, 13, 1-20.

Ohno, Hideshi. (1996a) "The Impersonal Verbs in *Troilus and Criseyde*: The Verbs Denoting 'Obligation' and 'Necessity'." *ERA*, 14, 1-15.

Ohno, Hideshi. (1996b) "The Use of Impersonal Verbs in Chaucer: With Special Reference to PLEASE/DESIRE Class." *Hiroshima Studies in English Language and Literature*, 40, 47-58.

Ohno, Hideshi. (1998) "Notes on the Use of *Remembren* in Chaucer." *The Bulletin of Kurashiki University of Science and the Arts*, 3, 297-305.

Ohno, Hideshi. (1999) "Personal and Impersonal Uses of *Meten* and *Dremen* in Chaucer." *Hiroshima Studies in English Language and Literature*, 43, 1-15.

Ohno, Hideshi. (2001) "On Variant Readings of *Liken* and *Listen/Lusten* in the *Canterbury Tales*." *Originality and Adventure: Essays on English Language and Literature in Honour of Masahiko Kanno*. Ed. Yoshiyuki Nakao and Akiyuki Jimura. Tokyo: Eihosha. 55-70.

Ohno, Hideshi. (2007a) "Impersonal and Personal Uses of *Ouen* in Chaucer." *Language and Beyond: A Festschrift for Hiroshi Yonekura on the Occasion of His 65th Birthday*. Ed. Mayumi Sawada et al. Tokyo: Eichosha. 353-66.

Ohno, Hideshi. (2007b) "Hininshou Youhou no Shusoku Katei ni Okeru Ichi Danmen." *The Rising Generation*, 153, 110-13.
Ohno, Hideshi. (2007c) "Chaucer Sakuhin no Shahon ni Mirareru Ninshou Hininshou Youhou no Shusoku." *The Rising Generation*, 153, 564-67.
Ohno, Hideshi. (2010) "The Impersonal and Personal Constructions in the Language of Chaucer." *Aspects of the History of English Language and Literature: Collected Papers Read at SHELL 2009, Hiroshima*. Ed. Osamu Imahayashi et al. Frankfurt am Main: Peter Lang. 111-26.
Ohno, Hideshi. (2013) "Variation in the Use of Think in The Summoner's Tale, Line 2204." *Chaucer's Language: Cognitive Perspective*. Ed. Yoshiyuki Nakao and Yoko Iyeiri. Osaka: Osaka Books. 79-98.
Oizumi, Akio. (2003) *A Lexical Concordance to the Works of Geoffrey Chaucer*. Hildesheim: Olms-Weidmann.
Oizumi, Akio and Hiroshi Yonekura. (1994) *A Rhyme Concordance to the Poetical Works of Geoffrey Chaucer*. Programmed by Kunihiro Miki. 2 vols. Hildesheim: Olms-Weidmann.
Ono, Shigeru. (1969) "Chaucer's Variants and What They Tell Us: Fluctuation in the Use of Modal Auxiliaries." *Studies in English Literature*, 45, 51-74.
Ono, Shigeru. (1982) *Eigo Houjodoushi no Hattatsu*. Tokyo: Kenkyusha.
Palander-Collin, Minna. (1996) "The Rise and Fall of METHINKS." *Sociolinguistics and Language History: Studies Based on the Corpus of Early English Correspondence*. Ed. Terttu Nevalainen and Helena Raumolin-Brunberg. Amsterdam: Rodopi. 131-49.
Palander-Collin, Minna. (1999) *Grammaticalization and Social Embedding: I THINK and METHINKS in Middle and Early Modern English*. Helsinki: Société Néophilologique.
Palmer, F. R. (1986) *Mood and Modality*. Cambridge: Cambridge UP.
Pearsall, Derek. (1985, 1994) *The Canterbury Tales*. London: George Allen & Unwin. Rpt. London: Routledge.
Pickles, J. D. and J. L. Dawson, eds. (1987) *A Concordance to John Gower's* Confessio Amantis. Cambridge: D. S. Brewer.
Pocheptsov, George G. (1997) "Quasi-Impersonal Verbs in Old and Middle English." *Studies in Middle English Linguistics*. Ed. Jacek Fisiak. Berlin: Mouton. 469-88.

Robinson, F. N., ed. (1957) *The Works of Geoffrey Chaucer*. 2nd ed. Boston: Houghton.
Robinson, Peter. (1997) "A Stemmatic Analysis of the Fifteenth-Century Witnesses to The Wife of Bath's Prologue." *Occasional Papers*. Ed. Norman Blake and Peter Robinson. 2nd vol. Oxford: Office for Humanities Communication. 69-132. 5 February 2008 <http://www.canterburytalesproject.org/pubs/op2-robinson.pdf>.
Root, Robert K., ed. (1926) *The Book of Troilus and Criseyde*. Princeton: Princeton UP.
Roscow, Gregory. (1981) *Syntax and Style in Chaucer's Poetry*. Cambridge: D. S. Brewer.
Ruggiers, Paul G., ed. (1979) *The Canterbury Tales: A Facsimile and Transcription of the Hengwrt Manuscript with Variants from the Ellesmere Manuscript*. A Variorum Edition of the Works of Geoffrey Chaucer. Vol. 1. Norman: U of Oklahoma P.
Saito, Toshio and Mitsunori Imai, eds. (1988) *A Concordance to Middle English Metrical Romances*. Vol. I. *The Matter of England* & Vol. II. *The Breton Lays*. Programmed by Kunihiro Miki. Frankfurt am Main: Verlag Peter Lang.
Sawada, Harumi. (2006) *Modality*. Tokyo: Kaitakusha.
Seymour, M. C. (1997) *A Catalogue of Chaucer Manuscripts*. Vol. 2. *The Canterbury Tales*. Aldershot, Hants: Scolar P.
Simpson, J. A. and E. S. C. Weiner, eds. (2009) *The Oxford English Dictionary*. 2nd ed. CD-ROM. Ver. 4.0. Oxford: Clarendon. [*OED*]
Sisam, Kenneth, ed. (1921) *Fourteenth Century Verse & Prose*. Oxford: Clarendon.
Skeat, Walter W., ed. (1919) *The Complete Works of Geoffrey Chaucer*. Oxford: Clarendon.
Skeat, Walter W., ed. (1924) *The Vision of William Concerning Piers the Plowman*. 10th and rev. ed. Oxford: Clarendon.
Stubbs, Estelle, ed. (2000) *The Hengwrt Chaucer Digital Facsimile*. CD-ROM. Birmingham: Scholarly Digital Editions.
Tajima, Matsuji. (2000) "Chaucer and the Development of the Modal Auxiliary *Ought* in Late Middle English." *Manuscript, Narrative, Lexicon: Essays on Literary and Cultural Transmission in Honor of Whitney F. Bolton*. Ed. Robert Boenig and Kathleen Davis. Lewisburg, PA: Bucknell UP. 195-217

Tajiri, Masaji. (1989) "Variation of Word Order in the Manuscripts of the *Canterbury Tales.*" *Journal of Osaka University of Foreign Studies*, New series, 2, 39-52.
Takamiya, Toshiyuki. (2004) "Ellesmere-Hengwrt Shajisei no Shoutai." *The Rising Generation*, 150, 490-91.
Tani, Akinobu. (1994) "A Quantitative Study of Word Order of 'Quasi-Impersonal' Constructions in Chaucer's *Troilus and Criseyde*: With Special Reference to the Order of 'Dative' Pronoun and Verb." *The Bulletin of Mukogawa Women's University*, 42, 31-37.
Tani, Akinobu. (1995a) "The Word Order of the 'Quasi-impersonal' Constructions in Chaucer's *Canterbury Tales.*" *Jinbungaku Ronsou*, 16, 1-16.
Tani, Akinobu. (1995b) "On the Quasi-impersonal Constructions in Chaucer's *Canterbury Tales.*" *Jinbungaku Ronsou*, 17, 1-13.
Tani, Akinobu. (1995c) "Variant Readings and the Study of Impersonal Constructions in Chaucer's *Troilus and Criseyde.*" *The Bulletin of Mukogawa Women's University*, 43, 25-31.
Tani, Akinobu. (1997) "One Determinant of the Choice between the Personal and Impersonal Uses of Impersonal Verbs *Like* and *List* in Late Middle English and Early Modern English: An Inquiry into the Possibility of 'Person Hierarchy'." *Studies in Medieval English Language and Literature*, 12, 45-59.
Thompson, Sandra A. and Anthony Mulac. (1991) "A Quantitative Perspective on the Grammaticization of Epistemic Parentheticals in English." *Approaches to Grammaticalization*. Vol. II. *Focus on Types of Grammatical Markers*. Ed. Elizabeth Closs Traugott and Bernd Heine. Amsterdam and Philadelphia: John Benjamins. 313-29.
Tripp, Raymond P., Jr. (1978) "The Psychology of Impersonal Construction." *Glossa*, 12, 177-87.
van der Gaaf, W. (1904) *The Transition from the Impersonal to the Personal Construction in Middle English*. Heidelberg: Carl Winter's Universitätsbuchhandlung.
Visser, F. Th. (1963-73) *An Historical Syntax of the English Language*. In 3 parts in 4 vols. Leiden: E. J. Brill.
Warner, Anthony R. (1993) *English Auxiliaries: Structure and History*. Cambridge: Cambridge UP.

Whiting, Bartlett Jere. (1968) *Proverbs, Sentences, and Proverbial Phrases from English Writings Mainly Before 1500.* Cambridge, Massachusetts: The Belknap P of Harvard UP.

Wimsatt, J. I. (1974) "Chaucer and French Poetry." *Geoffrey Chaucer: The Writer and His Background.* Ed. Derek Brewer. Cambridge: D. S. Brewer. 109-36.

Windeatt, B. A., ed. (1984) *Geoffrey Chaucer, Troilus & Criseyde: A New Edition of "The Book of Troilus."* London: Longman.

Windeatt, B. A. (1992) *Oxford Guides to Chaucer:* Troilus and Criseyde. Oxford: Clarendon.

Wischer, Ilse. (2000) "Grammaticalization versus Lexicalization: 'Methinks' There Is Some Confusion." *Pathways of Change: Grammaticalization in English.* Ed. Olga Fischer et al. Amsterdam: John Benjamins. 355-70.

Yasui, Minoru et al. (1983) *Imiron.* Tokyo: Taishukan.

Yoshikawa, Fumiko. (1999) "Impersonal *Remembren* in Chaucer." *Journal of Language and Culture*, 8, 57-75.

Yoshikawa, Fumiko. (2008) "Julian of Norwich and the Rhetoric of the Impersonal." *Rhetoric of the Anchorhold: Space, Place, and Body within the Discourses of Enclosure.* Ed. Liz Herbert McAvoy. Cardiff: U of Wales P. 141-54.

Index

Akimoto, M. 99n
Allen, C. L. 2, 21, 27, 171
as-clause 28, 61-63, 70, 92, 138, 167, 177n, 180
auxiliarisation 58, 61, 64, 163
auxiliary 59, 61, 64, 66, 69, 79, 112

Baugh, A. C. 29
Benson, L. D. 4-5, 29, 36, 68n, 78n, 104, 111, 113, 146-47, 180
Blake, N. F. 25
Brinton, L. J. 98-101, 123
Brown, P. and Levinson, St. C. 28n
Burnley, D. 76
Burrow, J. A. and Turville-Petre, Th. 95n

calque 76
Cause-Subject 2, 10, 32, 77
Chaucer, G.
  Anel 32, 52
  BD 12, 26, 91, 98, 104, 116, 122, 125, 127
  Bo 10, 56, 67, 75n, 77-79, 84, 86-87, 118
  CT *ClT* 27, 32, 36, 51-52, 61, 66, 89, 113, 161, 177-79; *CYT* 48, 71, 162; *FranT* 16, 19, 77, 103, 155; *GP* 26, 44, 105, 160; *KnT* 28, 35n, 40, 62, 114, 150, 155n, 158, 175-76; *MancT* 88n; *Mel* 44, 56, 57n, 71, 147n, 164, 167, 179; *MerT* 29, 33, 35, 49, 158, 177; *MilT* 40, 45, 170; *MkT* 10, 68; *MLT* 88n; *NPT* 37, 40, 103, 113, 117-18, 121, 126-28, 165, 170; *ParsT* 70, 84, 154; *PhyT* 159, 165; *RvT* 39, 149; *ShipT* 24, 33; *SNT* 69; *SqT* 24, 92, 104, 150, 156, 168, 175; *SumT* 50, 96, 180; *Thop* 100, 111, 113, 127, 169; *WBT* 10, 19, 23, 35, 40, 76, 82, 105, 117, 155, 162, 164, 169, 178;
  HF 39, 85, 92, 112, 116, 120, 126
  LGW 12, 17, 22, 24, 26, 50, 69-70, 78, 86, 128
  Mars 81
  PF 12, 18, 93, 106, 112, 127
  Rom 17, 51, 60, 71, 86, 104, 112-13, 121-22, 124
  Tr 10, 13, 20, 22-25, 28-29, 33, 36-37, 40-41, 66-69, 72, 80-81, 84, 89-91, 97, 103, 105, 111, 118, 125-6
  Truth 72
Chen, G. 171, 175
comment clause 99
Davis, N. et al 29, 37, 113
degree of control 171
Denison, D. 1, 72, 79, 112
Donaldson, E. T. 29, 68n
dream 85, 105-06, 109-10, 119-20, 122-28

Edwards, R. R.   110, 124
Ellesmere/El   97, 147, 167, 177n, 180-81
Elliott, R. W. V.   3, 26, 29, 58
Elmer, W.   9, 31, 47, 55, 145
epistemic   66, 68, 72, 123, 127-28
evidentiality   104
experiencer/Ex   1

Fischer, O.   21n
Fischer, O. C. M. and van der Leek, F. C.   2, 21, 110
Fisher, J. H.   29, 68n
focus of utterance   86, 120, 123, 126, 128, 139
French, W. H. and Hale, Ch. B.   111

Gower, J./*CA*   4, 32, 41, 46, 57, 61, 63, 80, 85n, 88, 90, 95-96, 99-100, 110, 117-18, 124, 169
grammaticalisation   98, 123
grounds   68-70

Helsinki Corpus   65, 98, 101-02, 143
Hengwrt/Hg   5, 48n, 57n, 97, 144, 146-47, 167, 177n, 180-81
Higuchi, M.   33-34, 75n
Hogg, R. and Denison, D.   143
Hopper, P. J. and Traugott, E. C.   98
Horobin, S.   3-5, 145, 181, 185
if-clause   28, 83-84, 87, 138, 174
imperative   33
impersonal use/construction   1, 10, 32, 56, 88n, 111
initiator   2, 21, 110

I-P variation   151

Jespersen, O.   2
Jimura, A.   3
Julian of Norwich   105
juxtapose/juxtaposition   12, 24, 44, 88n, 90, 160

Kerkhof, J.   48, 65, 114

Laing, M and Lass, R.   143n
Langland, W./*PPl*   4, 41, 63, 88, 90, 95n, 96, 99-100, 110, 114, 117-18, 125-26, 169
Leech, G.   176
Loureiro-Porto, L.   182

Mair, Ch.   81
Manly, J. M. and Rickert, E.   5, 48, 97, 144, 147n, 156-57
manuscript/MS   4-5, 48, 57n, 97, 143-45, 156, 162, 164, 167, 173, 177n, 180-81
Masui, M.   17, 20, 22, 25, 28, 61, 81-82, 95, 110, 138
McCawley, N.   22
McMillan, A.   50-51n
mental attitude   29, 49, 87, 97, 123
Miura, A.   76, 83
modesty   27
Mustanoja, T. F.   76

Nakao, T.   27, 57n, 64, 76, 110, 143n, 145, 147n
Nakao, Y.   101n
Nevalainen, T.   148
nothing/noght   36-37

objecthood   51

Ogura, M.   3, 39, 75, 77, 160
Oizumi, A.   35
Oizumi, A. and Yonekura, H.   17n, 63n, 82
Old French   75-76, 83
Ono, Sh.   144-45

Palander-Collin, M.   98, 101-02, 104, 168
Palmer, F. R.   124
parenthetical(ly)   92, 97-106, 122-24, 158, 167
person hierarchy   14, 50, 82, 96-97
personal use/construction   2, 56, 87, 111
Pinkhurst, A.   181
P-I variation   151
polite(ness)   28, 84-85, 87
pragmatic marker   98-99

range of variation/RnV   150
rate of variation/RtV   150
reflexive   39, 44-45, 77-78, 81, 113, 156, 159-63
relative (clause)   44, 120, 126
replacement of *ye* by *you*   148-49
rhyme clause   20, 46, 61, 138
Robinson, F. N.   97, 147
Robinson, P.   156
root meaning   66, 68-69, 166

Schmidt, A. V. C.   114
scribe   143, 145
Skeat, W. W.   97, 180
subjecthood   30, 51, 129, 180

Tajima, M.   59

Tani, A.   13, 64, 82, 146
Tripp, R. P.   20-21n

van der Gaaf, W.   12, 23, 55, 76, 109-10, 118
Visser, F. Th.   60
volition(al)(ity)   2, 4, 51, 129, 182n

Warner, A.   59, 61, 66, 72
what   35-36
Whiting, B. J.   105
Windeatt, B. A.   29, 68n

Yasui, M. et al   122
Yoshikawa, F.   76, 105

■著者紹介

大野　英志（おおの・ひでし）

1970年、岡山県倉敷市生まれ。広島大学大学院文学研究科博士課程後期修了、博士（文学）。倉敷芸術科学大学准教授。
主な著作物：『中世ヨーロッパと多文化共生』（共著；溪水社，2003）；"The Impersonal and Personal Constructions in the Language of Chaucer" in *Aspects of the History of English Language and Literature: Collected Papers Read at SHELL 2009, Hiroshima* (Peter Lang, 2010)；"Variation in the Use of *Think* in *The Summoner's Tale*, Line 2204" in *Chaucer's Language: Cognitive Perspectives*（大阪洋書，2013）；"*I preye/biseche (yow/thee)* in the Late Fourteenth Century: With Special Reference to Chaucer" in *Language and Style in English Literature*（Peter Lang，近刊）.

Hideshi Ohno is Associate Professor of English, Kurashiki University of Science and the Arts. He was born in 1970 in Kurashiki, Okayama, Japan. He received his D.Litt. from Hiroshima University in March 2011. His research areas cover Middle English language and literature and historical studies of the English language. He is a co-author of *Cultural Symbioses in Medieval Europe* (Hiroshima: Keisuisha, 2003). His recent publications include "The Impersonal and Personal Constructions in the Language of Chaucer" in *Aspects of the History of English Language and Literature: Collected Papers Read at SHELL 2009, Hiroshima* (Frankfurt am Main: Peter Lang, 2010), "Variation in the Use of *Think* in *The Summoner's Tale*, Line 2204" in *Chaucer's Language: Cognitive Perspectives* (Osaka: Osaka Books, 2013), and "*I preye/biseche (yow/thee)* in the Late Fourteenth Century: With Special Reference to Chaucer" in *Language and Style in English Literature* (Frankfurt am Main: Peter Lang, forthcoming).

Variation between Personal and Impersonal Constructions in Geoffrey Chaucer
A Stylistic Approach

2015 年 4 月 20 日　初版第 1 刷発行

- ■著　　者──大野英志
- ■発 行 者──佐藤　守
- ■発 行 所──株式会社 大学教育出版
  　　　　　　〒700-0953　岡山市南区西市 855-4
  　　　　　　電話 (086) 244-1268 ㈹　FAX (086) 246-0294
- ■印刷製本──サンコー印刷㈱

© Hideshi Ohno 2015, Printed in Japan
検印省略　落丁・乱丁本はお取り替えいたします。
本書のコピー・スキャン・デジタル化等の無断複製は著作権法上での例外を除き禁じられています。本書を代行業者等の第三者に依頼してスキャンやデジタル化することは、たとえ個人や家庭内での利用でも著作権法違反です。

ISBN978-4-86429-337-2